1

Cover Photo by Bobbie Kingsley

ISBN: **9781983052637**

MY EXTRAORDINARY LIFE

BY

STELLA JANSEN

4

Index:

5

BOOK I

1959 – 1977

~

As soon as I could write I began to write stories and poems, my first song I wrote when I was eight years old and on my tenth birthday my parents gave me a diary.

~

Chapter 1

A little girl on the verge of womanhood

1959:

I got a new petticoat and I finished the blue bathing suit   for my doll,
I named her after my mother: Sietske. It came out darling. Now I'm
working on a dress for her. My doll has got a couple of cloths now. It's
easier with this knitting-book. I won it with some wool in a competition.
You had to knit a scarf. This is the poodle prize.

Tonight I'm going to the movie *Alone in the world* with mommy and my
two sisters. She promised us last year already.

My first wish is a guitar or a ukulele, my second wish is that I become
a little singer; my third wish is that I may have a long healthy and happy
life. I hope my three wishes will be granted. On television you often see
rock and roll, I love that! I also value operetta music very much. I have a
notebook with songs that I wrote myself. Perhaps they're not so good but I
love them anyway. And I certainly like to write stories. I have notebooks
in which I write stories.

These are my three wishes. And I have many more.

I want to be a movie-star.

1959

My best friend is Kita, her mother is English and her father is Polish and she has a little brother who has fifteen names. Her last name is too difficult so I call her Kita Football. I like her so much.

1961

All the children are teasing Frits and me, the other day some stupid guys put my scarf around me and him and they pulled us, screaming: Frits goes with Stella, Frits goes with Stella! I hate them, stupid idiots!

1961

Poor Frits, he was looking over his shoulder at me when we were walking to school and walked straight into the lantern post, now he has a big bump on his forehead. I feel sorry for him.

1961

The head master was very angry with Frits but it wasn't his fault, he was teaching those stupid boys a lesson. I like him very much. He is Indonesian and very handsome. Why are Jim's parents so mean? He and his little brother were tied to the washing line for punishment and Jim always gets beaten, he has a bold spot on his head and all the children are mean to him because they say he is dumb, I hate that!

1962

I wish something happened. Suppose I was kidnapped by a darling Romeo who only does this because although he doesn't have to kidnap me, he can't get to me. It should be Frans or Frits although Frits doesn't have to kidnap me; he can talk to me whenever he wants and Frans too. I'm in favor of Frits. Shit, school is so stupid, always sweating over exams; however, staying home isn't all that great either. Having to help my mother with everything, she said that as sweet as I used to be as horrid I am now. She said she expects kids hate me in school. Not so! I told her to leave me alone.

1962

There's no one here who understands me. Daddy wants me to cut off my witches' hair. He has no idea about what girls my age like. And mama doesn't either, she always says: 'You're too young for that.' And Lilly is often in a bad mood lately. She's always complaining, like now again. What a drag! I wish I had pocket money. I guess I'm too young for that too.

Oh, I wish I was sixteen. Everything is so boring. I'm sitting in mama's room, watching myself in her mirror. How ugly I am! Lilly is the prettiest of the three of us I think though she's too skinny. Hell, I don't care that I'm ugly. Maybe I'm pretty, no, that's impossible. I guess I'm just plain. Dad says I shouldn't go on and on about boys.

April 1, 1962

For the first time in my life I have been very sad, that is to say, it is my first big sorrow. I'm over it a bit now but it has shocked me deeply. My closest and dearest friend, my great love Frits, died on March 19.

Monday morning at half past five he has passed away. Aunt Trijntje told us, she came in early through the backdoor and with her loud piercing voice, she said: 'Do you know who died? Fritsje Burggraeve!'

I was so shocked that I dropped the breakfast plates I was carrying from the kitchen to the dining table. I couldn't believe my ears. Frits dead, My Frits, dead? Mama was very shocked also. That dear Frits, handsome, sweet, darling Frits. He was my best friend and I always knew him so well, from first grade I knew him already. We were going steady then, well, that's what all the children said about us.

Oh, before, when he was still alive I was always so happy and in love with him. He always liked me too I think. We kissed once. And now he is dead. So suddenly that everyone who heard about it cannot believe it. Frits, Frits, Frits…I can't write anymore now.

April 23, 1962

We are always going to Fritsje's house these days, the whole gang, it's much fun, the other day we did a competition who could kiss longest, my sister Marjorie and Robbie won. Fritsje's mother is a dancer from Java and she dances sometimes too.

It seems already long ago that he died, the burial was awful, and Estelle's father made photos, Fritsje's mother put them in an album. I don't like that at all but they are from Indonesia so different from us of course. It's hard to forget what he looked like when all the children came by the house to pay our respect, farewell…so strange, he didn't look like Frits anymore, his ears were too big and purple, he looked much older than fourteen. His father I saw for the first time, he is a tall white man, and they are divorced from table and bed. I don't quite understand what that means. Frits his brothers were so upset especially Harrie, the youngest one, now there are only three of them. Everyone in the neighborhood calls Harrie Troelifer, I don't know why. It's terrible because Frits could've been saved. On Saturday afternoon he was playing soccer here on the field, Bertje van Marwijk, Frank Everts, Bennie de Jong, Jopie, Freddie and well, all the boys…then Frits got pain in his abdomen and later that night his pain became worse and worse. His mother and Jopie, the oldest son, went to Estelle's parents to use their phone to call the doctor. He refused to come because he said it was probably stomach flu and to give him an aspirin. But he didn't get any better, all through Sunday and then early Monday morning he passed away. How he must have suffered….I must stop now, it's too sad.

May 9, 1962

It's unbelievable but true! Estelle and I have found Frits his lookalike, he lives in Twello. We go there every day after school to observe him and we know that he plays judo, we saw him in a competition recently. We are so happy because now it is as if Frits has come back to us. His name is

14

Frank van Wijk, we don't talk to him of course, and he doesn't even know that we are following him.

June 12, 1962

Estelle and I had a fight and now we don't speak anymore. I can't remember very well what our fight was about.

We already stopped going to Twello, that boy is not Frits, how could we think that he looked just like dear Frits, absurd, he is nothing like him, so stupid of us.

1963

Scheisse, I'm sure I'll never let myself be taken by someone's mother again. Just when Josje called me an attractive boy wanted to dance with me.

Jesus, it seems I'm always talking about boys!

1963

I'm in a rotten mood today. I grumble far too much, says mama. This afternoon I had to go to town to take the prescription for big Lilly (she's one of my mother's younger sisters who lives with us) to the pharmacist. Right off I was angry because I wanted to go skating.

I think it's obligatory to stay in training. I never forget how surprised and happy I was when daddy presented me with the beautiful new white skates, it wasn't even my birthday!

I can skate really fast already and I love it so much. I have to train every day after school, it's absolutely necessary!

I'm so angry, why do I always have to do these things? Why couldn't Marjorie do it? I told her she wasn't allowed to use my skates while I went for the drugs for big Lilly.

When I was in town after crossing that horrible bridge over the IJssel River, I noticed it wasn't so bad after all. I even liked it, a little trip to town. I observed the people with great interest and counted the fur coats I passed. I criticized all the conspicuous types and then I bought licorice for 5 cents for my trouble, I figured I deserved that.

But when I came home Marjorie had gone skating, with my skates! Why didn't mama stop her! I am so angry, grr!

16

1963

I wrote a poem about my beautiful city, Deventer, the title is *My city on the river* and I really like it. I let Lilly read it and she likes it too.

1963

I'm in touch with Estelle again. For a while this winter she refused to greet me. My hair looks great, up with curls all over the place; this is a Bossa Nova hairdo. The Bossa Nova is a dance. There are many popular dances these days like for instance:

The Madison, The Twist, the Loop-the-loop, the Limbo, etcetera.

Walt Schenke left school. The boys that are left aren't up to much I think. Anna, whom I saw a lot lately, left school because she's pregnant. She's only sixteen. But Mandy is even younger, only fifteen and pregnant.

Just think - I see myself being pregnant. Just imagine! No, that's nothing for me.

1963

Recently there was a documentary on television about young people in America who still worship Hitler. Stark raving lunatics!

This morning my mother said she thinks it unnecessary that I'm already wearing a bra. 'I only started wearing one when I was seventeen,' she said. Something else again to die laughing.

Tonight mom and dad have a party of the factory my father works for. She made herself a marvelous emerald green dress. It's so beautiful, especially with mama's flaming red hair.

She made so many lovely things already for me and my sisters and everything perfect! I hope I can sew like that for myself and my children later on. I pity the children whose mother can't sew.

May 5, 1964

Today is Liberation Day. Yesterday it was the Remembrance Day for the dead. I forgot to watch it on television. Pity, I had hoped they would show the play The Diary of Anne Frank but instead it was The Last Train, disappointing.

Recently we went to an exhibition with class in the Munt Tower in Amsterdam. It was about the Resistance 1940-1945. I thought it very interesting.

I'm not speaking with Estelle. A few weeks ago two cousins of Frits were here. One of them, Erwin, often came my way and I sort of liked him. Later, when those boys had gone back to The Hague, Estelle was mad with me. Rainee had told her that I had something with Erwin. That was true. But how was I to know Estelle was going steady with him? Now all hell broke loose. I'm laughing my head off because she's making a fool of herself. She is so terribly jealous! Just when we had a good contact lately. Well, I suppose she'll be alright with me again some time. I don't give a damn!

I'm working on a story which I'm going to mail to a publisher. I'm becoming quite nervous about it because the story is almost finished. Two chapters to go and then edit a few things. I dare not think they'll accept it which they probably won't anyway. Mandy is big as a house. Later I expect they'll pass off the baby as her mother's. For her it makes no difference whether she has ten or eleven children.

19

Princess Irene is going to become engaged to a very unattractive man from Spain. There's been a lot of fussing about it and still but I don't want to get wrapped up in it because I don't give a damn.

I'd love to live in a cozy apartment, nicely decorated with pillows, stuffed animals, a record-player, many records and lots of tropical jungle plants. I will invite my mother over for tea in the afternoon and later, getting married, move into a small mansion and having babies, many lovely little mongrels.

Mama says the school years are the best. I believe her. I wish I never cross twenty. I'm only fourteen now, I'll be fifteen in May. Everyone thinks I'm older but I wish I could stay young forever.

As far as boys go, it's such a problem. Well, no, just inconvenient at times. Hans Kröner, Fidel, Harry, etcetera, etcetera.

I'm taking dance lessons. Antoinette and I are in all the classes, Julia too. It's allowed because there are not enough boys.

I adore dancing! But skating gets squeezed out a bit now and that's a deadly sin! So, I've decided to go skating on Sunday.

For your information: I'm wearing glasses now.

In dance-school they say I'm a French type and that I resemble Francoise Hardy. It's because of my long hair. Now they call me the Special Attraction in school because that's what is printed behind my name in the program of the school party.

1964

I sang and it was great! Everyone loved it! First things first: Bob! Bob! Bob!

I always liked him. He's the drummer of the Dixie Pipers. I will never forget; it was such fun! Harry was also much nicer than at the rehearsals.

Nancy was a doll for me at first but in the meantime she stole Hans Kröner away from me. She threw herself at him. Hans and his friend Tom are in my dance class, Hans is so handsome. I've got to get him back but how?

Harry is in the hospital, he'll come home on Friday. Hans has a rock and roll band, The Ruffians. Marjorie also likes Bob. Bob is a student.

Hans forgot all about me. I have to tell you I sang a couple of times with the Dixie Pipers after the school party.

I never saw Bob again after that time. Tom went steady with Marjorie but she broke it off because she thought him very boring. Nothing happens these days. I think they all forgot about me. I'm walking barefoot.

1964

I don't think myself anything special with that thick red hair, all those freckles, blackheads, pimples, rods for legs, thin arms, elephant ears and my big hands. But I'm not ugly.

In my stories the funniest things happen but when I have to do something myself I'm dumbstruck, why can't I be like Kita van Dalen in my book? I want to be me again.

I'm so stupid! To pleasure my mother I add that I am a fresh know-it-all. She's right. I'm a pain in the neck and I don't want to be such a louse! What happened to that sweet, honest, shy little chubby girl from Kindergarten and First Grade? I'm not me anymore, I'm all different now. Nobody likes me anymore. If you only knew how fresh I am towards mom and dad sometimes. I'm a rotten teenager!

May 29, 1964

I turned fifteen yesterday. In general I'm alright but I have few summer cloths, I grew out of everything. It's annoying but can't be helped. I've joined a folkdance group: Chaverim We Chaverot.

Friday, one of the last days in January 1965

It's been ages since I wrote but I've got so little time now that I have to do my very best to succeed. The thought of the final exam makes me shudder.

Tonight I broke away, I did bookkeeping quickly, it was a balance columns so I didn't do the counting because if I do and then tomorrow I've got something wrong I have to make a mess of it, it's such a mess already! Well, then I quickly did two German exercises, the third one I'll do during the break. Now that it's so cold, Margot and I stay inside secretly, we first go to the WC until everyone's outside and the teachers behind their coffee and then we quickly sneak back into the classroom.

I've got to wash my hair; thank God it's a lot shorter; I had it cut in December.

March 18, 1965

How stupid I am! That's why I waited so long to write.

Mom and dad are fierce opponents of Italians, French, Spaniards and Negroes. I can understand. They are right; they are a different kind of people, habits, and etcetera. Much more high spirited than us. Mama says: 'You don't know those people. They are not educated; they come here out of need because they can't earn a thing down there.'

She said this when Marjorie put out a feeler by saying that there's always such a nice Spaniard in Extase whom she really likes. Mama was furious by which I can safely assume that I need not dare ever to start about Erminio. I'm not at all saying that I was planning to marry him; I'm also not saying that I wouldn't want to. Okay, I agree that there are many disadvantages but there is one big advantage. Obviously I am far too young to judge this matter and if my parents are opposed to it nothing rests me but to break it off with him although that won't be easy for me. However, it can't go on like this. One day it will end. I'm too unsteady of character to restrain myself and won't go dancing anymore. Last Sunday we were early in De Buitensoos because it was incredibly crowded. Erminio didn't come until eight-thirty and I thought he wasn't coming and the night was already ruined for me. I came to life when I saw him. All the girls know it and also that my parents mustn't find out about it. I am so sick of it! It seems as if you live in a completely different world and I can't talk to them at all. I would like to yell! If only I could tell mama, nice and easy, that I'm going steady with an Italian and could talk about him to her.

Friday, June 4, 1965

I'm singing! I am singing, yes, it's true! With a famous band here in Deventer. This good fortune just fell into my lap. Marjorie's friend Mary used to sing with them and when she heard me sing one time when Marjorie and I were at her house, the leader of the band, a guy named Hans, came by.

We talked and an audition date was set on Tuesday, May 25, and I went there. It was the house of the manager, Mister Flipse. They are nice boys: Max, Tony, Hans and Teddy, the son of the manager and his wife. He was very nice, his wife too. I sang Tous Les Garçons and Pouppée De Cire and he liked it immediately. He let me listen to two new songs on the tape-recorder: Santo Domingo and Der Abendwind, fine numbers that in the meantime I sang on stage already.

Saturday there was a party of the Playground Committee. We practiced four times of which the last rehearsal on Saturday morning was a total disaster.

It was alright at night but Mister Flipse said: 'Singing on stage for the first time in the open air is the most ungratifying there is because the sound dissipates.'

That's exactly what happened but even so it was great fun. The whole neighborhood was surprised to see me singing there. There were a lot of people but it was frightfully cold. There was no tent and if you didn't jump up and down to stay warm, you froze to death. I danced crazy with Freek van de Wal.

I've got a terrible cold now. My mother called Mister Flipse to say I couldn't come to practice because of my sore throat.

Yesterday Mister Flipse came to see me. I half expected it already for it's like him to do something like that. He stayed and chatted a long time. Joke Damman* who used to sing with them and is in ballet class with Marjorie (the school of Ymkje Bloema-de Jager) acted very arrogant when she went to see mister Flipse on Tuesday to give him a piece of her mind about what a dirty trick it is that they now have me as their singer.

She told Marjorie that mister Flipse has asked her to sing with them again but that she refused because she'll start as a professional ballet-teacher in September. Ha!

- Joke Damman became known all of over Holland in the nineties as Yomanda, the amazing faith healer. Later on she was on trial; she was held responsible for the death of a Dutch television star, Sylvia Millecam, who refused to let herself be treated for cancer because Yomanda had convinced her she didn't have cancer and that she would recover. Sylvia Millecam had breast-cancer and died; Joke Damman lives somewhere in Canada these days I heard.

How ridiculous and what a blatant lie! She got her way though because Saturday the band will give her an official goodbye. Mister Flipse told me and mom that it became impossible to keep Joke. She sang dreadful, just awful, completely out of key and Mister Flipse had to swallow a lot of criticism from people because she was so terrible. He assures me all the time that he has a lot of confidence in me and that I certainly will become a valued member of the band because I have plenty of self-criticism.

I will take singing lessons because there is room for improvement in my voice. It still sounds too ordinary; it must become something beautiful, something special.

The band has their own club where there is dancing every Sunday afternoon and every Saturday night they perform by invitations in Deventer and surroundings. They even have a Fan Club. I'm going to become very busy: rehearsals, new repertoire and so on. I love it all! I want to do my utmost to be very good so that everyone is content about me. I'm still very unsure but that will change when I perform more I hope. What a pity I can't sing yet this Saturday, my throat hurts so much and I have a hacking cough.

I want to do great French songs like Dans La Neige of Guy Béart but also German and English and naturally not just slow songs.

We didn't talk about money but Marjorie says they put it into a pot and they save for better equipment. When Joke needed a dress or shoes she got them. I like that even more than money. Now and then we go out to dinner together also on Sundays.

July 14, 1965

You don't know how hard it is to get a job. Every time when I apply for a job I come back in a foul mood. I'm going to go to the Deventer News or the Deventer Post. Anyone who sees the marks on my diploma can see that I'm great in languages. It has got to be possible to do something with that. When I'm making money I'm going to save for a type-writer and then I'm going to write all night long. How wonderful that will be! Our manager is still on holiday, I guess they'll come back this weekend. I'll be glad when he is back, I miss him a little. As it so happens, I'm a bit in love with him. It sounds insane I know and it's not the same feeling as if you're in love with a handsome boy. Mister F acts as if I'm his daughter and he knows I like that. In a little while I have rehearsal with the band. Although Mister F ...oh, shit...Max, our lead-guitarist, keeps a tight schedule, we learned three new songs, perhaps four tonight; I must hurry.

Tuesday, July 20, 1965

I have to solve all my problems myself, no one to guide and help me. I don't know if that's right. Perhaps you grow strong and independent when you have to raise yourself. I made so many mistakes already. Thank God, no fatal ones! I'm thinking of Erminio. I'm proud of myself because I was really crazy about him but I withstood all the temptations. I will never forget him. He was so sweet and awfully handsome. Maybe it's because I don't have brothers that I fall in love too easily.

I…it's stupid I know but I am in love with Mister F but… I must be honest, I kissed him. It happened on the night he drove me home from the performance in Schalkhaar. I'm so ashamed of myself! I can't even put it into words! I don't know how it happened or why, it just did, suddenly….oh, it's awful! I am so ashamed! I can't understand myself, how could this have happened?

After that night he went on holiday so I didn't see him for three weeks.

Yesterday when I went to his business for rehearsal my knees were shaking, I was nervous as hell and thought I would burst into tears when I saw him again.

He opened the door himself and I amazed myself by saying, immediately: 'Hello, Sir, did you have a nice holiday? I passed the final exam.' He has said to me several times already to call him Theo but I can't do that.

He congratulated me and wanted to know my marks. Everything was normal as if the kiss never happened. I'm so relieved and glad because we go on vacation on Saturday so I won't see his wife for a while and don't have to make myself a nervous wreck about that. Mr. F must have pulled a joke on me that night of course. He thought I was in love with him but that's not true! It's ridiculous!

I just like him, that's all but I don't want to be in romantic involvements with him, that's logical I would say! He acts like a father to me, that's alright; he doesn't have a daughter so I can be his adopted daughter. Ha, that's funny! I must talk to him first chance I get. That night I was totally upset, couldn't sleep, shaking in my bed. I wanted to leave the band. I told Mr. F but he stressed that I must stay. Anyway, how was I going to explain my sudden departure to everyone? Furthermore I can't give up the band anymore. To be on stage and to sing is marvelous! I'm never as good at rehearsals as I am on stage. I just love to sing!

Mr. F thinks I'm special, he said so many times already. I'm glad I wrote about my false step and I will remember it forever. No matter how grave your mistakes are if you reveal everything honestly to yourself and everyone, people will take a milder view of you. Even if they don't, you

will be able to forgive yourself and the chance that you'll make the same
mistake again will be smaller or gone altogether.

Tuesday, August 10, 1965

We're just back from our fortnight vacation. I've got a nice color on
my back and my face and tummy too. I got a real nice bikini and daddy
took 36 photos, imagine!

I've had the best holiday in three years. I never thought I could fall in love
with Johnny, I always thought he was a sweet, nice, helpful boy. He's
only fifteen. And he loves me. He said so.

He said: 'When you smile I could just eat you up.'

He's so sweet and protective and strong and smart. I don't feel that I'm a
year older than him at all. I wouldn't mind marrying him, much later of
course, when I'm older.

Somewhere in 1965

I didn't put a date on purpose. This is my last entry, I will never write
in my diary anymore.

I'm different now. That's all I can say.

I would like to study psychology in University. I'm interested in what moves people, why do they act the way they do, what are their motives? Man, his thoughts, his feelings, that's what interests me!

I have a good life despite my many contradictions; I sing with a band. The boys in the band like me. I've got friends and always someone to talk to. I've got a good father and a sweet mother and my sisters. I have everything I could possibly want. I am happy! Later when I'm married and my children big, I want to write. Now I can't write anymore. It's all over!

Chapter 2

Young, carefree and ambitious

The manager of the band was short, about five feet two or thereabouts; he was chubby and his looks were that of the tired decrepit salesman. He owned a wholesale business in bicycles, motorbikes and their parts in the center of town. The forty-eight years old man had a flabby moon-face with slicked-down black graying hair and could by no stretch of the imagination be called a handsome devil, however, he had a certain charisma and my younger self was very much taken in by him.

Obviously it thrilled me that here was someone, a grown-up, who seemed to understand me, who recognized my singing talent, who believed in me.

After that first kiss more kissing followed, always on the sly so as not to alert the boys of the band and although I felt bad about it I also felt very grown-up and it excited me.

The Italian fellow, Erminio, who after four months had not gotten any further than first base with me, tried his luck one afternoon in the park. As if stung by a bee when I felt his hand sliding up between my

thighs, I bit his other hand. His painful howl echoed   through the
whole park, however, before he had a chance to do something, I had
already jumped up and got on my bike. That was the end of that harmless
affair.

The manager of the band took advantage of my innocence and my
adoration for him. One day he lured me into a nightly drive; parking his
car in some secluded area, he persuaded me to sit on the backseat with
him to neck and kiss.

'Come sit on my lap, darling,' he said while pulling my pants down.
Why did I not bite in his hand that time?

Before I knew what was happening he had stuck his hard dick into me
and, panting like a pig, reached orgasm within seconds. I screamed when a
flaming pain shot through me while he kept saying: 'Did you come? Are
you coming?'

I had no idea what he was talking about. What did he mean? Coming?
Where? I was completely in shock, full of guilt feelings and confusion.

I had to carry on as if nothing had happened but my attraction for him
had vanished instantly after he had violated me like that and a week later
when his son wanted to sing a Rolling Stones song I had set my sights on,
all hell broke loose.

'Egotistical bastard!' I shouted, 'I want to sing *I Can't Get Satisfaction!* Why do you always give Teddy the best songs! I'm sick and tired of it, you are such an asshole!'

I glared at him, mad with rage while the boys looked on stupefied. Without further ado I turned and stampeded out of the rehearsal room.

Still furious and terribly upset I ranted and raved inwardly while bicycling home and as soon as I burst into the house I gave my mother an accurate account of what had transpired at the rehearsal.

Instinctively my mother knew something had to be terribly wrong for me to be cursing the manager like that; she smelled a rat. Her grey-blue eyes widened, a strange look came over her face and almost simultaneously a veil of sadness shrouded her.

She quickly pulled herself together though; she sat me down and extracted the truth of what had happened out of me.

Our general physician examined me and quietly asked if I couldn't have kept my legs closed. I didn't answer, in fact from the time my mother alerted the authorities I withdrew into myself, only spoke when absolutely necessary and, as if I was in mourning, wore black garments for months.

The police were alerted and the officer told my parents that if I hadn't just turned sixteen they would have arrested the man immediately because they wouldn't have needed my parents to press charges.

The manager's wife and his brother-in-law came with sad and solemn faces to talk with my parents. Luckily for me the idea of a court-case was abandoned eventually. I shudder to think how awful it would've been for me had I been called to testify in court. My parents received the money due to me for my singing and put it into a savings-account. I felt stupid and guilty for a very long time, sad too, not only because of the shame of it all but also because my life in the spotlight had come to an abrupt standstill.

My glorious days of the pretty singer of the band - posters all over town, a Fan club, every weekend singing on stage, the club Sunday afternoons, articles with photos in the newspaper, being always the center of attention – it was all over now.

Resilience is one of the positive traits of the young and, in my case, falling in love easily, helped to ease the pain.

~

May 19, 1966

So much happened, I'd like to write a lot of things down but that's not possible. I have neuritis in my right arm. How did I get it? I don't know except that it's bothering me a long time already. It began two years ago. I'm such a fool for never wanting to go see a doctor. Now you see what happens!

Every day I have to go for an injection in my arm, now every other day. I can't type anymore; even playing the guitar is difficult. It hurts. I do it anyway but only one song at the time, I mean I play a song then I wait for a long while before I can play another song. I have to stop now, my arm hurts a lot.

May 30, 1966

First off I have to tell you that I sang for almost a year with The Skybolts. In the middle of January or thereabouts it was all over. It's something I absolutely cannot talk about, maybe later.

Evidently I haven't stood on stage for about five months!

I miss it terribly!

Tuesday, June 14, 1966

I was on television! Yes, I was! I entered a competition to sing like a famous star. I would've liked to do a song of Marianne Faithful (I can sing just like her) but in the end I did the song of Sandy Shaw with which she won the Eurovision Song festival. My parents and sisters encouraged me to enter; the pre-selection was in the Minerva Pavilion in Amsterdam. There were twenty contestants. I think I sang okay but my mom and sisters said I was the best. I won together with two other girls and two weeks later was the taping of the show.

It was nerve racking but it went very well. Mama bought me a new dress and I looked great if I say so myself. Everybody complimented me on my singing. What a wonderful experience.

August 17, 1966

I sang in Loosdrecht, the Cabaret Festival. I sang well, mama and Lilly confirmed it but unfortunately I didn't win.

I cried but later I thought that was quite silly of me, there will be other opportunities. That's what mama and Lilly said to me also.

September 4, 1966

The music season has started again. There was a big advertisement in the newspaper of the Skybolts. I thought about being back in the club, singing. It was all so wonderful then. Posters everywhere and everybody knew me and liked me. We had so much success! I was famous, not only in Deventer but all over the province. Everybody recognized me. And I always had so much fun with the boys, Tony, the drummer especially. When I think of all the misery that followed I shudder but I am not going to think about that anymore.

December 11, 1966

Mama says: 'It can't always be gloomy, fun times are coming again, you just wait and see.' That cheers me up. Mama doesn't half know how sweet I think she is.

March 10, 1967

God, it's such a mess in the world. Just take that war in Vietnam for instance. When I see all the misery on television and read the paper I feel like crying. I feel so meaningless, small, and impotent. I wish the devil would abandon people.

Hey, I've got a motor-bike! I saved and saved and saved and now I'm só happy!

May 18, 1967

We moved. We live in Alkmaar now. Marjorie and I haven't found a job yet but we're trying. Lilly stayed in Deventer to finish her last year of high school. She lives with big Lilly and her husband Jacob. I miss my little sister so much. Big Lilly is about to give birth to her first baby. I just practiced my guitar, now my fingertips hurt. It's lovely here: the dunes, beaches and...the North Sea of course!

August 1, 1967

I'm still going steady with Johnny or should I say I am again going steady with him. I love him but sometimes I can't stand him when he acts like such a child. It's the fault of his stupid family. I love him but I also don't know what it is with me, I guess I'm just very fickle.

This Saturday I'll have my first singing lesson with Bep Ogterob in Amsterdam. I'm so curious about it. Will I become a real great singer?

I want to marry Johnny and have babies. My sister Marjorie broke off with Koos. I hate that stupid guy! I worried so much about it last night; I thought I could write him a letter and maybe he will come back to her. But then I thought it's not such a good idea.

December 3, 1967

Johnny and I are engaged, on December 3rd. My arm hurts so much. I will be operated on in January in the University Hospital in Leiden. Can't write more, arm hurts too much.

May 9, 1968

Today Johnny and I are going steady for one year. Unfortunately he's not allowed to come here anymore. We've had a lot of fights and problems. It's me I think but him too. At times I just can't stand him!

In March I was operated on my arm by Professor Luyendijk. It was alright. The pain slowly went away.

Last Monday, Frans Peters who has a sound-studio here in Alkmaar did a recording of me. I accompanied myself on guitar and he loved it. He said he will let someone of Philips Record Company listen to it.

Thursday, June 6, 1968

Today at 1.44 p.m. Robert Kennedy died. On Wednesday an Arab fired three shots at him. One bullet went into his brain. He was operated on immediately but alas, to no avail. He is dead.

Just like Dr. Martin Luther King, who was killed about two months ago and like his brother, President John F. Kennedy four and a half years ago. It is so shocking!

Society appears to be rotten to the core and not only in America. All around us it's nothing but misery! The war in Vietnam continues.

I felt like crying when I heard that Robert Kennedy got assassinated too. It is so awful!

What possesses people? He is dead; another senseless act of violence.

I'm cold; I'm sitting in a skimpy baby-doll on my bed.

Johnny is allowed into our home again. They don't like him very much around here I think; he's boisterous, he spends too much money…anyway, who cares? I love him. My sisters hate him.

I hate him too sometimes.

Frans Peters says he really likes my songs but I don't trust him, he's windbag I think.

I have a teddy bear that I still take to bed with me; I'm a certified nut, eh?

July 29, 1969

Oh, I forgot to tell you, on July 20 1969, man set foot on the moon. Idiotic, isn't it? Or should I say wondrous?

It was exciting and at the same time so touching to see Andrews and Armstrong walking around on the moon. I find it amazing. Thursday, tomorrow, they'll come back to earth. It's wonderful to experience something like this.

October 28, 1969

First, I've got to tell you that we've been there! Where?

Ibiza of course! Johnny and I went there on vacation, that amazing beautiful island in the Mediterranean Sea.

As soon as I got out of the plane the little island conquered me. You could call it love at first sight.

I want to write a story about Ibiza, yes!

Nowadays you see many hippies! They dress queer and extreme and come from all over the world to Amsterdam. Their vision of modern life and our society is new and they express themselves openly. Fascinating I think.

I'm not so happy because at night I'm too tired to do the things I love doing most and in the daytime I'm doing office work that doesn't interest me in the least. It bores me to death in fact. I feel as if I'm not living the life I should be living. I'm becoming a person without substance.

October 8, 1970

I sang on the radio four times already, it's going well. I perform in Amsterdam in the Zodiac, the Cloppertje and I'm part of shows for old folks in homes.

I went to the Music Fair and met a lyricist with whom I made an appointment to visit him in Loosdrecht. I'm in contact with Ruud Jacobs (brother of the jazz pianist Pim Jacobs); I've been to his house several times already. He works for CBS Records. I'm also in touch with Nico Knapper who promised to come listen to me in the Zodiac.

Fashion is great these days: mini, maxi, midi, wigs, make-up. It's all fabulous! I long for Johnny. It won't be long now before we'll have our own place. That will be so nice.

June 1, 1971

Lilly and I went to Paris in May. It was great! Paris is a city to fall in love with at first sight! We walked so much and saw everything and we had so much fun! I turned twenty-two on Friday.

December 10, 1971

Johnny has got his flying license. He always wanted to become a pilot but his eyesight isn't perfect.

Last year I went with him to Zestienhoven, he had a flying lesson and I was allowed aboard.

It was a Cessna and it was wonderful! We flew over Zeeland and I loved it.

Johnny has many hobbies like photography for instance. He built his own underwater camera and because I'm his favorite model I have to go with him to the swimming pool and swim under water all the time so he can take pictures. I have a lot of great photos of myself now. Last year he was into model planes; that was so much fun! Daddy really liked it too. And then the race-track of course and the trains, toys. Daddy has a whole train contraption set up in the attic. It's too bad for daddy that he doesn't have a son. He and Johnny get on so well; they are compatible, they love to tinker with electronics and that sort of thing. And they both have a great sense of humor.

Daddy has always liked Johnny, much more than my mother who thinks Johnny is not the right man for me, she once told me that she thinks he is overpowering me too much. I think she has a point there because I always seem to go along with what he wants.

December 12, 1971

I'm going to move out of my parents' home. Perhaps when I have my own place I'll start writing again.

Johnny is in the army and doesn't come home much anymore. He's stationed on the island Terschelling, the Air Force; he loves it.

I went there a couple of weekends ago; there was a big party. We drank like swine.

I've got my driving-license. Lil is going to move also.

December 17, 1971

I met someone special. I was with Johnny the weekend and we didn't go out Saturday night which was okay but Sunday he was in his dark room all day and paid no attention to me whatsoever. I felt lonely. I asked him to go for a walk with me but he didn't hear me because he was totally preoccupied with his first color prints.

I got angry with him and left, slamming the door. I thought I'm going to sit on the terrace of the Victoria Hotel and if I see a nice looking guy I'm going to flirt.

I didn´t but instead walked through the Kalverstraat looking at the shop windows. When I came to the Rembrandtplein a young man approached me. I saw that he was a hippie right away but he seemed sympathetic. He was Mexican and gave me a piece of hashish. He said I should heat it and crumble it into tobacco and roll a cigarette, a joint they call it. He said I really should try it because it was very nice. I accepted it, smiled at him and said goodbye.

I haven´t smoked it yet but I put it in a little box. Maybe I will smoke it one day.

~

Not one diary entry in 1972 which is a pity because in that year I met a man who would become a major influence in my life.

Actually, before I met him Lilly and I met another man with whom I fell in love instantly. Piet Hein was his name and he never went anywhere without his Martin guitar that he played very well. He invited us to a farm in Brabant near the Belgium border one weekend and what a great time

Lil and I had there. Aside from Piet Hein there were six other young men, musicians, artists and loafers, most of them with long hair and mustaches which was in vogue those days. We took a walk in the surrounding countryside, chased cows and later cooked a meal together. Afterwards someone chopped wood for the fireplace, guitars and flutes and recorders came out and one of them rolled a giant joint that went around. I sang too but felt rather inadequate because my guitar playing wasn't as good as the other guitarists especially Piet Hein.

'Don't worry about it,' my sister told me later when we were in stitches because we were afraid to put our heads down on the dirty pillows on the bed, 'you sing better than anyone of those boys.' Piet Hein and I were an item for about two months, however, after the weekend in Brabant I never heard from him again except years later when he wrote me a very sweet letter in calligraphy which I always kept.

My sister Lilly and I moved out of my parents' home to Amsterdam at the same time, in the beginning of 1972. Lilly had rooms with an elderly couple and I with newly-weds.

After a few months we discovered it was possible for us to get an apartment in a newly developed suburb, the Bijlmermeer, for less money that we each paid to our landlords added up. It made a lot of sense to move especially since Lil was getting pretty fed up with the nosiness of the old people who didn't shrink back from showing her room to visitors while my sister was lying in bed. I also had my stomach full of the lovebirds; every morning I had to sprint out of bed to beat the guy to the bathroom or else I'd be late for work again.

My sister Marjorie and her very nice, funny and attractive boyfriend Ben got married on December 27, 1971 and consequently my parents had to say goodbye to their three daughters within three months time. It was especially hard for my mother.

Lil and I now worked for a temporary agency in Amsterdam and were placed with the same company in Sloterdijk. I had first worked for the taxman in Alkmaar, then with a cranky, crazy dentist, then at the shipping office of Holland's largest steel mill in IJmuiden before I switched to taking various jobs via the temporary jobs agency.

Living together with Lilly in our cozy brand new apartment in the Bijlmer was great and remains in my memory as one of the happiest periods of my life.

My romance with Johnny that had lasted off and on from 1966 till 1972 had run its course. We fell in love while camping in the dunes near Bloemendaal with our families but eventually, over the years, we outgrew each other.

When Johnny had to join the army and was stationed on the island Terschelling I lost him to the games young men play and when he told me one day that he thought he was falling in love with a girl he met on the island my world collapsed.

Johnny, who had a black belt in judo at sixteen, loved and excelled in several sports; with his dark looks and ingratiating manner coupled with the masculinity of the Air Force uniform, he became quite the ladies man.

At first I was pretty naïve, thinking he just stayed in during weekends to play tennis, however, reality forced me to face up to the truth. He failed to show up for stretches of more than six, seven weeks and although I at first didn't believe he was in love with another girl (I thought he was just saying that to make me jealous) things weren't the same between us anymore.

I met other men; at work, in the music scene and although we kept up the pretense that we loved each other and were supposed to get married, we never talked about the trousseau, the wedding, the honeymoon and our own place anymore.

In fact when he did skip a weekend at 'Terschelling with the boys' to be with me, we either fought and consequently stayed in each other's company without speaking or we were still not talking since the last fight and ended up in another terrible row. Obviously the zap was out of it and the affair was slowly but surely bleeding to death. And then there he was: the poet.

~

Chapter 3

A married woman

Amsterdam, December 6, 1973

I love seeing myself in the newspaper; I still have all the clippings from my time with the Skybolts.

I keep looking at this photo, I look só pretty! I'm looking over the head of the photographer mysteriously into the distance, wearing a red turban; it looks so professional, refined, like an arrived celebrity. The piece written about me is grossly exaggerated, like that style of sensationalism of Henk van der Meyden of the Telegraaf but never mind, I'm flattered.

I received five large photos of myself; very nice of the photographer.

My husband says they're good enough to try out as a model. I don't know. He's sleeping now. I'm trying to put his poem *Modus Operandi* to music and I think that what I came up with is very good. Another poem of his, *Emptiness,* I put to music already and I've sent it to the BUMA.

I'd like to sing it right now but I won't, it's late and I don't want to irritate anyone. I only practice well when I'm alone.

The course I'm taking with the Amateur Theatre School is very interesting. My group is taught by Gelijn Molier.

Since I'm with Lee and especially since our marriage something is happening; my whole personality seems to be changing. I have such lovely dreams.

I feel as if I'm entering a different dimension; Lee is the ideal man I think. He is warm, of high moral caliber, he is wise and his spirit is vibrant, soulful, and resonant. I'm very happy with him. He's a real friend to me.

Hamlet, my grey tragic cat and his brother Othello, my naughty, affectionate black cat are pooped, one in front of the fireplace and the other one curled up on the couch.

I shall read the newspaper and let's see what's on television.

I must get myself another good gig: I did three months in the Hilton Hotel which was super but now I am without work for two months already. I write many letters with copies of the articles about me but alas…so far nothing has happened yet.

I did register with the Sylvain Show Theatre Office and the man there seemed very positive about getting me work in a nightclub. I have little faith in it though…so often things seemed promising only to fall through later on.

Lou van Rees (theatrical agent) wrote me a letter asking me to be patient a little longer. Hope is what gets me through the day.

December 8, 1973

Yesterday Lee and I saw *Rosemary's Baby,* shocking. Afterwards we went to Eylders Café on the Leidseplein. We saw many acquaintances, Roland also. He's a young poet and plays the guitar as well. Lee knows his father a long time already.

Lee said I should act better. He said that I flirted with Roland and that I don't have much personality and inner strength and that's why people don't respect me. He says that I'm still very young and have a lot to learn. Bull!
He's just jealous because I'm twenty-two years younger than he is. Ha! I have enough personality. He ruined everything just as I was in a loving mood. He was rude, said that he had other things on his mind. Well, I can understand that because we are indeed pretty broke.

We married on May 4, 1973, at 9.30 in the morning. The fourth of May is the national remembrance day of World War II victims; it was a Friday, drizzling but when the justice of the peace recited *The Marriage* from *The Prophet* of the Lebanese poet Kahlil Gibran, the sun broke through full force and the rest of the day was glorious. Ben and Marjorie and mom and dad and grandpa and grandma were present as well as a few friends. After the ceremony we had coffee and cake at the Krasnapolsky Hotel and later we walked through the Vondelpark. We dined in Bali, the Indonesian Restaurant on the Leidseplein. Ben made photos that came out lovely Lee and I went on honeymoon to Copenhagen for three days that was wonderful, I especially liked Tivoli Gardens.

Too bad Lilly couldn't be at our wedding; she works as a tour guide in Spain these days. That was the only setback as far as I'm concerned. I wore a black and white beautiful dress with a great hat with voile and Lee had a black and white suit made by his tailor Tjerk Kok. Lee is very handsome...I adore him!

Ah, there he is, time to have supper now!

December 9, 1973

I just heard that the record industry will have to press fewer records because of the oil crisis; p.c.v, a by-product of oil, is necessary in this process.

Beginning artists like yours truly will be the losers according to the newspapers and television.

What is going to happen? Will this oil crisis jeopardize the world economy? I don't know but everybody is complaining and it doesn't look very bright.

Lee and I want to go south.

Omar called and asked if he could stay with us for a few days. Helen and he are having problems. Helen is a Dutch writer, a bit of a strange type if you ask me. I am twenty-four now and Lee and I have been married for seven months. We live in a furnished four rooms flat at the Amstelveenseweg overlooking the Vondelpark. We have a great view with balcony in front as well as in the back where you can see the canal. It's so lovely here.

Lee has come up with an idea to make money. It's called Afro American Special Tour

Service. He has already registered it with the Chamber Of Commerce. We've had several tourists already, it's going well. We have brochures for which Shouki did the layout, really great.I'm madly in love with my husband and want to write about him. He's forty-six, a Gemini like me and tall, slim, well built. He is a black American and liked by everyone. He's always very charming and sympathetic. He knows a lot of people, has had many women. I'm his first and only wife. He told me that when he was eighteen he said to himself that he swouldn't marry before forty-five.

He's a sharp dresser and designs most of his clothes that are made for him by his tailor Tjerk Kok, a very amicable man. People think he's only thirty-five; he lied to me in the beginning when he told me he was thirty-nine but I thought he was around thirty or thereabouts. I don't care about him being so much older than I; I love him, that's all that matters to me.

My parents were upset about it at first but later, after they met him that was no issue anymore.

He's poet, a very good one I think but I'm not objective and my English isn't up to par yet. Some of his poems are too difficult for me to understand. He published a lot and also wrote a book. He's a realist I think, he abhors politics. He also has a great sense of humor, of the utmost importance in a man as far as I'm concerned. For me he is the sweetest and most handsome man in the world.

Another thing, I'm a month late with my period. Lee and I would love to have a baby, Lee especially.

December 16, 1973

Well, my period came so…I feel rotten. I'm waiting for a   phone-call from Lee.   He's in Germany.

I went to my parents over the weekend and took Hamlet and Othello with me. It was nice being home again.

Lee calls me every day. The first time he called I was so nervous I just laughed. Silly me, I wanted to ask him a million things.

The phone rang, it wasn't him but Ger Akkerman; she is the mother of Jan

Akkerman, the guitarist. Anyway, she told me she left her husband Jacob

and asked me if I knew of a place where she can stay. I'll make some

phone-calls tomorrow; I hope I can help her. What problems people have!

They've been married for years and have two grown sons. Jan wants

nothing to do with his parents anymore; they were the ones who got him

started. They used to travel to Austria and Germany with Jan, their

prodigy.

 Ger has booked me many times already, she is great, and I also like

Jacob. Their house on the Transvaalstraat is an open house for musicians.

 My sister Marjorie is very heavy with child now, about six months. I

can't wait to welcome their first baby! Lee and I went to visit them; their

house in the country is so beautiful!

We've had some people over on Sunday. Joyce and Theo with their two

kids, Liam and Tess who brought some others, Harry and his girlfriend

and Shouki. Keith didn't come; he and Shouki are having problems and

want to separate. Omar came too of course. It was nice although I'm not

your ideal hostess yet; I intend to do better next time.

December 30, 1973

Another year almost gone. New Year's Eve we're going to a party at The

American Disaster; the group Sail are going to play. I'm sure it's going to

be a regular riot!

I performed in Deventer both Christmas days. I had a lot of success. Lee and I visited my parents before and exchanged gifts while eating fondue, it was so cozy.

Ger Akkerman is back with her husband. She came here and we had a lot of fun. After awhile she decided to call her husband; he came and I went to bed. They went home together. All is well that ends well but in the morning I saw that the Makkumer plate (a wedding gift from my grandparents) was lying on the floor. It's s pity because it's chipped. Ger and Jacob say that it suddenly sailed off the wall and landed at Ger's chair. She thinks it's black magic because Jacob wouldn't let her be my witness at our wedding. She told me she will pay for it. We'll see; it's rather expensive.

On January 12, I have to sing in the Student Club Lanx, Ger booked me there.

Oh, I suddenly remember, Lee and I should have gone over to Le Bon Marriage for the radio show, Ronnie Potsdammer invited us. We forgot all about it. Well, we'll go next week. Trio Louis van Dyke will play then. I invited mom and dad so they can go with us. I'm sure they will like it.

I have a nice little Christmas tree; the cats keep crawling under it.

Lilly is doing well on the Canary Islands.

January 9, 1973

I feel lonely, I wish Lee was here. Sometimes I feel like meeting a new man. In 1972 I had three lovers: Huub, Fred and Klaas. Huub Soudant was on television Sunday, he conducted the Broadcasting Orchestra and Willem Duys interviewed him. I always called him Soudant instead of Huub which is a bit strange. I really liked him in the beginning. And Daniel who used to perform in the Ognibeni with me. He is from Mozambique and was mad about me. He cried when I told him I was getting married to Lee. Ger took care of him for awhile; he uses mescaline and she gave him an ultimatum to quit doing that or leave. I never knew; that goes to show you!

Soudant was so charming especially because he stutters; it's very cute when a man stutters I think.

Lee never told me he loved me but now he's crazy about me. However, he has kept up his life of a bachelor, I hardly see him; he's never home!

We went to Le Bon Marriage last Sunday with mom and dad. It was nice and I believe they enjoyed themselves.

Tuesday my friend Vicky came from Wassenaar where she works as an au-pair with the Canadian Ambassador. We met when I did a performance there, I really like her, she's a Gemini like Lee and I.

There was another exhibition in Eylders. It got very late but we had so much fun; Omar, Liam, Laura, Vicky, Lee and I went to the Bamboo bar afterwards and Liam went home with us. He and Vicky slept together in the guest room.

January 23, 1974

My performance in Lanx went terrific.

Lilly is back, I'm so glad. I spoke to Hans Boskamp yesterday, he said he'd like to help me and introduce me to Lou van Rees, the man for me according to him. Well, I know Lou van Rees already and so far…nothing.

Hans Boskamp is a well-known actor and is in a play in Rotterdam at the moment.

Nothing happens lately. I'm studying medieval songs for Tourist Shows of Call Tiffany together with the Hilton.

They had a delay because of the renovators of the warehouse on the Rechtboomsloot. I'm not too keen about it for it pays little and no contract, black money but something is better than nothing. Vicky is coming to stay with us this weekend.

January 27, 1974

The end of the month and bills piling up. How we live! Boy, it's crazy yet somehow we always seem to manage.

Ger has been here again. Jacob threw her out. I couldn't believe all the stuff she hoisted up here; suitcases, bags with shoes, a sewing machine, hair rollers, sheets, towels.

Lee stored it all in our attic room.

Well, what a mess! Telephone calls, Jacob rummaging about in the neighborhood. Jesus!

Ger absolutely didn't want to talk to him; however, she left the next day to another   friend in Landsmeer. Last Sunday she called to say she's back with Jacob and if they could come by to pick up her things. They brought us a bottle of jenever. I feel sorry for Jacob who seemed so embarrassed. It's sad when people are together for almost thirty years and have these kinds of problems of not understanding one another anymore; it happens all the time.

Vicky and I spent hours on the flea market on the Waterlooplein. She bought two blouses and I bought silk flowered pants, only ten guilders.

I saw Hans Boskamp again in Eylders last night. He said he'll listen to my cassette over the weekend.

February 19, 1974

I was in a movie, via Call Tiffany, something else that was! A medieval caper, ferocious looking Viking men, distressed maidens with pigtails in low-cut dresses. It was a Norwegian commercial for beer. Such fun! I'd like to be in other movies.

Anyway, Jos Stelling is making another film again. I was in his first

movie, Mariken van Nimwhegen.

Someone called from World Wide Pictures in Haarlem about a movie

they're doing about World War II. They got my number from Gelijn

Molier, my drama teacher.

Unfortunately Lee was ill during the beer commercial shooting so I

worried a lot about him and quit early the last day. His fever was so high.

I also got an offer from KRO radio to sing two songs in the program

Between Twelve and Two.

I sang Lee's poem We'll Go On and Farewell of Brendan Beehan

translated into Dutch by Cees Nooteboom.

When I came home the next day there was a telegram from Dureco

Record Company.

They are very interested in me and asked me to call them. They want to do

an LP with me with only Dutch songs.

Hymie, a South-African sweet big man, an acquaintance of Lee, wants to

introduce me to Hans Kellerman, he's with Negram Records.

I spoke with Dino D'Ellena Productions who want to hear me sing.

Today Mister Zwart of the Okura Hotel called. He heard about me from

Pepa Hollander from Call Tiffany. They are looking for a singer so we

made an appointment.

Those women of Call Tiffany, Pepa and Genevieve, are very nice to me.

Never heard from Hans Boskamp anymore, that figures!

Genevieve called just now. I have to go to the Warehouse for a photo
session for Holland Herald Magazine.

Oh yes, on February 2nd, my grandparents had their 50th wedding
anniversary. Lee and I went to Friesland and stayed in hotel De Kroon, at
least that was the plan but when we returned from the party at three
o'clock in the morning, we couldn't get in. We went next door, to the
Oranje Hotel which was more expensive.

Lilly is staying with us. Unfortunately she's going abroad again.

February 25, 1974

Out of seven nights a week Lee is gone five or six. I'm always alone.
He rarely takes me with him. We had a fight about it on Saturday.
But he won't talk about it; he says he can't change his habits. He was so
mean to me. We made up later but he never said sorry. Well, what can I
do?

I knew he was a man who goes his own way when I married him. I love
him anyway. I was always waiting for him to call me when I still lived in
the Bijlmermeer with Lilly. And no matter at what odd hour he called, I
hurried to go to him whenever he wanted me to.

Once when Johnny visited me shortly after we broke up, to get something
or bring something, I can't remember, I was in the shower. Johnny waited
for me to come out and when I did the phone rang while I was drying my
hair; it was Lee. He asked me to come right away because Keith and

Shouki were getting married the next day. Naturally I apologized to
Johnny and left immediately.

Keith and Shoukie are separated. At the moment she's in Ibiza and he in
Surinam.

February 26, 1972

Lee dreamt of me last night. He was in a theater with me watching a
play but I kept going on stage to act in the play and he was so afraid for
the end when the man would kiss me and I would leave with him.
And that's what happened and Lee kept searching for me trying to get
close to me but he didn't succeed for there were too many people.
Darling Lee.

February 27, 1974

I've been hired to sing in the Okura Hotel, I'm so happy!

March 3, 1974

I was in Haarlem this afternoon. I saw Fred Hilberdink to talk about
that war movie. It's about a woman who hid a lot of Jews during the war.
She was sent to Ravensbrück but survived. She's a spry, eighty-year-old
woman and her name is Corrie Boon.

I think it's so interesting. I have to play a girl who gets drunk with two German soldiers. It's an American Film Company. It doesn't pay very much, only fifty-five guilders a day.

Today I started at the Okura. It was okay, a little tough later when a large group of Spaniards arrived.

Henk van der Meyden of the Telegraaf came by; he said he'll send someone to take my picture for the newspaper.

April 1, 1974

Today I got a call from Paris from Mister van Dam of the Inter-Continental Hotel there. He said the Inter-Conti of Abidjan, Ivory Coast, are looking for a singer/guitarist. He said it's for a couple of months and pays five hundred dollars a month. I said yes immediately but after talking to Lee about it later I realized I can't go without him.

So I called Mister van Dam and explained to him that my husband will have to come along. He said he'll send me a telex. It's very exciting, imagine Africa!

Lee and I are still trying to make a baby. I had bought a book called Astrological Birth Planning. Very interesting.

I was so foolish to tell Lee days in advance about the key hours when we should make love.

This month it was Friday at one o'clock in the afternoon. I had drawn the curtains, lighted candles and incense; we drank some wine, smoked a joint, did a couple of lines, we even had some hash candy. All of this we thought would get us into the right mood while Marvin Gay sang in the background and we lay down on the pillows in front of the fireplace. Alas, Lee couldn't perform which is to be understood with all the pressure I put on him and, to make things worse, we knew my uncle Jaap was going to ring our doorbell at about three o'clock. His wife, Aunt Tonnie is in the hospital, she has been operated on - her uterus that was full of cancer has been removed – and he always visits us after he sees her and before he goes back North. So, we stopped and got dressed again. Sure enough, at exactly three the doorbell rang. What foolishness, eh?

I have to keep important fucking hours to myself from now on. Last night there was a riot at the Warehouse. A group of students demonstrated against the Hilton throwing extravagant parties there whereas the warehouse should be used to house the homeless, they say. I guess they have a point. So, we couldn't perform. It got quite ugly actually.

April 23, 1974

My sister Marjorie just gave birth to a son. All is well with her. Lee and I are aunt and uncle now. I'm so happy for her and Ben. Mama thinks his name is Roelof Jurriaan but isn't sure.

May 4, 1974

Today we're married a year. Lee gave me pink tulips. He has gone out, he had an appointment he said but promised to be back soon.

May 7, 1974

Mister van Dam of the Inter-Continental Hotel Paris called. I wasn't home. He told Lee Abidjan would like me to start on the 27th of this month. Unfortunately their conditions are unacceptable. So, Africa is out for the moment.

May 23, 1974

I had my hair cut and look like Maria Schneider from Last Tango in Paris, all curls. It looks great!
Just now I called Joop van de Ende; he's a producer/impresario. He said he doesn't need new people at the moment.

May 16, 1974

I visited Vicky last week in Wassenaar. She lives in this huge mansion with the Canadian ambassador and his family; she's the children's nanny. We smoked pot in her room, with an English friend of her.

May 17, 1974

Roelofje is an adorable baby. I love his little shrimp fingers. Lee and I went there on Saturday. Mom and dad were there too, they're staying for the moment. Marjoric is still weak from losing so much blood from that terrible delivery.

Their house is beautiful and the garden exquisite with all those wonderful plants, trees and flowers but Marjorie is lonely there and she's happy mama is with her now.

~

Chapter 4

Never a dull moment

When we moved from Deventer to Alkmaar I wrote a letter with a publicity photo of myself to Gabriel Schmulowitsch, a cabaret artist whom I met a year earlier at the Loosdrecht Folksong Festival which he won. He was a funny guy who liked my singing. My mother was with me and bought him a coke.

We exchanged addresses, Gabriel became a popular performer and we never met again until many years later.

One day, in March 1972, I received a telephone call at my job in Sloterdijk from an English speaking man who was looking for a singer to join his poetry group. Gabriel had given him my number.

Lilly and I were working at the same company in Sloterdijk, Hoekloos, and of all the office jobs I've had this was the best because we, the young secretaries, were a great group of fun-loving troublemakers. I could type very fast and consequently was always finished with my work

for the old geezer in the shipping department way before it was time to

leave and, therefore I and the other fast and precise working girls went

downstairs to create havoc with the telephone operator/receptionist Meike;

a redhead with clownish capabilities. What fun we had, for instance by

calling in to Radio Veronica, a pirate radio station in the North Sea, and

sending absurd telex messages to them and other radio stations.

One day when I had partied the night before way into the wee hours

I decided to take a nap underneath the telex machine figuring nobody

would find me. The head of the department, Mister Stener, walked by and

apparently saw my legs sticking out from underneath the desk. He took a

closer look and couldn't believe his eyes; I was summoned to come to his

office and there he told me that my rebellious spirit was totally out of

order and I was sacked on the spot.

When Lee called that conspicuous day I agreed to meet him at

Central Station in Amsterdam. I never forget the sight of him; a good

looking black man dressed in a long brown leather coat, wearing yellow

sunglasses. He had me mesmerized instantly.

We got into a car with two friends of his, one a light skin black

grumbling filmmaker and the driver a ferocious looking white man with an enormous mustache who kept saying: 'Motherfuckers! The dirty mortherfuckers!' I sat quietly wondering whatever the word motherfuckers meant.

The first time I sang with Lee's poetry group went very well and pretty soon we were booked all over town.

Already dissatisfied with Johnny's indifference towards me, I had become loosely involved with three men simultaneously, none of whom I was seriously in love with. I still loved Johnny and thought that I could get over the loss of romance by playing around.

There was Fred who also worked at Hoekloos but whose heart was into jazz music and who eventually became a well-known jazz saxophonist. We never went beyond flirting and necking, for lack of opportunity but also because I had met his wife who seemed to be quite nice and really in love with her husband.

Then there was Klaas, also married, about forty, a music teacher at Lilly's high school in Bergen and conductor of the Light Opera Company I had joined. In retrospect I'm sure Klaas never cheated on his wife before; I think I was his midlife faux pas because whenever we met he seemed to be skittish and ill at ease as if riddled with guilt. He was terribly attractive, he resembled Sean Connery, however, I pretty soon lost interest in him when I discovered he had the same old fashioned ideas as my parents and was appalled at the Che Guevara poster in my room with the newly-weds. No going all the way with him either. And then there was my adorable stuttering friend the classical conductor Huub whom I made love to once.

When I met Lee I was lost, fell head over heels and dropped my fiancé and toy boys like hot potatoes. He wasn't like any man I'd ever met; a black man, a poet, a world traveler, an American living abroad.

And I wanted to be close to him all the time; I sat quietly next to him when he played chess with his cynical friend the filmmaker in one of the five in-crowd bars: the Pool, the Pels, the Prins, the Prinses and the Pieper strewn around the Jordaan area except for the Pool on the Damstraat. I gobbled up everything he said and thought he was the most fascinating, interesting man alive.

Lee said to me: 'You have a lovely voice but if you really want to become a great singer you have to go for it. Quit your job and become a professional. That's the only way if you don't want to linger in mediocrity.'

Nobody had ever spoken to me like that and as if it had to be, two weeks after I met Lee, I was sacked at Hoekloos. I went to the artist

department of the municipal employment office the very next day and met
with Mister Andriessen. He was so kind to take me to the little Italian
restaurant Ognibeni on the Reguliersdwarsstraat to audition. They hired
me and thus I landed my first regular singing gig, making more money
with two hours singing every day except Mondays and four hours on
Saturday than my salary at Hoekloos. Lilly said that since I had nothing to
do all day I now was in charge of keeping our spacious apartment in the
Bijlmer spic and span; forfeiting the fact that in order to give a good
performance one has to practice and learn new repertoire.

Lee lived on the stately Oranje Nassaulaan in Amsterdam South
where he had a big lovely furnished apartment where I came to visit him
almost every day and before too long we became lovers.

Lee's lawyer, Mister Bennekom, was busy trying to get his residence
permit for him and told him it would be easier if he was married to a
Dutch woman. When Lee told me I immediately loved the idea and
wouldn't leave him alone until he agreed to marry me because at first Lee
had many objections. He argued that he was too old for me, that he was
too much set in his ways and that I would be better off with someone my
own age, etcetera, etcetera. However, I couldn't be talked out of it and
eventually he began to like the idea so after knowing each other for about
a year we decided to take the big step: we got married.

My parents were not pleased, to put it mildly, my mother tried to talk me out of the marriage until she saw blue in the face. My father suggested we try living together first but…I couldn't be stopped. As far as I was concerned he was the man I had been waiting for and it was nothing but destiny we met and were going to be husband and wife.

Lee Bridges, born the 31st of May, 1927 in Thomasville, Georgia, USA, was the leader of a group of poets who read from their work in small theaters and tea houses all over Amsterdam and I was now their musical interlude.

After my eight months stint at the Ognibeni, Lee wrote a letter to the direction of the Hilton Hotel where I was hired for three months.

Life with the poet was totally unpredictable and very exciting for me, the naïve country chick.

Meeting famous poets, writers, intellectuals like among others Simon Vinkenoog, Remco Campert, Bert Schierbeek, and Henk Hofland. And jazz greats like Johnny Griffin, Archie Shepp, Art Taylor, Memphis Slim and lesser known artists; it impressed and excited me to no end. It was just like I had always wanted my life to be: living like a real professional artist amidst artists who were important at that time, changing things, making a difference, being at the center of the universe.

There was no financial stability in our life; everything was always in flux, not one day equal to the day before or the day after.

The years of the times they are a-changing, the seventies, freedom, drugs and sex and rock and roll.

I plunged in, saw it all and did it all. What crazy times they were indeed!

~

May 23, 1974

Today is grandma's birthday. I made a new song, it's called Restless Soul. Tuesday afternoon Shouki visited me, she's so much fun.

June 3, 1974

I'm studying very hard because I have to pass the exam to be admitted to the Sweelinck Academy of Music.

Sunday we went with a group of friends to the Machine and guess whom I saw there? Fred! I hardly recognized him; he lost a lot of weight but looks great. He's a jazz musician now. I sang My Funny Valentine. Nedley Elstak gave me his phone-number; he said he likes my voice

June 14, 1974

I didn't make it to the team of the Oostende Song Festival. My agent, Frans van Klingeren, said I chose the wrong repertoire. I don't agree with him. I sang Angelitos Negroes and Some Other Spring, a Billie Holiday number.

Shouki and I studied so hard on it, she's a good pianist but I wasn't allowed to use her, I had to be accompanied by the house pianist, so ridiculous! My mother was in the audience and said I was great. I wore an adorable vintage black little dress and had a gardenia in my hair.

Well, idiots, what do they know? I got an ovation, doesn't that mean something? I'm so fed up with Holland, Lee also. We're leaving in October. Oh, next Wednesday I'm rehearsing with the Nedley Elstak Combo. On the 21st I have to do the exam for the Music Conservatory. Bep Ogterob, my vocal coach, doubts that I'll make it. I think I will. I'm working very hard.

Lilly has a great time in Spain.

July 3, 1974

Shit, we're completely broke! What will happen now? I took an LSD trip on Sunday, for the first time in my life. It was magnificent! I loved it! Lee was with me. But I think I used up a lot of energy because I feel so tired.

Listen, I passed the exam for the Sweelinck Music Conservatory, isn't it wonderful? It starts September 2nd. My main course will be singing, then also piano, guitar, and solfege, Italian, German, French and Choir.

Jeanine Knapper (she divorced Nico) is on holiday now. She wants to help me with my career. She likes my own compositions very much and says I should continue to write.

I'm so poor it's insane! I've got to get a job that pays soon! I hardly have money to buy food. Lee is working on something, I don't know, a lottery for handicapped children in Surinam. I'm going to Rotterdam on Friday.

A boy called. He wants to start an all girls group. He's got a bass player, a violinist, a pianist and he's a drummer himself. Now he's looking for a singer.

July 4, 1974

Rain, rain, rain but... we're working on a beautiful project.

We need a holiday and new shoes and to do what we want. Lee isn't home. Vicky went to London; she's coming back on the 27th. Then she goes back to Canada, I'll miss her.

July 7, 1974

Holland lost the World Championship Soccer! What a shame! West Germany won; I can't believe it, what a disaster!

I was in Rotterdam on Friday. I had a nice time with the group and would like to work with them but it's a bit far away for me.

After the soccer game that we watched with friends in Café Hoopman on the Leidseplein, I walked home through the Vondelpark. Lee stayed in town. It was pleasant and I was daydreaming, looking fabulous in my ochre yellow silk dress made for me by Tjerk Kok, it has a pelerine! And, crossing the little bridge I bumped into Matthew. I blushed, don't ask me why but when Lilly, Rita and I were in jazz ballet classes with Helen Leclerq, I had a crush on him. He's married to Helen. He smiled and we both stood still. 'I know you,' he said. He used to accept the payment for the lessons.

'Yes, me too,' I said. We started talking, about the dance school and his scholarship to study guitar, about astrology. He asked if I wanted to go for a drink. I said: 'No, I'm on my way home, I'm going to prepare dinner.' He has a studio/apartment near the park. He's ridiculously handsome, light skin, slim and very tall with beautiful light brown eyes. He knows Lee (who doesn't?) and asked how old I am. I told him and he told me he's twenty-nine. He said he would like to see me again. I just smiled. We said goodbye to each other.

I wonder why he married Helen; she's much older than he is. Well, people probably wonder why I am married to Lee. Age, it means something after all.

It's nice to know someone is interested in me. I wonder if we'll meet again by coincidence.

August 3, 1974

So much has happened. Matthew (he likes to be called Mat) and I made love two weeks ago. We had met a few times before that. There was something between us right from the first time we looked at each other even back at the dance school. It was so fabulous! I don't know where to begin.

The work for Committee Friends Overseas is well on its way. I arranged for interviews in the newspapers Het Parool and the Echo and last Sunday Lee and I talked on the radio about it. Today someone from the magazine Viva came to see me. We write a lot of letters. I'm busy now, visitors are about to pop in but I have to write soon because things aren't going so well anymore between the poet and I. We had a terrible row on Wednesday, very strange and Thursday I slept all day, I took too many sleeping pills. I don't know anymore, oh God, I feel sick.

August 20, 1974

The poet hasn't come home. It's a quarter to five in the morning and he isn't here. I was with Tess and Shouki all afternoon yesterday, then I went home, the poet wasn't in. I had rehearsal for the musical I'm in. I'm with Theater Amsterdam now. When I returned at ten thirty he still hadn't come home. I wasn't worried because he often stays out late. But I just woke up. What's happening?

I'm afraid he's with another woman. Since I was so stupid to confess my faux pas with Mat he has changed. I guess that despite his enlightenment he's just plain jealous.

A few weeks ago he came home late with some people. I was in bed but not asleep yet. He came into the bedroom and said: 'Go to sleep' and then: 'Do you want to come out?'

I said no but I couldn't fall asleep because of the music and voices talking; I distinctly heard a woman's voice. The cats were running around like crazy. At some point I got up and locked them in the kitchen. I was angry and slammed the kitchen door. I heard him call out: 'Hey!'

I finally fell asleep but woke up again when Lee came into the bedroom. I had no time to speak because he struck me twice across the face, not so hard, but still. I was shocked of course and said: 'Have you gone mad?'

He said something about unbecoming behavior, called me a bitch so I tried to hit him. Then he twisted my arm behind my back and pulled my fingers. That really hurt but I didn't say a thing. I guess he hoped I would beg for mercy but I never said another word, I was totally perplexed. He let go off my arm, went to bed and was asleep instantly. I got up and sat crying in the living room, took two sleeping pills and went to sleep in the guest room. I hear him, he's home. Shit!

August 31, 1974

Things are much better again, thank God. I'm dead on my feet.
We're working very hard, organizing the first show of Committee Friends
Overseas. It will be on the 21st of September. I can't think about it, it's so
much work!

October 7, 1974

Artistically the show in the Tropen Museum Auditorium was a huge
success. The program with about 25 artists went like a bomb into overtime
about 40 minutes. We had too many performers. Financially it was a
disaster; the Surinam guys who did the food and beverages robbed us.

I'm in the Sweelinck Academy of Music now since a month. I'm
looking for a second-hand piano. I'd like to take composition lessons too
but my knowledge of solfege isn't up to par yet. Mister Heppener saw two
compositions of mine (Lee noted them down for me) and encouraged me
to continue writing songs. If I do my best maybe I can make the
composition class of mister Heppener next year because that's what I want
most.

Lee helps me by giving me rhythm dictation.

Like I said the show was great. Milly van't Veen and Dwight Thompson were the MC's but I announced a few performers also.

We had: Oscar Harris, the classical guitarist Julien Coco, Judith de Kom, Trille Bedarrides, Ben Brouwers, Simon Vinkenoog, Wim Overgaauw, Natasha Emmanuels, Ria Snijdoodt, Mnine Houcine, Danny Mahony, Donald de Marcas, Sonja Berndt, Cabaret Group Tweeter, Saskia Martijn, Bobby Reid, Louis Armsville, I and... the famous blues singer Memphis Slim. He came over from Paris, Lee and he knew each other when Lee lived there, and visited with us on the Amstelveenseweg. They almost closed the curtain on him; thank God we could stop them in time. The Show had started at five o'clock in the afternoon! It was quite a happening and much fun!

We should have made more publicity and longer but never mind, we won't lose heart and are planning the next happening, on a smaller scale, already.

My health is poor lately. Three weeks before the show I was out of commission for a week. I had practiced the Cancan with Theater Amsterdam a bit too fanatically and torn my leg muscles; they looked like tree trunks! I went to hospital with a taxi and was brought back by ambulance. I had to stay completely off my feet. The poet was very sweet and carried me everywhere. I was lying on the sofa in the living room with the telephone close at hand to expedite the publicity campaign.

Then, last week my whole body was covered with red spots suddenly. I thought I had scarlet fever. The doctor gave me pills and I'm fine again.

The other thing is that I've had three periods this month. My doctor gave me pills to make it stop but now it has started again. Wednesday I'm seeing a gynecologist.

I also have anemia and got pills for that too.

Yesterday we went to Alkmaar; it was my father's birthday. It was nice and little Roelof is such a sweet little piggy!

October 24, 1974

Oh, dear Lee, I love you so much, I wish we didn't have such financial difficulties.

Lee is a great poet; he always sells his poetry books in the Amsterdam café scene. When he was younger he played clarinet and saxophone and later he had his own band and traveled all over the States with them. Their singer was Esther Philips. I am so proud of Lee and very much in love.

I practice the piano at school every night; it's a beautiful restored building on the Keizersgracht. Next Monday I'm in a radio broadcast and on November 2nd I have to sing in Monnickendam. Today someone called about a gig in Edam, preliminary act for the group Sail. They only want to pay a hundred guilders, ridiculous, however, I agreed.

I went to see Jeanine and felt bad because I only came up with two new songs since I last saw her two months ago. I've got to be more productive.

In December I have a couple of gigs also, thank God. This weekend Lee and I are going to Friesland for a little holiday. Monday night we had company; Shouki, Jill and a couple from Ibiza came by. Pepe Madrid, the son of the famous Pepe Madrid, played on my guitar, classical and it was fabulous. However, they stayed for a very long time and I was so glad when they finally left.

November 14, 1974

I work hard, Conservatory is nothing to be sneered at but I do my very best. I still suffer from too many periods; I'm tired all the time. I'm under treatment with a gynecologist now.

There was an exhibition of Shouki's paintings in Eylders on Tuesday. Liam and Tess gave a party for her. I fainted there. I hadn't eaten much but that's another problem I have, no appetite. It's a good thing Tess caught me or I would have slammed my skull against the kitchen counter. Well, anyway, Lee isn't home; I wish he was here.

Romance seems to slip out the backdoor when you're a married lady.

We're very busy with organizing the next show for Committee Friends Overseas. It's going to be on the 7th of December in the American Hotel.

Billie Holiday sings In My Solitude. I feel like crying and my shoulder hurts.

November 23, 1974

I'm trying to write a song. I don't want to disappoint Jeanine but it's not coming easy!

I've got to make a move on. Shouki and her lover Tim are picking me up at nine thirty, we're going to a party of Milly van't Veen and I still have to change.

God, our finances are at a terrible low, how are we going to manage? I worry about Lee.

November 24, 1974

I saw Matthew again. Lee and I were walking in the Leidsestraat. I was so surprised to see him. I thought he was in the States.

Lee said: 'Aha, so that's him!' Shit! Is there anybody out there who doesn't know my husband?

~

Chapter 5

Travelling Together

Lee had met Mister Curiel, a former minister of Economy in Surinam who had a Charitable Organization together with two friends, a banker and a minister, that could do with some extra promotion.

Already two schools for handicapped children in Surinam were built but more was needed and that's why the idea was launched to organize variety and jazz shows.

The Afro American Tour Guide business that was going so well at first was dwindling and therefore the organization of musical extravaganzas was very welcome indeed.

Lee knew many artists personally; Dexter Gordon was a close friend with whom he had spent time in Copenhagen, Memphis Slim, Kenny Clark, Johnny Griffin, Art Taylor and Kenny Drew he knew from when he lived in Paris and since he came to Amsterdam in the mid sixties (his first place of residence was with Provo Movement Leader Robert Jasper Grootveld) he had met everybody on the scene; always selling his poetry books and small pieces of hash and marihuana in the bars.

He left me alone a lot and it's understandable that his behavior began to eat away at me. I was busy as a beaver; doing all the publicity for the shows (we did seven shows in seven months!), going to Music Conservatory, studying piano, solfege, dictation, etcetera, singing gigs and performing with the Theater Amsterdam, hanging out with my girlfriends (painters mostly), composing new songs, practicing my guitar – it just never stopped. My health was deteriorating and my general physician, a young guy, was not helping the situation by giving me prescriptions for valium and sleeping pills.

My life with the poet was turbulent, often balancing on the absurd and catastrophic when bills piled up; you never knew from one day to the next how problems were going to be solved. I remember one time when the bailiff rang our doorbell; Lee was busy baking pancakes, wearing my flowered apron. He sat the bailiff down with a plate of pancakes and a cup of mint tea; the roly-poly taxman was eating away heartily and left us with two weeks postponement of payment. Theo, our accountant, was a good friend who got us out of dire straits more than once.

I worked hard and brought home the bulk of our income, however, the poet had his genial moments and through his inventive spirit and creativity we made money in unexpected ways. The work for Committee Friends Overseas, helping the handicapped children in Surinam, brought a lot of satisfaction. Lee went 'round to businesses like KLM, Coster Diamonds and others to sponsor the show and people could win prizes like a 7-day round trip for two persons to Surinam, a Hi-Fi stereo-set, a portable television, another 7-day round trip for two persons to New York and some smaller prizes as well with their admittance tickets.

In my interview with the Viva magazine I said among other things: 'Many children in Surinam don't get the attention and encouragement that they need. That's what causes their frustration and perhaps they also become aggressive because of it. Their own identity has to be stimulated because these young people will have to bring Surinam to development after the upcoming Independence.'

Lee was rather erratic, he could easily spend a couple of grand at his tailor or buy an expensive watch or shoes that would put us right back into the hole again.

We argued about his crazy spending thrifts now and then but I began to realize that trying to change him was useless so I overlooked his shortcomings; I never stopped loving him, however, I never stopped fooling around either.

~

January 26, 1975

The jazz show was a huge success. We didn't have enough tickets and they were standing outside trying to still get in.

We'll have two big shows on the 1st and the 2nd of February, here in the Concertgebouw and in the Doelen in Rotterdam.

We have fantastic artists lined up, namely: Kenny Clarke, Johnny Griffin, Art Taylor, Jimmy Gourley, Pim Jacobs, Ruud Jacobs, Kenny Drew, Wim Overgaauw, Koos Serierse, Evert Overweg, Oscar Harris, and The Helen Leclerq Dancers.

Milly van't Veen will be the MC here and Michiel de Ruyter (famous Dutch radio personality) will be the MC in Rotterdam. We're doing a big publicity campaign this week.

February 23, 1975

The shows were a financial disaster; I get sick thinking about it. We're ruined!

In Rotterdam I did a speech about the handicapped children in Surinam we're trying to help. We just didn't have enough people in the audience, such a pity! The shows itself were beautiful; Rudy Koopmans raved about them in his review in the Volkskrant of February 3, 1975. He wrote that it would be hard if not impossible to top these two jazz shows this year!

Lee is at the end of his rope. I worry about him. Thank God it's almost springtime.

My sister Marjorie is pregnant again.

The Rolling Stones were at our Concert in the Doelen in Rotterdam. They were recording there in secret. Everyone talked with them; they were in awe of those jazz legends like Kenny Clarke and Jim Gourley and the others. I heard Keith and Mick were doing coke in someone's dressing room.

My god, the dressing rooms in the Doelen are something else, grand pianos and spacious but unfortunately since we didn't have enough people in the house everyone had a great time except Lee and I, busy and worried as we were.

March 16, 1975

I'm working very hard each day on my music studies. Naturally the poet isn't home again. He showed me his extensive wardrobe this morning, asking my opinion about every possible combination; then he finally left and hasn't been back since. I applied for a job with the Dutch Opera Choir, also with NOS television.

Our next show is on April 11 in the Concertgebouw. We'll have: Ramses Shaffy, Simon Vinkenoog, Sight and Marken (two rock groups). Then there will be another show on May 16 in the Concertgebouw. We don't have artists for that one yet.

Our life is a succession of fan mail from the taxman and the most enterprising fantasies like a long vacation in July and August. I very much look forward to that. I've got to get money together to pay Charles to make me a new fabulous creation to wear in the April 11th show. Actually I'd like to get new shoes also.

The poet threw a glass of sherry in my face on Saturday. He said I was making him nervous. Anyway, I'll be asleep when he gets home, whenever that may be, a sleeping pill will save the day.

Lee is a sweet child and sometimes a nice grandpa! Oh, I shouldn't write such mean things. It looks like I don't love him anymore but I do, really I do. It's just that I long for our romance of the first year. Oh, Lee, please come home.

March 29, 1975

Today is Lilly's birthday. I called her in Austria but she was still asleep. They had a big party for her last night.

We've got a group for our next show, seven black American beauty queens, The Love Machine. They're touring Europe at the moment.

I spoke with Albert Mol (actor/comedian) on Wednesday in the American Hotel; we'd like him to be the M.C. for the April 11th show. Lee and I met Matthew last night in café Hoppe. I still like him; I wish…well, never mind!

April 21, 1975

I spoke with Pieter Schellevis, he's the president of Phonogram International; when I performed for the employees of Phonogram a while back and the M.C. told me the president was there I asked him to introduce me and that's how I met Pieter. Anyway, I asked him if it wouldn't be a good idea to tape our Show with The Love Machine to be released as a special LP for Committee Friends Overseas.

'It's a possibility,' he said so…who knows, that would be something, wouldn't it??

I hope the poet comes home soon, I long for him. We're totally broke. I don't have money to buy toilet paper and we're out of shampoo also. However, I know how to make my own; just mix green soap with a few drops of olive oil et voila! I did it on Sunday and it works fine.

Shit, I've got my period, I hate it! Lilly is back. She's got a boyfriend, Werner. This weekend she's off to Hamburg to see him. I'm happy for her. On Wednesday our darling baby Roelof will turn one, he's such an angel.

April 25, 1975

The telephone has been cut off. It's nice and quiet but rather inconvenient especially since we're doing another show again.

May 27, 1975

Tomorrow I'll turn twenty-six, God willing. I go to Conservatory every night to study till about nine-thirty. Then I go home, watch television or study some more.

Lee is never, hardly ever home.

Mat and I see each other now and then, we've become good friends. I like him a lot and he likes me too.

Oh Lee, come home! Don't leave me alone all the time, not every single goddamned night!

Think about me sometimes! I need you! Come home, please Lee!

June 10, 1975

I want peace, rest and peace. Maybe I'm starting to lose my mind. I'm so tired. Valium makes me indifferent and sleepy.

I sang in a village near Helmond, Lierop, on Saturday. It was great fun, I had a lot of success and afterwards there was a party. I stayed with a young couple on their farm; it was heavenly, such nice people! In the morning we had a hearty breakfast outside on their terrace. What a nice weekend!

June 25, 1975

Today is mama's 50th birthday. Lee and I are planning to move south, probably the south of France. Perhaps a holiday will bring us closer together again. Meanwhile…I wrote a song for Mat; I think I am in love with him. I just called him, he's not home. I don't feel like sitting here all by myself again, miss Lonely Heart.

Mat loves my song for him, he's so sweet.

Lee gave me nothing on our 2nd anniversary, not even flowers.

We're both very tired, we want to leave Amsterdam.

It's Monday morning, June 30, 1975 and today Lee and I are going on holiday, yes!

It's 6.30 p.m. and we just arrived in Luxembourg, we are going to spend the night in Hotel des Ardennes in Rue de la Liberté where I'm now lying on the double bed after a great shower and putting on other cloths.

The room is lovely, clean, and rather large with nice old furniture and from our window we look over the streets into green hills and valleys. It is breathtaking and all this for only twenty-three guilders.

Lee is changing money at the bank. We got up very early.

He just came back with wine and Chinese food, olé!

We're going out in a little while to get information about our next train and then we'll go into town to look around and keep the camera ready, Lee's present to me.

We didn't sleep in the train only towards the end of the trip we dozed off. The landscape of Luxembourg is beautiful; when you enter the city with its old fortified walls and fortresses, spires, houses, bridges, hills and

valleys you're awestruck. Lee and I dashed from one side of the train to

the other, fantastic!

Thursday, July 3rd, 1975

We're in Barcelona. First siesta but I'll be back!

Our hotel is the Tobogan at the Plaza Real; I'm sitting on the balcony

looking out over the square. It's lovely weather and there are so many

people. Lee is hunting for socks and a bottle of gin or cognac. Switzerland

disappointed us, not the landscape for that is magnificent but it's rather

expensive and the people in general unfriendly and cold.

Montreux is a beautiful city and situated splendidly. We went to the

Jazz Festival there and met with Charles Mingus, the bass player and an

acquaintance of Lee; I gave him my booklet that Shouki made for me, it

has photos and a couple of songs of mine. Unfortunately the weather was

overcast and cold so we decided to leave for Barcelona the next day. We

hung out in Genève for awhile because we had time to kill before the train

left for Barcelona.

Sunday, July 6, 1975

We are now four days in Barcelona. I'm a little ill, caught a cold. Lee
is getting powders for me at the pharmacist. Last night I had a high fever.
We went to the beach yesterday and swam, it was great! Lee is mailing
postcards and searching for something to eat. Friday I did a lot of walking
looking for a singing job but I didn't succeed. I love Barcelona!

Monday morning, July 7, 1975

Today we're leaving Barcelona, probably direction Paris. At the
moment there's a film crew here busy filming on the Plaza Real. The
actors are wearing clothes from the twenties. It's a German movie. I took
two pictures of the main characters, unfortunately they're not famous. I
feel much better though I'm still coughing. Our money is almost gone. I
hope we run into some luck elsewhere.

July 9, Wednesday

We are in hotel Saint Paul on the Rue de Monsieur Le Prince on the Left Bank in Paris. The room is very small but okay. We arrived here yesterday at nine o'clock.

First Lee and I went for a cup of coffee and afterwards we went to the tourist office on the Champs Elysee to get a hotel. Last night Lee treated me to a great dinner in a couscous restaurant on the Avenue Montparnasse and then we saw many friends of Lee in the café's.

It was a great night and I had a good time, especially the dinner was fabulous!

July 15, 1975

We are in a nice hotel in Dijon, Hôtel de La Provence. We have a big room with a bathroom and it's magnificent. Lee bought delicacies so I'm going to eat now.

July 27, 1975

We're back in Amsterdam. Wednesday we arrived and found our key didn't fit the front door anymore. The landlady changed the lock and everything has been taken out. However, we are in our house now; we have a lawyer and we'll have to wait and see.

Paris was fabulous again! I sang in the Inter-Continental Hotel on Rue Rivoli and it was great. The general manager, Mr. van Dam, is Dutch and very nice. Perhaps I'll get a contract for September. I hope we can travel again soon. We would like to spend a few days up North, in Friesland.

August 5, 1975

It's tropical weather for a week already. I went to my parents this weekend. On Sunday Lilly and I went to Bergen aan Zee on our bikes. It was heavenly. I got a nice color. Today I sunbathed in the Vondelpark but I got too hot after an hour and went home. The hippies from all over the world that used to lie around there are all gone; now they have set up camp on the Dam in the center of town.

We still don't have our things back. Well, patience will save the day. I took a shower now, cold because that bitch also took the geyser away. Ah well, it's alright with this heat.

August 19, 1975

We're still in Alkmaar, Lee and I. Mom and dad are on vacation and it's so nice being here, not having to face all those problems we have in Amsterdam. Marjorie and Ben both have the flu and they're bringing little Roelof in a little while. They're throwing up all the time, I feel so bad for them, and I especially pity my sister who's going to have her second baby in six weeks. But I can't go there to help them because Lee is in Amsterdam and I have only two guilders. So…I'll be a mother for a few days and Lee a father. I can't wait till he's here.

Little Roelof is asleep in his cot. Before when I looked in on him he was still awake playing with his teddy bear. I feel very responsible suddenly. I think that with a child you only have time for that child. As a mother you're always busy and have to be alert at all times. Roelofje is beginning to discover everything now. He can almost walk solo and my sister is having another baby soon.

Jean-Pierre Bergdorf called me back. He's going on holiday for two weeks but he wants me to wait for him because he's interested to go into the recording studio with me. I hope he means it because I don't intend to let him string me along the way Ruud Jacobs did for such a long time. I do need a good tape in any case; we shall see.

September 9, 1975

I'm in the train from Alkmaar to Amsterdam. Nice lazy weekend with mom and dad. Mama gave me a lovely dress; it was too tight on her. Nice eh? I saw the movie Lenny Bruce played by Dustin Hoffman on Friday, very good film.

Two days ago some nut tried to kill President Ford; It's a crazy world filled with crazy people!

November 29, 1975

Today I brought something to the pawnshop for the first time in my life; my gold ring with a diamond. We had to pay a lot of bills. Lee pawned his ring too, he got much more money for it.

December 4, 1975

So much has happened, where to start? On September 18th my sister Marjorie gave birth to another son, his name is Jordi Benjamin; he's dark and looks like his brother Roelof.

December 9, 1975

Our holiday and business travels have taken us at a fast pace through Europe: Belgium, Luxembourg, France, Switzerland, Italy and Spain. We were in Paris five times.

However, we're still broke or should I say broke again? Paris was much fun though.

I made a demo-recording there with Phonogram through mediation of mister Pieter Schellevis. I hope something comes of it.

Russell Triest is my manager now and so far got me a couple of good gigs.

The poet signed two contracts for books, great! I'd like a drink right now but there's not a drop in the house and I'm dead broke. I am so sick and tired of never having enough money!

I wrote a letter to Vicky, she's in Bali now on her way to Australia.

December 30, 1975

On this day before the last day of the year I'm in a good mood. I just cooked spaghetti which I'm going to eat now. Mm…delicious! We have a darling little Christmas tree and the room looks nice and cozy. On Christmas Eve we gave a dinner party for Desiree and Norman who were so hospitable to us when we were in Paris. Lilly was there, the count and countess Vijlbrief, Shouki and Tim (Keith is back in Surinam, he loves it there) and Christmas day we spent with our friends Ellen de Thouars (I know her from the acting class of Gelijn Molier) and her husband Jack Kröner, a translator and good friend of Lee. There we ran into the Vijlbriefs again. Ellen, she's a real baroness, prepared scrumptious hors d'oeuvres and pastries. Later we did word games and before too long Ellen, Jack and the Vijlbriefs were stoned out of their minds, they always are.

Second Christmas day I had to perform in Take Five. Friends came to cheer me on. Russell was very pleased. We drank champagne and had a great time.

On Sunday mom, dad, Marjorie, Ben, Roelof and baby Jordi came to visit. The babies are so cute!

I did something very stupid a couple of weeks ago. Lee hasn't gotten over it yet. The Irish blues singer Sean McGauly shook me, saying over and over: 'But baby, you've got it all! You've got it all, silly girl!'

I'm going to work with a guitarist, Joost. Lee is working on a new book of poetry. We want to go to America next year

~

I did something very stupid indeed. One night when I had been left to my own devices once again and consequently drank too much, feeling sorry for myself, I cut my left wrist.

A rather halfhearted act because if I really had wanted to take my own life I would've used a knife instead of a razorblade. The little scar is a reminder for the rest of my life, however, seeing blood floating out I panicked and quickly bound off my arm. When Lee finally came home he found me asleep on the floor with the bloody rag wound around my wrist. Naturally he was shocked and appalled and showed no compassion whatsoever. Committing suicide was something for idiots and losers in his opinion. He didn't speak to me for several days and since I hadn't taken any of my girlfriends into confidence either I had to get over it all by myself. Evidently Lee had told some friends or else how would the Irish blues singer have known about it?

For years I had tried so hard to get somewhere with my singing and although people had promised me this, that and the other thing nothing ever came of it.

Ruud Jacobs, producer with CBS records, kept me on hold for several years, always telling me not to sign with any other company, saying that he would come up with songs and what not; I was often at his house and helped his wife doing the dishes even! Promises, promises; I never lost heart, I kept believing in myself and my music.

The Dutch record companies Dureco and Negram had offered me contracts but I didn't like the repertoire they wanted me to sing; I was determined to stay true to myself and, unperturbed, I pressed on.

However, the disappointments coupled to being left alone by my husband most of the time and the continuous financial problems weighed me down.

Pieter Schellevis was a very nice and attractive man in his mid forties who invited me to his office after I had spoken to him at the employees evening where I was one of the performers; he really tried to do something for me that would further my career. He made valuable suggestions and arranged for me to do a demo-recording at Phonogram in Paris. He was the president of Phonogram Worldwide and discovered a.o. Demis Roussos and Gypsy Kings. After I did the demo-recording in Paris nothing happened for a long time but after Mr. Schellevis intervened I was asked back for another try-out in Paris. However, it never materialized into a record deal due to the fact that the producer there wasn't confident that I would become a commercial success and once again my hopes were dashed.

~

January 6, 1976

I just sang in The Other Place. It felt good! Russell has booked quite a few gigs for me already. On January 12th I have a radio broadcast with the Metropole Orchestra. I just came home and had a piece of apple cake Lee baked; he's a great cook!

Tomorrow we're off to Paris. Nat Dove wants to arrange my music.

I had a bad experience the last time I went to Paris by myself. I did a recording again with Phonogram in the afternoon and I just didn't feel like staying overnight. I ate supper with Norman and Desiree who live on the left bank. I watched a bit of television there and left to take the night train back to Amsterdam. I ran into Bobby Reid (jazz bass player and close friend of Lee) at Gare Du Nord. He and his skinny girlfriend Jane (he's big as a house and Lee and I always make jokes about how the two of them make love, only possible if little Jane is on top) were on the same train, first class though. I sat with them for a while but later I went to my own compartment leaving my guitar with them. I had hidden my passport and money between my cloths. There were two elderly men in the compartment with me. I stretched out and went to sleep.

Suddenly I woke up when I felt something. A man was standing over me getting ready to snatch my purse. I jumped up and made a lot of noise. I wanted to run out of the compartment, the two elderly gentlemen were gone, but the man pushed a pistol against my stomach. He told me to sit down. The other guy threatened to throw me out the window; they spoke French.

Luckily the man with the pistol called the other one and they left.

I immediately ran back to Bobby Reid and Jane in first class, told them what had happened and stayed with them.

Later at the frontier I told the border patrol what had happened and I had to go with them through all the compartments looking for the crooks.

There was another Dutch girl who had been bothered by them also. We did find them and they were taken off the train, the girl and I had to come along. We had to sign a statement and then we were allowed back on the train.

Lilly told me later that she read in the Telegraaf newspaper that there are indeed many robberies on the night train to Paris. What a rotten experience, they could've killed me.

Anyway, I'm over it already.

Lilly and her friend Welmoed are going to Austria on Thursday.

Lee hasn't come home yet. I wonder where he is now again.

January 12, 1976

Tonight I have to sing in a radio program. Last week Lee and I went to Paris for a couple of days. This is going to be a great year for us I think.

January 22, 1976

I just heard on the news that civil war broke out in Lebanon. The world is a madhouse; a bloody mess in Angola, England and Iceland are at each other's throats in a fishing war and in Spain tension is rising since Franco died last year. Portugal is full of trouble too.

And I read in the paper that my country is teeming with CIA agents.

This morning Lee and I heard on the BBC that America has a new kind of weapon, a missile that can operate by itself and that can't be traced by radar. It has a range of 3000 miles. And Russia developed something else, deadly of course. We won't even start about the Middle East. Kidnapping has become the order of the day.

Last year around Sinterklaas, 5th of December, two kidnappings occurred simultaneously: a train near Beilen (three deaths) and at the Indonesian Consulate in Amsterdam.

Well, what else? The weather is okay and sales are on. I need boots so I've got to make my move.

February 2, 1976

I just sang in De Kroeg and am about to go to bed. I did a lot of typing for Lee's book, it's ready now.

Lilly comes back on Sunday. I'll go to Alkmaar on Saturday. It's a rough winter, snow and ice. Last Sunday mom and dad came, they brought my skates. I skated Monday, Tuesday and Wednesday in the Vondelpark, that was great!

February 21, 1976

Strange, I always took it for granted that I would get children. Well, I haven't given up hope. I'm going back to the VU Hospital next week.

There's a big exhibition in the Stedelijk Museum (museum of modern art) and Lee's poem Oh Amsterdammers is part of it, printed on seven meters of paper. It's so nice!

There are works of painters, sculptors, engravers and so on and so forth.

April 12, 1976

I went to the Eurovision Song festival in The Hague with Mary Bosman, Marjorie's old friend from Deventer. I sang in a Spanish radio show and also at the party afterwards.

Mary and I also sang in Manfred Langer's new place, it was great. Manfred is such a cool guy and his place on the Amstel is very popular with the in-crowd.

I went to see Jos Stelling's new movie in Utrecht about the life of Rembrandt van Rijn. I played a little part in his first movie, Mariken van Nimwhegen.

Saturday night Lee and I went to the birthday party of Ellen de Thouars; I really like her a lot, she's a great actress.

Tonight Mary Bosman, Lee and I are going to Ronnie Potsdammer's radio show in the Koepel Café of the Sonesta Hotel.

I forgot to write about the offer I had from the Inter-Continental Hotel in Bali. They offered to pay a thousand guilders a week. I was a fool not to grab it with both hands but how could I? I just started at the Sweelinck Academy of Music!

Lee bought me a lovely ring, I keep looking at it.

Lilly is in Spain, she's a tourist hostess in Ibiza for six months. My sweet lucky sister!

I'm going over to Mary's. She's the one who got me started as a singer with the rock group The Skybolts back in 1965.

She's had a hard life, last year her husband died.

May 28, 1976

Today I'm twenty-seven. The poet isn't home. Shane and Joke came to see me. Joke plays the flute and Shane guitar so it was a musical night.

We've got a new apartment. Hopefully we'll be able to move in soon. It's at the Oosterpark. We go there regularly to paint everything.

Lee received a sensitive blow; his publisher went out of business. I hope we go to the States soon.

I've had a little affair, I was in love, with a West-Indian from the island Lucia for awhile. He plays the guitar and sings.

There's a black dance group here, old buddies of Lee, they call themselves The Hoofers, nice old men.

Ellen's husband Jack gave me twenty-seven red roses today, how sweet, especially now that I'm sitting here all by myself. Ellen and Jack are the sweetest people.

We met Mick Jagger and Keith Richards in front of La Coupole on the Boulevard Montparnasse in Paris. Mick especially was super nice, they had just come back from a Santana Concert, his girlfriend Bianca too and, I couldn't help myself, I kissed him right smack on his big fat sensuous lips! Lee sold him a book of poetry.

The Stones are doing a concert in The Hague this week.

May 29, 1976

Jippee! I'm packing; we're going to Maastricht for a few days, yes!

~

Chapter 6

Change is gonna come

June 4, 1976

I look terrible! Lee hit me last night when we walked back from theater Carré on the Amstel where The Hoofers danced in the Cotton Club Show, right on my eye. I never received such a hard blow in my life.

We had an argument, both tipsy I must add, about that woman of Call Tiffany, Genevieve; I thought he paid too much attention to her.

For a few seconds I was stunned; then I got so mad I kicked and slapped and scratched him wherever I could. He pulled my long hair. It was a ridiculous complete fight in the middle of the street. What a ludicrous scene! Cars stopped, people looked out their windows. At some point I just ran away and took a taxi home on the Rembrandt square. The driver was so nice, he gave me a cigarette and said: 'Go on, it's alright', because I was shaking.

At home I took a handful of valiums so I slept like a log. My eyes look a mess, all red and purple. Lee doesn't know how to act, he feels terrible. I'm not mad about our stupid argument but he shouldn't have hit me.

This is the fourth time he misused his strength, it's too much. I know we both say horrible things to each other in anger. Lee can be very sweet and nice at times and call me all kinds of endearments but, hell; he says such things also to Hamlet and Othello, our cats.

I need more. Most of all I need him to not leave me alone all the time. It's too bad, I love him so much.

What my mother warned me about before I married him is true; there are too many years between us.

I won't let him hit me again!

I put a lot of eye make-up on but still, now I look weird so I put on sunglasses.

Maastricht was fun. I helped sell Lee's books, I'm good at it. Yesterday they took photos of my uterus, a rotten feeling that was.

In two weeks Lee and I have to come back and they'll give us the result of all the tests.

I wish Lee was here to comfort me.

June 30, 1976

This lovely hot weather continues and is great! So is our new house and all my family have been wonderful and helped us a lot. I feel much better now that Lee and I are closer since that nasty fight. Perhaps all will be well.

July 7, 1976

Lee's German former girlfriend Wiltraud called today; she's coming to Amsterdam. I happen to know she still loves him very much, I read it in a letter she sent him a few weeks ago. I never pry but this letter was lying on the table, just like that.

I'm not jealous because I'm sure Lee loves me, at least more than he loves her. They're just friends. I wouldn't feel this way if she was young and gorgeous of course but Wiltraud is forty or thereabouts so, I need not worry although I must say that she looks alright for her age.

August 2nd, 1976

I've got a contract to sing three months in the Inter-Continental Hotel in Tehran from January till April 1977. They pay everything and $400 a week. I called René van Nie to ask if he had something for me in his next movie, he said he'll know within a month.

I'm going to call my sweet mama.

August 13, 1976

My sister Lilly was on television last Monday, in an interview of the TROS about the tourist industry. She looked fabulous!

I have an interview with someone at Phonogram on Monday. I'm performing a lot lately but I am so tired. I also started typing Lee's new book and Conservatory is taxing.

August 18, 1976

It's lovely weather and I'm lying on my mattress on the floor in the sun. Why and how does my money disappear always? I ate the last biscuits with mayonnaise and tomato, delicious! When I get hungry again I can eat chicken soup or bake pancakes. There's honey and molasses. There's milk and a little bit of tea. There's no coffee. In a minute I'll smoke my last cigarette. I have one guilder and a few quarters to my name. For the moment I'm lying okay here and when the poet comes home I'll expect he'll have something. He was going to pawn his ring. The rent is due and the telephone bill.

I hope to go to Cyprus. I want to leave. I have got to get out of Amsterdam or I'll go stark raving mad.

This life in poverty is killing me. It looks like it was always like this and it'll stay like this too. It's like being dead alive. I'm going to practice with a group on Monday, the Milestones.

Wiltraud didn't come. Lee called her. He told me that he didn't feel like being with her an entire weekend.

'My life is built around you, puss,' he said, 'it's what's most important to me and I want to keep it that way.'

I feel the same. There's no one like my Lee, I will love him forever.

September 2, 1976

If everything goes well I'll be on Cyprus Sunday night. I don't have a contract yet but my agent, Mr. Kok, promised I'll get it by telex tomorrow. I'll get $40 a day and it's for three months.
It sounds good to me especially since it's raining every day here. Mister

Curiel gave me 750 guilders today, great! I have a cold. It'll be the first time I'll be so far away, on my own, without my Lee.

But what the heck, I have myself and my guitar! Cyprus is a lovely island and they speak English there. My sister Marjorie is so worried, she doesn't want me to go. I have to stop, I'm tired and my nose is running.

Sunday, September 5, 1976, Limassol, Cyprus

What a delight finally to be lying in a soft clean bed although the peace is being disturbed by what seems to be political propaganda but perhaps it's news about the Palestinian airplane kidnappers.

My flight from Amsterdam to Athens went well but in Athens the delay began. It seems some Palestinians kidnapped a KLM plane that was on route to Tel Aviv; then they wanted to land on Cyprus and have circled the island a couple of hours. Athens was beautiful, a paradise of lights, really breathtaking! At Larnaca Airport it was chaos; I never saw such a thing. The Bank was a shack where you could, if you were so inclined, grab the money and a roguish looking young man almost indifferently threw the changed money in an open drawer.

I was driven to this hotel by a chauffeur of Mister Linkinopulous, my new boss. I'm dead on my feet. The drive from Larnaca to Limassol seemed to take forever.

My first impressions of Cyprus by night: hazy, bare, woods, beautiful, boring, and Limassol: a village with one big nightclub. There's the sound of music outside and a car with the motor running; it gives me an impression of rural boredom.

I'm thinking of Lee. I will try to call him tomorrow, collect; I want to let my sweetheart know that I'm alright.

~

Who suggested I try out the agent Kok to me? I can't remember. I believe it was Bobby Something, a Canadian pianist/singer. This Kok character saw nothing wrong with sending me to Cyprus to work in nightclubs there. What I do remember is that his wife/secretary kept saying that it was a shame and that he shouldn't send me there.

Why not? I thought, why does that woman not want me to go there? Silly old cow!

The prospect of singing on a beautiful Mediterranean island seemed like a dream come true to me.

What did I know? I had never set foot in a nightclub and had no idea of what I was getting myself into. Lee, being unworldly in many respects, gave his permission, with the idea that it would be a valuable experience for me to sing abroad. I quit the Sweelinck Academy of Music, silly in retrospect but I was fed up with everything and longed for adventure.

As it so happened I soon found out that singing my lovely songs accompanying myself on guitar was not all that the Linkinopulous brothers expected of me.

On my first night, while having a drink at the bar of my hotel, a young man's melodic voice said: 'May I keep you company?' I turned and looked into the most handsome face of a young man. He was absolutely gorgeous; I almost fell off my barstool but got hold of myself. We got to talking and later I agreed to go to a disco with him. We danced the night away and when he took me back to the hotel and kissed me I had fallen in love irrevocably.

We became lovers overnight and he took me over to meet his family a few days later.

I had a diary with me but never wrote in it after the first entry above mentioned.

I was on Cyprus three weeks and those three weeks had an enormous impact on me. I wrote a short story about it, Bittersweet, and a novel later on, Facing the Music.

Michel and I stayed in contact for more than four years and I will always remember him, his sweet mother, his teenage sister and his handsome proud father.

They had been kicked off their orange plantation in the North of the island in 1974 when the Turks invaded Cyprus and took over the Northern most fertile part of the island that remains so today.

With Michel's help I eventually succeeded to flee because I had been so clever to leave my passport with his mother and therefore was able to get aboard a cruise ship to Athens. The Linkinopulous brothers ran practically every hotel and nightclub in Nicosia and Limassol and entertainers like me were supposed to sleep with clientele of the clubs. At first I didn't know but it wasn't hard to find out something was amiss when I was asked to sign a paper stating I owed the Linkinopulous brothers a large sum of money. I refused to sign it, went back to my hotel and brought my passport over to Michel's mother. I also went to the Dutch embassy in Nicosia where I was told that it was safer for me to leave the island immediately. The civil war was raging in Lebanon and so much was going on, however, I was in love and thought that I could keep men who wanted to be with me at bay. I succeeded more or less but in the end I had to get the hell out of there when the Linkinopulous brothers got fed up with my refusal to do as they told me to. It was and most likely still is nothing less than modern day slavery.

Chapter 7

The Middle East

Monday, September 27, 1976

Left with the boat Apollonia from Limassol, Cyprus, to Athens; a beautiful trip. Arrival at Piraeus on Wednesday morning nine a.m.

My suitcase was much too heavy. In Anthens I first took a taxi and went to the American Express Company. No message from Lee; I left my steel monstrously heavy suitcase there and off I dashed to the American Embassy, again no message from Lee. I left a note for him that he can reach me via the Dutch Embassy. No message from him at the Dutch Embassy either. I thought he was going to meet me in Athens. He told me when he called me in Limassol that he was going to leave for Athens.

I was so disappointed. I waited in my hotel but left at two-thirty because I was tired of waiting for his call. I sent him a cable, saying: I'm going to Milano, will call you from there.

I ate well in Athens before I left. The trip by train took two days and two nights, very tiresome but beautiful; straight through Greece, Yugoslavia and Italy.

I called Lee from the hostal where I am now here in Milano, no answer. Where is he? I'm going to sleep now. I'm so tired, and lonely, and sad.

I'll try to get work in the Hilton Hotel here tomorrow. It's near here.

~

October 6, 1976

It's my father's birthday today. Happy birthday, daddy!

I arrived in Maastricht yesterday after a hard trip from Milano. It was hard because after about one hour on the train I got terrible stomach cramps that became worse all the time. I felt so cold and even though I took two valiums I couldn't sleep, not even a little.

October 7, 1976

My Cyprus adventure was a financial failure. It's not so bad considering the state of affairs in the world: overthrow of governments, earth quakes, toxic gas poisoning, wars, dictatorships, corruption, exploitation, floods, droughts, moral degenerate indoctrinate destruction processes....

I can't stop thinking about Michel. He and his family are Greek-Cypriot refugees. They come from Xeros at the Morphubay, the part that was invaded by the Turks after the overthrow of the Government and ousting of President Markarios in 1974.

It's Saturday, October 9, and I'm lying in bed with internal bruises and black and blue spots all over my body, bumps on my head too.

I fell down the stairs at Ellen and Jack's; I regained consciousness at the Binnengasthuis Hospital. Nothing was broken according to the X-rays. Lee was afraid I had broken my neck. He's very sweet and taking good care of me.

I can only think of Michel, Michel and Michel.

His father owned an orange plantation; they were rich, had two houses but lost everything with the Turkish invasion. Michel is tall, well, about 5 feet 11, dark curly hair, beautiful light brown eyes with the largest lashes I ever saw on a man, a big full mouth, an irresistible smile and a set of strong, even, white teeth. My Michel, I'm still madly in love of course. He is so sweet and sings beautifully. And he is an athlete; he can do somersaults forwards and backwards without touching the ground! I wish I was in his arms again.

Monday, October 11, 1976

My whole family visited me yesterday. Mama brought beautiful flowers and grapes. Lee was disappointed they hadn't called because he would've liked to cook for them.

Lee went to say goodbye to Shouki who left for New York this morning. She wants to stay there for awhile and do exhibits of her art work.

I had written her from Cyprus about Michel whom I call Apollo because he is indeed like a Greek god; he called me Aphrodite. Shouki couldn't believe I was back already, me neither but as it is I'm lucky to be here.

After my family left yesterday I called the Apollonia Hotel in Limassol, a personal call to Michel and God, I spoke with him. Hearing his sweet melodic voice I couldn't believe it.

He was so happy and told me that he wrote me an express letter. I need to go to sleep.

I still don't understand what happened out there to me. I love Lee, I do love my husband and want to stay with him till death do us part. How could I fall so totally for Michel? I don't know. I long for him, I miss him so much. It was so special. I just don't know what happened to me. My darling Michel, I will never forget you. It's in the past already.

Lee and I are going to Groningen on Wednesday. I wrote a letter to the Ministry of Foreign Affairs about what happened to me on Cyprus.

Kok says he's going to do everything he can to get my money from Linkinopulous but he's full of shit. He should never have sent me there. Anyway, I'm back in one piece and at least I met Michel, my unforgettable Apollo.

Sunday, October 17, 1976

I can't find my driving license. I suspect little baby rascal Jordi ate it when they were here, if so, it's my own fault for leaving things lying around.

November 3, 1976

At least I'm singing quite often but still, money is very tight. Tonight we'll go to The Rose Tattoo of Tennessee Williams to see Ellen de Thouars.

Monday, November 15, 1976

We have a gas heater and that almost broke our back, financially speaking. I'm so glad we've got it though because it's getting cold.

I finally feel a bit better, no, I feel a lot better. After Cyprus and that nasty fall – Ellen and Jack have a cozy apartment above the Athenaeum Bookstore on the Spui but it's got those typical steep Amsterdam stairs – I was rattled for quite a while, not myself anymore, crazy and paranoid, however, I have taken hold of myself again.

December 3, 1976

I'm reading Dante in English. I have a long way to go still.

December 12, 1976

I pawned my ring, necklace, bracelet and my camera to pay bills, I had to. I try not to think about it because I'll go nuts if I do.

Michel's mother wrote me, she says Michel is very unhappy and they're all afraid of the threat of war. Michel hasn't written me anymore. I'll send them photos.

December 30, 1976

I worked a lot this month but because of all the bills there's nothing left over. No Christmas presents for anybody. I feel so bad. My grandfather is very ill, he's in hospital.

I was cheered up just now because there's a lovely card from Michel in the mail.

January 14, 1977

My grandfather died on January 3rd. I'll miss him, I really loved him. And I feel so sorry for my grandmother. But I believe in reincarnation. So, I wish you all the best, dear grandpa!

Vicky wrote to me from Toronto. She lives there with her sister.

Lee just came home, very cheerful. He said he spent all the money and is going to cook a special meal for me. Oh, sweet man!

Tuesday, February 1, 1977

Yesterday I arrived at 7.30 p.m. at Tehran Airport. The trip was okay; the plane went via Frankfurt and was continuing on to Tokyo. From the airport I took a taxi to the Inter-Continental Hotel. They were very surprised to see me. Kok didn't send them a cable about my arrival, however, what's worse, I have no visa! Kok told me that I would get it at the airport in Tehran, no such thing! That man is a real stinker! Anyway, today I'll meet Mister Etazumi who's going to try to arrange for it as fast as possible. As long as I don't have the visa I can't work.

I'm staying at the Elizabeth Hotel situated behind the Inter-Conti, about ten minutes walking distance.

The ground is covered with snow here but it is lovely weather, the sun is shining. This is a beautiful hotel even though I didn't even see everything yet. I am enchanted and now I'll go for a walk until my meeting with mister Etazumi.

February 3, 1977

My visa hasn't come through yet, perhaps Saturday. So, I'm having a little holiday in the meantime. I'm going to write a letter to mom and dad and the poet.

I met a nice American and I'm having a jolly good time.

The weather is lovely and the snow is melting now.

February 5, 1977

Yesterday it was Friday and that's Sunday over here. I hope I can start today; I don't understand why it's so complicated to get me a work-permit and visa. I didn't come here to hang around. It's a bit boring and I'm already imagining how great it will be to return to Holland in May. It is really wonderful weather here; perhaps I can get a tan when it really gets hot in a month's time. I'm having a good time with the American, he reminds me a bit of Johnny, playful and witty.

He's also an Aquarius. I've got an appointment at one o'clock about my visa. If I'm allowed to start work today I can get an advance on my salary.

Thursday, February 10, 1977

I'm working since Tuesday; long hours, from eight p.m. till one a.m. with a break to eat.

I've had a bit of bad luck though because I fell Tuesday afternoon; running, dodging cars, trying to cross the broad boulevard in front of the Inter-Conti (there are no zebra crossings and drivers act like they're all in a Formula I car race together) I jumped over the sewer ditch (how these ditches must stink in the summertime!) but I miscalculated and my left leg went down in the ditch causing me to lose balance and, in trying to fence off the inevitable I severely bruised my right hand thumb.

I had some scratches and grazes on my legs but my thumb swelled up and I was in so much pain playing the guitar for five hours, it was sheer agony. It's still bad but I carry on of course.

I received a letter from the poet on Monday. He's looking for a cheap flight to here. God, I miss him so much and am beginning to feel lonely. I haven't seen the American joker for three days either.

Friday, February 11, 1976

Today is my day off. I saw Scott again last night, the nice American. He stayed home two days because he was out of money, he said. We kissed and I would've liked to make love to him but I'm not allowed to take anyone to my room in this backward hotel, so frustrating.

Tonight I have a dinner date with Alain, a Frenchman who seems to be chasing me. I like him alright; he's the Ibiza jet set type and brought me a good joint twice already while I was working.

Scott is so jealous; he dislikes Alain who, by the way, is a nephew of the famous writer Albert Camus.

See what happens, Lee, when you let me go off on my own to faraway lands? This place is infested with yearning men but I long for my own darling Lee.

Monday, February 14, 1977

Last night Mohammed (chief of the waiters) gave me a letter from Lee. He was very worried because he hadn't yet received my letters. And there also was a telegram; he needs a thousand guilders to get here. I asked my boss for a four hundred dollar advance.

On Thursday, Wibo Welters, an employee here, is off to Holland. He offered to take the money; that would be the fastest way. I sent Lee a cable this afternoon to meet with Wibo at Schiphol airport. So, if all goes well Lee can be here Friday or Saturday, I hope so.

Scott is beastly annoying because he's upset that Alain took me out to dinner and comes in often to listen to me. He can go to hell; he's just like Johnny indeed! And he doesn't come that often to listen to me.

February 15, 1977

Today my boss told me that I can't get an advance until the 21st. I'm sick to death of course; I had sent a cable to Lee already. So, I sent him another one today. What misery! I can't stand it! I wish I'd never come here!

Wednesday, February 16, 1977

If my Lee doesn't come soon I shall go mad from loneliness. All the time I have to brush off dogs in heat! A group of American high ranking military men come in every night and one evening the Supreme Court Judge Thurgood Marshall was with them; he complimented me on my singing.

He is the first black American Supreme Court Judge and a fatso but very nice. One of the military men said he would like me to sing for them at their base. Ha! I don't think so!

I don't feel well; I wish I had sleeping pills with me. Today I don't have to work; it's a religious holiday.

No sign from Scott anymore, ah, so what, c'est la vie!

Thursday, February 24, 1977

Since Saturday I'm in another hotel, the Keyan, it's fine. Friday a guy tried to break into my room at the Elizabeth Hotel. I stayed in the Inter-Conti for two days.

In this hotel are six Israeli boys, they're fun. I slept with two of them and that did me a world of good.

I sent money to Lee's bank account, perhaps he'll be here tomorrow or Saturday. I hope so. We are separated from each other more than three weeks, it seems much longer. Okay, I'm going to wash my hair and play the guitar. My boss said I'll get off to pick my husband up from the airport.

Sunday, March 6, 1977

Lee is here! Thursday night he stood in the lobby of the Inter-Conti. The reunion was joyful. He flew with the Russian airline Aeroflot, very cheap, and stayed two days in a hotel in Moscow, all included in the trip complete with a sightseeing tour. He brought me a beautiful Russian scarf and dolls that fit into each other; I believe they are called Matrushkas.

I'm in another hotel again and this one is much better than the first two. My room is on the 7th floor with a magnificent view of the mountains, it is the Royal Gardens hotel.

I do miss my Israeli friends a bit, especially Zwi, a young architect originally Romanian. He's a Gemini like me and I adore him. He gave me an original Persian skirt with blouse and a beautiful book about Iran, so sweet of him.

Lee and I spent almost the entire day in bed today. I'm so glad he's here; it's so much nicer now. I told him about Zwi who wants to take me to a Harold Pinter play. Lee says that he has no intention of curtailing my freedom; however, it is different now of course. Oh, well, I'm glad Lee is here anyway. He's busy as a beaver; he wants to do something, teaching perhaps. I hope he can because Tehran is an expensive city. Lee wrote a lovely poem for me, really very special and I am deeply touched by it.

It's time for a nap.

April 1st, 1977, Kabul, Afghanistan

I shall buy another book to write down everything we experienced so far.

April 2nd, 1977

From Tehran we rode (first class, super!) the train to Meshad, the Holy city. We had to leave behind our faithful little dog Wiggy on the sidewalk of Hotel Pars. I hope she's alright. She had been our faithful companion for the whole time we were in Hotel Pars; one day she was sitting there and followed us to the corner of the street and then she walked back. When we returned she was waiting for us again and so it was all the time. She was just a puppy, no older than four months I guess, I named her Wiggy because she was always wagging her tail as soon as she saw us. I shall really miss her.

We shared our compartment on the train with a nice couple with their two-year-old son.

We slept well; it was the most comfortable train I ever was on. In Meshad we continued our trip with a private car and chauffeur which, in retrospect, was a mistake because the driver, a student, was off his rocker. We had to be at the border no later than five o'clock because we were told they close up at that time. When we were almost there the driver decided to have his tires checked, at a quarter to five!

We managed to convince him to drive on and arrived at the Iranian border just in time. We were supposed to cross the piece of no man's land and drive to the Afghan border by mini-bus but that took some doing and the Hindu boys who went by bus from Meshad arrived three quarters of an hour later. So, we spent extra money and gained nothing by it.

The Afghans squabbled for hours; it was on the bus and out of the bus, with all their worldly possessions on their backs. Fascinating experience, that's true.

We were the only Westerners and I the only woman. Naturally I wore the Persian cloths Zwi gave me and my hair covered completely by the Russian scarf; I don't want to cause trouble.

I was so glad when we finally left; the bearded men with their turbans, dressed in pastel colored baggy pants, decided to let us get on instead of the two sour looking Afghans who were left standing in the sand. Hospitality to us, foreigners, was more important to the men evidently, how nice. It was freezing cold there in the middle of nowhere, the desert, bare sandy plains, hills and high snow topped mountains in the distance.

At the Afghan border we had to stay in a hotel, well, you could hardly call it that. We were asked to lie down on the floor in the main entrance room there which we refused and then a man took us outside on a long path that led to a shack. When he had left we could hear howling wolves in the distance so Lee and I walked back to the main building and settled ourselves as best we could on thin mattresses on the floor. We slept remarkably well and left early with a bus to Herat. We arrived there at two o'clock. Herat is a quaint little town with decorated horse drawn carriages serving as taxis. We stayed in Hotel Mustafa for 50 Afghans; nothing to write home about, a little room with two shabby beds but okay; we could rest and freshen up a bit at least.

Since Tehran we didn't have a hot meal anymore just fruit, nuts and cookies. We are scared to eat just anything without knowing what it is or if it is any good. One has to be so careful out here.

From Herat we went south the next day by bus to Kandahar. That trip took seven hours. We slept in a clean hotel for a change and had a wonderful hot meal. Kandahar is a lovely, picturesque little town with lots of shops and handicrafts.

We continued our trip north to our final destination: Kabul.

We are here one week now. Since two days in a magnificent room overlooking the city (tucked in between the snow covered mountains) in the Inter-Continental Hotel. I am booked here for the month of April.

If I hadn't landed this job we would have been forced to go back to Holland because our money is starting to get low. I only make $300 a month, however, all our expenses are covered and it's very comfortable indeed. Each morning breakfast is being wheeled in with whatever we want: pancakes, Canadian bacon, marmalade, jam...etcetera. This is a great holiday for us. We bought soft very good quality leather bags and boots, all handmade, beautiful and dirt cheap.

Now I'm going to write a letter to Marjorie. I only have to sing two hours a night, piece of cake!

April 3, 1977

Every morning we are up with the crack of dawn because we don't draw the curtains at night, we refuse to do so.

Since two days we have pancakes for breakfast, so delicious! They roll in our meals three times a day, with fresh flowers, silver spoons and forks and knifes, the works, it's great!

This healthy mountain air, the peace and quiet, the beautiful panorama; it is like an elixir for us.

Singing in the Nuristan Bar and later on in the Pamir Super Club is fine, not many people but nice.

I've added eight songs to my repertoire since I left Holland and I'm adding two more.

April 4, 1977

In the Kabul Times newspaper there's a big add about my performing in the Inter-Continental Hotel with my picture. How nice! I'm reading an interesting book, Future Shock by Alvin Toffler. Lee went into town. I've got Besame Mucho down pat, well, almost. It's a bit cold today and strong wind.

April 5, 1977

Today is my day off. I wrote a letter to Ben Dull, he's the journalist from Het Parool who wrote little pieces about me several times. I also wrote a letter to the Sheraton Hotel in Tehran. Who knows, maybe I can land another singing engagement there.

The weather has changed, rain and rather cool. It's unbelievable, the quiet here.

April 9, 1977

I've decided to have something done to my hair and made an appointment with the hairdresser in the hotel for Saturday morning. My hair is a little over my shoulders now and practically even so quite nice but I can never let it hang totally loose because it sits in my face too much.

At night when I'm performing I wear artificial flowers in diverse colors in my hair; it's a classical look and nice but somehow I feel old fashioned.

I wrote letters to the Inter-Continental Hotels in Tokyo and Hong Kong. Now I'm going to tape Besame Mucho.

April 13, 1977

My hair is much nicer now, smoother, and more modern. It's just a little shorter and cut straight.

I have to start at six p.m. in the Nuristan Bar till eight o'clock and then later another half an hour from ten till ten thirty in the Pamir Club where the Esquire Set, a band from Shri Lanka plays, I'm the intermission attraction.

I think that pretty soon I'm going to buy my first fur coat and that definitely will be a milestone in my life although that sounds rather exaggerated.

I never made so much money in only a few months time. It feels great! I write to kill time and I read a lot these last couple of days. I wonder when a new song will flow out of my pen, soon I hope. I long for a letter from my mother and my other relatives, maybe Friday?

April 15, 1977

At last a new melody sprouted from my brain, however, writing good lyrics for it is hard but it's a start.

April 16, 1977

I have talked to some nice men since I'm here. Yesterday I bought a great little fur coat, a gold fox. I didn't pay yet because it's being made for me. Not one with little pieces like most of the foxes they sell here but a jacket with only the backs and of the best winter fur quality.

Kabul is boring, we haven't received any mail and the weather is not what it ought to be. At night there's more going on since about a week, more people. I met a couple of French doctors, tonight I'm having dinner with them. Last night we had a nice time in the Pamir Club after my performance. I had a ball dancing. The band from Shri Lanka is very good. The drummer, Niha, is cute and falls for me; I know because he stops by the Nuristan Bar all the time when I sing before he has to start and, whenever I see him he always has something to say, the rascal.

In a little while I have a date with one of the French, he's a professor and surgeon of vertebra injuries. He's here to operate on the son of the President and he is director of the Hôtel De Dieu Hospital in Marseille, well, that's what he told me. He somehow intrigues me, don't know why, it's something about him, can't put my finger on it. Though not particularly handsome he appears boyish with his forty-three years. Oh God, I'm an incurable teenager when it comes to men. Perhaps that's what keeps me young. His name is René.

April 17, 1977

I'm becoming quite a celebrity in Kabul; with advertisements with photo of me all the time and posters everywhere. I saw one yesterday in Goblen Lotus where I ate a scrumptious delicious meal with René and another younger doctor Bruno and Paul (anesthesiologist). To be continued.

~

Chapter 8

A long journey back home

What a promiscuous little devil I was in those days way back when. You may wonder why and how my husband put up with all my escapades.

I think that Lee felt it was best to let me be free and unencumbered by conventionalities; he knew that he was almost twice my age and, he always stressed that giving each other space was of the utmost importance in a relationship.

'Do what you want, baby,' he used to say, 'as long as you always come home to daddy.'

During the first years of our marriage our relationship grew ever stronger and, despite the arguments and fist fights now and then we became real soul mates.

I had always loved reading and through him I became acquainted with English literature. Charles Dickens, Jane Austin, Madame Bovary, Crime & Punishment, The Plague, The Painted Bird; the list was sheer endless but I loved it and in the process, with the dictionary at hand, my English improved rapidly.

Lee was also very funny; being a keen observer of human behavior coupled to his sharp wit, he often had me in stitches. I simply loved being around him; my romantic outings on the side could not rupture the strong bond Lee and I had, of that I was absolutely sure.

He was my anchor, my guide and tutor and I couldn't imagine ever living my life without him.

In the lobby of the Inter-Continental Hotel in Tehran hung a large portrait of the Shah and Farah Diba who would be forced to flee the land only two years later. I talked with a lot of people; everyone complimented me on my singing. I also met a Dutch woman who had married an Iranian meat wholesaler; with her I went to an orphanage one day and fell in love with a lovely three-year-old girl that made me think about adoption. I wrote my sister Marjorie about it which caused her to panic and urge me not to do such a thing.

There were a couple of female students who told me they were against the reign of the Shah and that they were working on a revolt against him. I often wondered later what became of them when the Shah and his family were ousted and Iran turned into an Islamic State.

When Lee came to Tehran we moved to another hotel, the Pars and on the day we arrived there a little adorable doggy was sitting on the sidewalk in front of the hotel. I wanted to take him up to our room but that was impossible of course. The little dog waited for us each morning and walked with us to the corner of the street. He walked back and was waiting for us again when we returned.

Something had gone awry in the Inter-Continental Hotel; I had been sent to the police office with a student for my working permit. The young man didn't speak more than three words English; I was asked what I was doing in Tehran and answered that I was working as a singer. Wrong! I should have lied I was told later by a very annoyed food and beverage manager, a German. He proceeded to tell me that I was fired because I had caused the hotel to be fined a large sum of money. Naturally I was in shock but fortunately I had made friends with Tallulah, an American singer/pianist in another bar of the hotel (the Inter-Conti in Tehran had five rooms with live entertainment) and she spoke to her friend, a lawyer. I had enquired with the Dutch embassy first but those idiots suggested a lawyer to me who was also the lawyer of the hotel.

Tallulah's lawyer friend got everything settled because a few days later I was summoned to the office of the General Manager, a Swiss; he apologized to me and gave me the rest of my salary according to my contract. The nice lawyer wanted no money from us, an added bonus; however, Lee and I went shopping and bought him a beautiful silk tie and a luxurious after shave.

Now I was free to do as I pleased and that's when Lee and I decided to travel on to Afghanistan.

In Kabul we took a room in a small but at least clean hotel and I immediately went over to the Inter-Conti there. I was hired on the spot and Lee and I moved into a lovely large room overlooking the valley with Kabul and the mountains alongside, in the Inter-Continental Hotel. That month in Kabul was fantastic! We went down to Kabul center every afternoon and sat with our friend Mohammed who had a shop of leather goods (you could lend foreign books there also) on Chicken street. I can only say that our trip to Iran, Afghanistan and Turkey remains to this day one of the most exciting and wonderful trips of my life.

~

April 26, 1977

Saturday will be my last day here. We still haven't heard from Marjorie or mom. Lee and I are busy buying presents.

René gave me a heavy silver bracelet with a design of leaves in it of lapis lazuli, very lovely indeed.

Last night was our last meeting. Bruno, René and I went to a show of Afghan music. It was wonderful, especially the old man with sparkling bright blue eyes and a very high piercing but joyful voice, full of enthusiasm while fiddling on a sort of... I don't know, a box, some sort of Afghan musical instrument. It was a pity that we couldn't understand the words for the audience often burst out in spontaneous laughter and applause. It was a splendid gay evening.

Afterwards René and I ate in an Italian restaurant where the pasta crunched like sand between my teeth. I couldn't bring myself to eat the next course, steak and vegetables, salad and French fries, this to René's great dissatisfaction who said: 'If I can eat it so can you, it's fine. Just leave the salad over.' But I wasn't hungry at all anymore. René is a wonderful man who taught me a lot about my body. He's sweet and I think we'll remain friends.

I read The Life of Vincent Van Gogh, very beautiful and now I'm at the end of The Glass Inferno, fascinating.

Wednesday, April 27, 1977

I'm sick to my stomach from the moaning flute downstairs, I mean somewhere in the valley. The whole blessed afternoon the musician is at it already, so annoying!

April 28, 1977

I passionately long for a letter from mama; I catch myself lately thinking about her all the time. I feel her delightfully soft plump arms around me and I would like to take a bite out of them. I long for all of them, Marjorie, the children, Lilly, daddy, Ben, grandma. But most of all I long for my mother.

I read her letter again today, the only one that I received from her dated February 15.

I'm not well; I have diarrhea and a nasty cough. Lee has had the same earlier this week. Both of us are sick continually, it's got something to do with the climate in Kabul. René said people call it Kabulitis. The weather still isn't great either, a lot of changes in temperature.

April 29, 1977

The Afghan outfits for Roelofje and Jordi are ready; how cute they will look in them.

May 1, 1977

Our bags are packed, the bus leaves at nine-thirty. Mohammed, our friend from the leather shop, he also lends out foreign books and we spent many an afternoon there, sipping tea, exchanging a sentence or two now and then;

he is a wonderful, tranquil man and his wife who came with him to the Inter-Conti one night to hear me sing, gave me a ring with huge amber off her finger when I admired it. I had to accept it from her, impossible not to. They are real sweet people, so anyway, Mohammed will see us off.

Now, we're sitting on the balcony of a restaurant at the bus center of Kabul, drinking Fanta.

The sun is blazing and below swarms the business life. I won't forget this sight. Afghans with turbans, little shops, vegetable stalls, Afghan music, artisans, the loafers, the hustlers, the majestic mountains around us, the mud, the dirt, the carpenter hammering away, claxons of the cars; it's a cacophony of sounds and smells and children's shrieks as well...so typical Middle Eastern.

The bus is supposed to leave at nine-thirty but that will undoubtedly be an hour or an hour and half later. Never be in a hurry in the East. We take our time, we are waiting for Mohammed.

Seven-thirty that night

Afghanistan is a trip! We have a little room near the hotel we stayed on our way going to Kabul. I'm now in the restaurant of that previous hotel, drinking tea after I freshened up in the bathroom.

After a bus trip of seven hours through desert-like country you get tired, dusty, clammy and sticky. Kandahar is in the South and very hot. Flies swarm everywhere, the wind is blowing and a film of dust covers you the moment you're outside.

Lee just came back. We are going to take the bus, it leaves in an hour. Ah, that suits me just fine. There are no trains in Afghanistan, no television either and because of that you feel as if you've stepped back in time, a century or so.

In Tehran people watched the same American soaps as we do in Holland, Dallas and Dynasty. But here it's a whole other ballgame.

Monday morning, May 2nd, 1977

Now we are in Herat again. The mini-bus to the border leaves at half past twelve. We slept in another small room and kept our clothes on. It's a pity that it is so dirty in Afghanistan, always wind and sand. I'm curious about Istanbul.

I heard from several business people in the Inter-Conti in Kabul that Istanbul is quite nice.

An Afghan female singer's music resounds through the street and mingles with the city noises of carpenters at work, merchants praising their ware, the horse and wagons decorated with pompoms and bells, those are taxis, you don't see that in Kabul but you do in Kandahar. I have also noticed that in Herat and Kandahar almost all the women wear those horrible burkas whereas in Kabul you also see women in ordinary cloths. That's the one thing I don't like in these parts, the way women are treated. To have to go about like a ghost, invisible all your life…it's terrible I think.

I'm tired, if all goes well we'll be in Meshad tonight. There we can wash up and have a good rest. Our destiny is Istanbul. I have three chances for work there. I'm full of courage.

Tuesday, May 3, 1977

There's nothing to do about it, you can only comply with it. Yesterday the jerk policeman didn't want to stamp our passports because our visas expired nine days ago. There was no going back on his decision; the man was a typical bureaucrat. We tried to slip onto the mini-bus to the

Iranian border, helped by four Europeans who took pity on us but, no such luck. Some official prick checked the passports and we had to get off.

There we were, in the middle of nowhere, barren plain, with our luggage. Luckily we caught a ride back to the Iranian border, in the loading platform of one of those fantastically painted Afghan trucks.

The trip back to Herat by rickety mini-bus was a never ending story due to the fact that the maximum speed of the overworked little bus wasn't more than sixty kilometers per hour. And, naturally the whole gang stopped to eat in one of those filthy wayside restaurants. We drank tea; since it's boiled water there is no poisoning danger.

At last we arrived at eleven o'clock at night in Herat. Our taxi (horse and wagon) treated us to a tour of the town; the driver didn't know where the Mowfag Hotel was.

Finally we got there and we slept well; the room is clean and that's a great luxury here. It costs two hundred eighty Afghans per night including breakfast.

This morning we went to the police office. It is three hundred Afghans each for the extra visas that are only valid today and tomorrow. Afterwards we also went to the Iranian Consulate to ask if our visas are still okay. The official there assured us four times that everything is in order.

Imagine; we don't want any more hassle at the border. Lee and I were cheerful and said to each other that everything wasn't as bad as all that, it was after all our own fault. We should've extended our visas in Kabul; we had plenty of time to do so. We gaily strolled to the ticket office for the bus to the border. And there we got to hear the next setback: there's no bus today! Not enough passengers! What can you do? Nothing! I'm beginning to get pretty fed up with this fucking country! I'm going to sleep.

Lee is still outside. We just ate in the restaurant of the hotel, Lee chicken with rice, and I French fries with fried eggs.

Tomorrow is our anniversary, the fourth of May: four years.

Lee said at the table: 'Close your eyes.' I obeyed without hesitation and when I was allowed to open my eyes I had a lovely ring on my finger with lapis lazuli. How wonderful!

It's a sweet little ring and it goes well with the bracelet I received from René.

We are having our siesta now and later when it's cooler we're going to take a look at the minarets of I.

It is Wednesday, May 4, 1977

Lee, I, a German boy, a Canadian and a Palestinian are in a hospital twenty km off the Iranian border; we are in quarantine.

Our cholera shots were not valid anymore; the border physician was implacable, we got a shot and have to stay in this hospital one day.

I say some hospital; there are no towels and no hot water. Earlier today I wanted to wash my dirty feet in the sink but I lost my balance and the water basin came off the wall. Lee and the Canadian were outside in the garden and heard the racket. Luckily I have only a few scratches; no harm done. For lunch we got an omelet, bread and yogurt, and tea. It is alright but not enough, we are all starving. And all of us are feeling a bit droopy; I guess it's from the shot. We ate rice with meat, nothing special.

The Palestinian is so annoying; he goes on and on about why we don't know much about Arabic history. We told him several times already that we're not into politics. At some point the Canadian asked him why he doesn't know anything about Canadian history. Ha-ha!

We are the only patients in the entire hospital, quite amusing. There's a television set but the picture runs and besides, it's an American Hospital flick synchronized in Farsi so…that doesn't help. All of us are rather withdrawn.

Lee and I share one room, there are eight beds.

I expect we'll run into John and Maggie again along the way, they are an American couple we met in Kabul and bumped into again in Herat. Their destination is Istanbul also. They are fun people, we smoked a lot last night in their hotel of which the owner is a brother of Roman, an Afghan we met on our way coming, in Kandahar.

Roman works for one of the bus companies, Fayaz, he repaired my sunglasses and on our way back we saw him again in Kandahar. He bought two cucumbers for us for the nightly trip to Herat and gave us his brother's address but we took the first hotel we saw when we arrived; we were dead on our feet. It was a coincidence that we recognized the name of the hotel, Yadin, yesterday afternoon and also that John heard Lee's voice and called after us.

We were on our way to see the minarets that we didn't visit because we hung out with them; it was so cozy and comfy.

Today at the Afghan border we saw the Afghan who gave us a ride the day before yesterday in his truck. He invited us to his room there for tea. He showed us a large piece of hash but naturally we are not going to buy hash while we have to cross the border; we threw away our last piece in the garden of the Inter-Continental Hotel. Then the little man with rickety brown teeth smiled mysteriously and gave Lee *tombok,* greenish, grass-like stuff which the Afghan men carry with them in a little box. You have to keep it under your tongue for a little while and then spit it out.

I understand now why I saw men spitting all the time, nasty.

At first Lee didn't feel much but about fifteen minutes later he was very enthusiastic and said: 'It's like a trip!'

I didn't try it, I was stoned enough as it was.

Goodbye Afghanistan! The Afghans are beautiful people!

May 8, Mother's Day

We're sitting in a small shitty restaurant in Turkey, in a small village thirty-five km from the border. I don't know the name of this hamlet; we arrived here last night.

So much has happened. Now I'm going to drink my Turkish coffee.

At night

We are in Erzurum. We left this morning at ten by bus, a long trip straight through the mountains.

Since we were released from the quarantine hospital we have had no other opportunity to wash ourselves.

We feel dirty, hungry and exhausted but we'll eat first now.

This reasonable hotel has a Turkish bath; it costs fifteen Lire a person. Our room is sixty Lire. It's a hustler-dealer-wheeler hotel. Oh well, shit, that figures! Lee just found out that the Turkish bath is only for men. Now that stupid idiot owner tells us! Anyway, he promised to bring me hot water.

Lee is now in the Turkish bath! Fuck, women are second class citizens in these parts! I am so angry!

Monday morning May 9, 1977

With difficulty Lee managed to get a can with hot water last night so that I could wash off the worst dirt but I still don't feel nice and clean. Naturally the Turkish bath was great for Lee.

Changing money is complicated and time consuming in these countries. Erzurum is situated in the mountains that are still covered with snow. Evidently it is very cold here. People wear winter cloths. The bus to Istanbul takes twenty-four hours but it appears to be perilous. Every day people perish in traffic accidents. By plane it's only two hours but, alas, no more seats available. That leaves the train. By train it will take forty-eight hours, terribly long but we can take a sleeper and perhaps we can catch a flight in Ankara. These countries are immeasurably large. Oh well, we'll see.

In Turkey men wear caps and the women colorful skirts and blouses. And no chadors or burkas here thank God!

Monday night, May 9, 1977

We're in the train to Istanbul. I'll continue my story about the past couple of days.

So, we were eating Mexican (very good) in the Steakhouse on the Villa Avenue in Tehran. Mike, the German boy, wasn't feeling well and only had salad and tea. We got a ride in a Mercedes mini-bus to the station. There were a lot of people, it was some sort of market and we saw policemen who dispersed the crowd while nonchalantly raining blows indiscriminately with a chain. It was so shocking to us, we couldn't believe our eyes!

The train swings rather; I just started a good book, The Fan club by Irving Wallace.

Saturday, May 13, 1977

We're in Istanbul since Wednesday morning and enjoying every minute of it. This is a gorgeous, wonderful, beautiful city!

Sunday, May 14, 1977

I'm in the train; it's a quarter past five. Lee is looking for oranges and a chicken for the ride. We will travel via Munich this time. God, it's so hot here.

Istanbul was a fantastic experience. I would have liked to stay longer but our finances are slim now and we really have to head home.

I'm curious about Munich, they say it's a happening place.

Traveling is so fascinating; I haven't had enough of it yet, not by a long shot! Everywhere we go we meet nice people, an asshole now and then too but that's to be expected.

We sent mom and dad, Marjorie and Ben and Lilly a card from Istanbul.

Monday, May 15, 1977

Lee is knocked out, sleeping like a baby, a book lying on his stomach; mouth ajar, my darling angel. The train is rushing along through the lovely countryside in Yugoslavia.

The compartment is empty, very few people on this train.

Last night we were rudely awakened by the Bulgarian customs clerks. They wanted thirty-two US dollars, no less, for a visa. We thought it a bit too steep and informed the man, Lee did actually, that it was far too much, ridiculous in fact. We offered them five dollars. They took our passports and motioned us to get dressed and follow them. However, we were in no hurry, we've about had it with this authoritarian and rude behavior of custom clerks in these parts.

Anyway, after about a quarter of an hour one of them returned, threw our passports on the seat and left without another word. We expected them to come back and fetch us but nothing happened.

I just spoke with an elderly American couple while standing in the passage way admiring the countryside and they told me that they paid thirty-two dollars each. Imagine that, what crooks those custom officials!

I guess they figure that all Westerners and in particular Americans are rich so they try and grab what they can.

Our supplies are down to one cucumber and two oranges. It's stifling hot in here.

Tuesday morning, May 16, 1977

We're in Austria. Snow-covered mountains all around, what a
magnificent land!

Though we managed to catch some shut eye, we're terribly tired and
stiff.

Nine p.m.

Now I'm sitting on a terrace at Mozartplatz in Salzburg. Sunshine,
lovely weather!

The poet is changing money at the American Express Company. Our
money is almost gone.

Many women wear dirndl dresses, carrying wicker baskets; a damn
parade if you ask me but funny in a way. Salzburg is beautiful and so
clean! If the weather is as nice as it is here in Holland we cannot
complain.

Eleven thirty p.m.

We're in the train again, on our way to Brennero, a little place just
over the Italian border. We have to transfer in Innsbruck. I feel good and
am enjoying everything, the countryside is so lovely.

Wednesday, May 17, 1977

We are in Innsbruck, in a nice little hotel for two hundred twenty shilling with breakfast. We slept delightfully here, took baths, put fresh cloths on so…today we are vivacious and ready to take on the last part of this trip.

If all goes well we'll be in Holland tomorrow or Friday. I'm a bit tired and I must admit that I long for home now.

Once back in Europe one is shocked to see the difference in living expenses. The Middle East is dirt cheap in comparison. I hope to stay with my mother for a couple of days or with Marjory. I long to hug my sweet darling nephews. Lee wants to go to Groningen to pick up his books.

May 21, 1977, Amsterdam

Everything is alright. We are unpacking. I have a splitting headache.

~

Chapter 9

Restless Soul

Being back home after our amazing trip in the Middle East took a bit of getting used to. I felt that Lee and I had become closer and decided that my fling with the French doctor in Kabul (who once, after we made love in his apartment, showed me a video of a vertebrae operation of his which I abhorred) had to be my last infidelity. Good intentions that got me nowhere because nothing changed; Lee was away every night, leaving me alone as usual and I felt neglected and lonely again.

~

June 8, 1977

Now I've been hit in the mouth by Lee again! It's true we all drank too much and it was a bizarre evening but still. How can I make him stop doing that? My lower lip is swollen. It doesn't hurt but I feel insulted and I think that he'll forget it all too soon and one day, perhaps a year from now, perhaps a couple of months, he'll do it again when he's in a bad mood. I feel very low. I thought about leaving him for awhile so that he can think about what he's doing to me. But where can I go? The only one I can think of is my little sister Lilly, she's in Mallorca. If I had money I would go there.

June 10, 1977

I'm in Hotel Fortia in Rue Fortia in Marseille, France. I arrived this morning with the eight o'clock train. I'm alone, Lee is not with me.

I got a cold; it came on very suddenly last night on the train, shit! Marseille is beautiful and warm. This afternoon I have a meeting in Hotel Sofitel with the director. I'm going to try my luck with other big hotels as well.

In Istanbul I sang in the Hilton and the Inter-Continental Hotel. Oh, I have to write down about all our fun adventures there and I didn't tell what happened at the Turkish border. Never mind, I'll get to that.

The idea to travel down here came up the day before yesterday; I received a payment of $125 in my bank account and saw an opening. Lee didn't object and wished me luck. He hit me two days ago and I am seriously thinking about leaving him.

However, now that I'm here, alone, with a cold, I wonder what in God's name came over me.

Anyway, whatever, the weather is great!

Saturday, June 11, 1977

I've got no luck so far. One secretary of a large hotel was so rude to me. She said: 'I've got no time for you, miss,' and slammed down the phone.

I will call The Meridian in Nice and perhaps one or two other hotels but if it is all so negative I've had it.

From here to Barcelona isn't too expensive, maybe I'll have more luck in Mallorca? Lilly is there and she may know something. Alone is just alone. I keep thinking of Lee and I dream of him every night.

I still cough like crazy. I think I'll read for awhile because if I call now everyone has their lunch break.

Yesterday I called five hotels.

Sunday, June 12, 1977

It's half past three and I'm in the train that's about to take off for Cannes. There I will try my luck once more.

Yesterday afternoon René called, the French professor I met in Kabul. He came to my hotel and greeted me a bit stiff as if he was shy. He's sweet but rather bourgeois I think. He took me in his fast BMW on a fabulous trip over a high mountain a little past the resort town Cassis. At the highest point we got out and enjoyed the beautiful view over the blue Mediterranean. From the point where we stood there was a sharp drop; an ideal spot for suicidal types. It was a nice relaxed afternoon.

Last night I went to the bar of Hotel Sofitel with my neighbor from room six. He's an American whom I coincidentally met in the little lounge of this hotel. He's having a week's vacation in Marseille and was a rather entertaining talker, Richard is his name. Afterwards we sat on the terrace of a bar in the old harbor and we closed off the night with a cup of coffee in another bar closer to the hotel we're in.

Anyway, now I'm on my way to Cannes and we'll see how it goes.

Monday morning.

What misery! It's raining cats and dogs and I don't know but it looks like my trip here is a disaster. I'm constantly thinking of Lee and I want to go home.

I sang in the street, with my guitar, walking over the terraces filled with people. I have never done that before! What a lovely town this is, a boulevard filled with roses and palm trees and all those luxurious hotels and restaurants, jewelers and fashion shops. You sense that wealth all around you, the rich and famous throwing away money by the buckets, living a life of leisure and luxury. I tried to get work in several hotels but no luck. I picked up thirty nine francs with my singing on the terraces; that felt a bit strange at first but what the heck, nobody knows me here and I don't know anybody either.

I'm in Hotel Des Voyageurs, it's forty francs a night, more expensive than in Marseille, I paid thirty two there. I went by four other hotels which were all more expensive or the same so it's okay. I ate very well, not in a tourist trap but in a real French pub with a movie on television. When I walked back to my hotel over the busy colorful boulevard a greybeard addressed me. He was strolling with his young girlfriend and they asked me to have dinner with them in Juan Les Pins. They also gave me their address in Nice and said I should drop by if I went to Nice. They have an apartment at sea there where I could sunbathe nude they said, like Francoise who 'never wears a bra' said the greybeard pointing towards her proud round tits of which the peak nipples shimmered through her thin blouse. Ha!

Sunday, June 19, 1977

I'm home again. I ran out of money but picked up enough for the train by singing on the terraces. Lee was happy to see me but surprised that I didn't continue on to Barcelona.

He didn't miss me I guess.

I think I'm going to get an offer to sing abroad again very soon.

This afternoon we're going to an opening of an exhibition of work of Keith.

Wednesday, August 10, 1977

My father has had a heart attack. It was such a shock to all of us. He's fine now with mama by his side, grandma came right away also and stayed with them for a fortnight. Dear darling daddy, I love you so much.

I did get two offers, one form Dubai and one from Abu Dabi, both Hilton Hotels, however, they want me to send them a cassette of my music and that's a bit of a problem because I don't have a tape-deck anymore. I can't bother daddy now to help me.

John, the Italian/American we met on our way back from Afghanistan is in Amsterdam.

Saturday night, August 20, 1977

I went to see a play last night in De Brakke Grond: *Ramses in de Nes.* It was nice although a bit chaotic. Ramses is such a dear, he moves me even though I don't always understand him back stage.

I typed Lee's new poetry book, such beautiful poems. I don't know anyone like Lee. I've got to make a professional tape, that's my number one project. Lee hasn't been home, I wish he would come.

September 23, 1977

I got an offer to perform in a club in West Berlin, to be the MC and to sing, seven nights a week from nine thirty till three in the morning, for one hundred fifty German mark a day of which I have to give 10% to John Wardell, my new agent. I'll get an apartment there which costs five hundred and eighty German mark a month that I have to pay and I also have to pay for my living expenses. I think I would like to accept, am curious about Berlin.

September 30, 1977

Tonight I'm leaving for Berlin by train. I'm a little nervous but also excited.

Berlin, Saturday morning, October 1, 1977

I'm in restaurant Kanzler at the corner of the Kürfürstendamm. It's raining cats and dogs. I had a good trip. There are several art exhibitions in Berlin this weekend. I have to start work tonight. What a pity that the weather is so bad, I would've liked to walk around a bit. Well, we'll see.

Afternoon, October 1, 1977

I just rehearsed two songs with the band in the Acheron Club. Although I have to announce the whole show tonight I have not a clue who the artists are and what they do. I guess it'll be alright. It's a beautiful club, a bit like the Blue Note in Amsterdam.

~

My work in the Acheron Club in Berlin, presenting the show and singing a couple of songs each set, turned out to be a failure. The management was not pleased with the way I presented the show. My agent flew in and explained to me that they wanted to let me go. Naturally I was quite disappointed; I was just getting started and why hadn't the management given me a little bit more time to adjust?

'Don't worry about it,' said my agent when he gave me an envelope with the money owed to me for the days I sang, 'I'll get you work in one of the clubs in Amsterdam, no problem.'

The other artists hated to see me go, they said, they organized a farewell party in a café near our apartment complex on the Bundesallee. The next day I packed up my belongings, took a taxi to the train station and got on the train.

~

October 11, 1977

Wardell hasn't found me work yet. He's working on it he says and keeps asking me to call him.

I wonder how it is with my little dog Wiggy in Tehran. I miss him.

Sunday, October 16, 1977

I went to see my folks. Papa looks well, much slimmer. Grandma is with them. Mama gave me a very nice sweater and grandma put a twenty five guilder note in my hand when nobody was looking. She's so sweet, she has done it before.

Bills are piled up again and the electricity is still cut off, I've got to do something about that. Candlelight isn't what it's made out to be, nothing romantic about it if you ask me. Lee and I watch Roots each week at Ellen and Jack's. It's very good but it makes me so sad each time.

October 23, 1977

There's a lot of terrorism these days. I got a positive letter from a hotel in Portugal, they're asking for a tape of my music. I'm going over to Jack and Ellen to see Roots. We're still living with candlelight.

November 3, 1977

The stove purrs...Jesus! There's always something! We keep hearing noises lately, what is that? Mice? A rat?

Something's got to be done about it!

I wanted to start off romantically. The stove purrs, tea is hot, the raisin bread that tastes delicious, the room neat and clean and everything dust-free, hallelujah! The floor lamp is on and it's so cozy! Since yesterday we have at last light in our darkness, electric ingenuity at our disposal, refrigerator, vacuum cleaner, oven, coffee maker, iron, boiler; it's fantastic! We were without electricity for nearly six months believe it or not. I went after it for three days like a maniac because Monday somebody came (without warning) and cut off our gas supply. What misery! Being without electricity is no fun especially since autumn and winter have started but having no gas! Good God, it seemed like war! I

was especially pissed off because I just had made an arrangement with

somebody by phone to pay off the bill each month with two hundred

guilders. So I went to City Hall yesterday in the pouring rain and I

probably walked in a side-entrance for personnel because to my

amazement I suddenly found myself at the department for Art Affairs and

thought: Hey, that's just where I ought to be. After two empty rooms I

encountered one with three gentlemen and one lady. I said: 'I'm so and so

and I'm a singer so I'm at the right place here. My gas has been cut off

and that's insane. I had intended to catch the mayor but I expect that won't

be easy, however, I've got to see someone, an alderman perhaps, because

I've got to be helped.' They seemed to be baffled and remained mute until

one of them tried to brush me off by saying that I had to go downstairs to

some department or other, I don't even know which because I cut him

short and said: 'No, you're the department of art and I'm an artist so that's

perfect.' I told them I had just arranged for terms of payment with lawyers

Kuper and Vulsma and that I didn't think they would agree with how

things were handled and would certainly try to do something about it.

Silence again but the one who had spoken before then said: 'It seems best

to me that you speak with the highest man with the Energy Company,' and

he proceeded to look up the number for me.

I asked to be allowed to call that man right then and there.

To make a long story short I obtained an appointment with the man who loosened up splendidly when I told him I had been at City Hall and that Mister Vermaak (in English this means entertainment so rather fitting) from the art department sent his regards.

Then I rushed over to my friend Ellen and later to Theo, our accountant and, between them I got three hundred guilders to pay the first installment of payment agreed with the Energy Company; all is well that ends well. I feel human again, there's warmth and light in the darkness.

November 11, 1977

Lou van Rees offered me a gig in an elegant restaurant for Christmas. Great!

November 19, 1977

Today, President Sadat of Egypt visited Israel; they say it's a historic event. Tomorrow Ben and Marjorie are coming with the babies and Lilly also. I'm so happy!

Lou van Rees wrote me an urgent letter to call him on Monday. I wonder what's up.

November 25, 1977

I heard that daddy has to go back to work for half days. Poor daddy, all his life working in that stupid factory and he could've been so much more if only he hadn't been taken from school to work when he was only fourteen. He had such a rotten childhood, with that witch of a stepmother and his own father who didn't lift a finger for him.

~

My father's mother died when she gave birth to him and Aunt Annie, his twin sister. Daddy was shipped off to his grandparents who doted on him but unfortunately when my grandfather remarried six years later those happy years came to an abrupt halt.

And the horror my father went through when he was sent to hard labor camps in Germany during World War II. He escaped, came back home but after only three weeks his stepmother said that it was too dangerous for them and his father's work with the post office to let him stay so he was back on the street and caught and shipped off to Germany again. He worked at the Messerschmitt airplane factory and once he and others sabotaged; consequently my sweet daddy was sent to an even more horrible camp. At the end of the war he escaped again and lived between the front lines; he had an affair with a German girl who wanted him to take her to Holland. Her mother cried and begged my father not to take her only daughter. I heard all this years later when I spent five weeks with him, in the summer of 1982.

~

December 1, 1977

We're collecting as much information as we can about Nigeria. It's so exciting! Perhaps Lee and I will be sweating on the back of an elephant next week. Lee is full of enthusiasm and I am too of course. Nigeria is the richest country in Africa, the fourth producer of oil in the world.

What a great opportunity for Lee, he went to the embassy a while back to present his plan of a poetry tour in Nigeria and now it looks like it's going to happen! All my life I've been dreaming of going to Africa!

December 6, 1977

I said goodbye to Lee this morning at the Central Station in Amsterdam. He has to go by the Embassy in The Hague to pick up his passport and visa. He'll arrive in Lagos Thursday afternoon at five p.m. His flight is leaving from London. I hope I can follow him next week.

He will send me a cable on Tuesday or Wednesday. It's better this way, he can put out feelers and I have of course full confidence in him.

It snowed; a majestic white blanket covers everything, so beautiful.

December 7, 1977

It's very cold outside and very cozy and warm inside. I slept alright but I miss Lee. I think of him constantly. It's eleven o'clock, I just heard on the news that a plane crashed on Cyprus. I haven't heard from Michel in ages. I wonder how he and his family are; I will send him a Christmas card.

Sunday, December 11, 1977

I miss Lee so very much; the house seems so empty without him. I played the guitar all afternoon. I don't know what it is, I've been with others off and on but that's just sex and I'm as empty after as I was before.

There's no one who can hold a candle to Lee, nobody; he is everything for me and I'm so lonely without him.

December 15, 1977

Help! I need somebody! Help, not just anybody! I've had visitors, I went out to visit friends, I wrote a short story that I tore up and I made a Christmas song that I like so I won't destroy it. But I go crazy with longing for Lee and I still haven't heard from him.

Thursday, December 22, 1977

I still haven't heard anything! Two weeks he's gone, I'm getting worried. I can hardly eat anymore. I miss him so much. I've got to work in Muiderberg on Boxing Day; I'll make five hundred and fifty guilders so that's nice at least. And I received a lovely Christmas card from Michel from Cyprus. He writes just as sweet as he is in my memory. In total I have five Christmas cards now. I was with the family in Alkmaar last weekend, Marjorie and her husband and the little rascals were there too, they're so cute and adorable my sweet little nephews. I hope that Lee is successful with his tour in Nigeria. I pray that I will hear from him soon. Ellen and Jack invited me for dinner with Christmas, so nice of them.

December 27, 1977

Finally I received word from my darling husband. Friday, the 23rd I found his letter on the doormat. My heart leaped for joy. He wrote it the 12th of December already. All is well with him. Lagos is a terribly dirty and expensive and criminal city. I had heard that from other people already. He resides on the campus of the University there which is probably one of the safest places in town.

Today I received a second letter from him. He wrote it on the 16th after his first recital which was very successful. He wrote that he has reserved a seat on the plane back on the 29th to London. So, I can expect him Friday or Saturday. I´m ecstatic with joy! I´m knitting a scarf for him, very pretty, grey stripes with black. He writes such marvelous letters, God, how I love that man of mine. My Christmas performance was great, wonderful audience and the owners gave me a little vase with beautiful flowers as a Christmas gift. I am so relieved since I heard from Lee.

December 31, 1977

This will be the first time we won´t be together on New Year´s Eve. He´s still in Africa; I´m sad but I guess it can only mean that he's been asked for extra performances.

I met a fun guy in café Hoppe on the Spui last Thursday, his name is Willem, he's a physician and nuts. I had a great time, lots of laughter. He's an acquaintance of Ellen and Jack.

It's been a while since I had a little adventure, I like him but I won't do anything with him 'cause Ellen told me he's married and has two children.

If Lee isn't coming home next week, I'll leave. I'll go to Formentera or something.

~

BOOK II

1978 – 1980

Chapter 9

Chasing my dream

January 5, 1978

I'm not well. I can hardly eat and evidently I feel like a wet rag. Mentally I'm instable as well. I went to the station last week to pick Lee up from the train. Today is the last valid day for his flight ticket. I received two postcards with a few cheery words.

I'm worth nothing anymore, totally washed out. I'm in Hoppe every day. I have sort of fallen in love with the blond doctor and against my better judgment I slept with him. What a stupid mistake! And now I'm angry with Lee. He shouldn't have left me for so long, it isn't fair. Now I'm afraid that he won't come back at all. I'm restless and tired and I want to leave. I am thinking of going to Formentera.

Wednesday, January 11, 1978

I'm back in balance, eating till I burst, singing up a storm, planning like crazy, in short: I'm my own positive self again. Lee is back. Saturday morning, at about nine, I was still asleep, he stormed into the bedroom. What an excellent surprise! Life is so much nicer. We're so happy to be together again at last. He missed me very much also and he's cooking up a storm already, every morning a cup of tea in bed for me. He bought a beautiful grey overcoat for himself and he had a great time in Nigeria. He met lots of wonderful people and wants to go back there with me. That would be nice, we'll see. He gave me a lovely snakeskin handbag. He's got more, of crocodile skin as well. He wants to sell them. He loves the scarf I knitted for him. I forgot to mention that I made a bed last Tuesday, all by myself, sick and tired as I was of sleeping on a mattress on the floor so…I went and bought the wood and put it together. I'm very proud of myself and Lee thinks it's great. He has got two left hands and aside from writing wonderful poetry he's pretty useless but I love him anyway. He gave me Roots, a beautiful book. Oh, nice, I've been invited to sing two songs in 'Magic from Studio One' a radio program, on February 11th. Lee said: 'We won't be here.' Actually I wouldn't mind being in the South somewhere myself.

Saturday, January 21, 1978

It's about nine at night and I exist of a thousand little pieces that have nothing in common with each other. I feel rotten. Nothing comes off right, I can't say a sensible word, can't think of anything sensible, or sing one single note. I am lost, mad as a hatter, totally nuts!

I should try to become pregnant maybe then I'll recover. God, I'm utterly depressed.

Wednesday, January 25, 1978

I'm working on taping songs of myself and of others. It's a very good exercise. Sean McCauley's friend Marjan is going to book me. I feel optimistic about my career and I have an idea for a new song. I made one recently.

Saturday, January 28, 1978

I gave a cassette plus photo to Rob who's going to give it to Aad van den Heuvel of KRO television. Marjan is my manager now and she's got me one gig already, on February 26, in Muiden in Count Floris the Fifth. I'll get two hundred and fifty guilders; she only gets 10%, I think I should give her a higher percentage when things get going.

Sunday, February 5, 1978

Mama called, jubilating. She heard an announcement about my performance on the radio. I noticed how excited and proud she is and I'm delighted. She said they would like to visit us soon. I long so much for them and told her to come soon like Tuesday or Wednesday.

Ellen put in a good word for me with the big producer Joop van de Ende who told her he wants to hear and see me sing to experience my charisma. Fine, I sent him a note saying that I perform for radio with a live audience on February 11th. I knew him a long time ago, via my friend Ger Akkerman and nothing ever came of it but, what the heck, you never know, do you?

I think we'll really go to America soon. I look so much forward to traveling again.

Lately I've been thinking of my grandfather who died a year ago. It was hard to part with life for him. I guess it always is. He still had so many words of advice to all his children and grandchildren. He expected much of me and said that I would move in the highest circles. Who knows; God knows I am giving it my all.

February 16, 1978

The radio show went fine. I got a stormy applause and beautiful flowers. Joop van den Ende wasn't there; that figures! Lee is in The Hague, I hope he comes back soon. I wish I had a child, I think I wouldn't feel so lonely but I also think it would be difficult, the responsibility I mean.

In May we will be married five years. And we're always poor. Even so we've been in many places in those five years: France, Switzerland, Spain, Italy, Iran, Denmark (in Copenhagen on our honeymoon), Cyprus, Luxembourg, Belgium, Afghanistan, Germany, Turkey, Greece and we've done many fabulous things. My life with Lee is a life full of surprises.

We get along splendidly, he is my best friend, we laugh a lot together and Lee has taught me so much, which books to read for instance. Life is good despite the hardships. Everybody likes Lee, he's very popular. He has published his poems extensively a.o. in the prestigious Negro History Bulletin of Washington D.C. and in countless other magazines and he's got several poetry books out. I always type for him and his publisher is Willem Klein, a dear friend of ours.

I'm going to take a nap now.

Monday, February 20, 1978

We're going to London for a few days. We're going to take the boat from Vlissingen tonight. I got over three thousand guilders from the Government. Wonderful, it is unemployment money retroactive from May 23rd, 1977. Great, isn't it? I bought a new second hand stove that looks beautiful and burns great! Isn't life a gas?

Tuesday, February 21, 1978

Hurrah, we're in London, in the Grosvenor Court Hotel, a nice and very comfortable room with bath, shower, television, radio, an electric kettle to make coffee and tea; it is so lovely and costs sixty three guilders a night.

It's foggy here but it's supposed to be, we're in London after all. Lee and I are happy like children. Thank God I brought my camera this time. I regret that I don't have any photos of our trip in the Middle East.

Wednesday, February 22, 1978

Lee and I are watching television from the bed. It's so much better than Dutch TV.

I bought a lovely grey suit today and a silk blouse, beautiful and not expensive. I've got to get shoes to match and I'll be in a fine feather for springtime.

I've got a meeting with the manager of the Hilton here tomorrow morning, a mister Peper. We saw Lee's gay friend Teddy today in his gorgeous shop on King's Road. We'll take a tour of the city tomorrow. The weather is quite nice, mild with some rain now and then.

February 23, 1978

I bought beautiful black shoes today and a red sweater. We didn't do the tour yet because a friend of Lee came by and stayed so long. We've got to do it tomorrow then.

Tuesday night we went to a Super Club here, Morton's, Bobby Relax played the piano, it's an elegant place on Berkeley Square. We want to visit Shouki's sister Tammy also.

Bobby took us to another place when he was finished playing and I rode in a double Decker bus for the first time in my life. Lee and I gambled on the boat coming over and lost fifty guilders.

Saturday, February 25, 1978

We're in the train from Vlissingen to Amsterdam. It was a great little holiday. I loved the tour of the city, to see the Tower where so many historical figures were kept prisoner and beheaded: Thomas Moore, Anna Boleyn, Elizabeth I and so many others. We visited Teddy, Lee's homo friend and I thought I would die laughing; the man is full of hilarious anecdotes. I hope we can go back soon and we absolutely have to do the Theatre next time.

Sunday, February 26, 1978

Not a dog listens to me when I sing and play the guitar in Count Floris V in Muiden; babies scream, the microphone distorts the sound horribly, beer-mats flying around, stamping, yelling, laughter, taunting remarks…it´s a fucking disaster! I keep singing as if nothing´s the matter but little by little, minute after minute I die, I shrivel up, now and then I revive, I won´t put up with it, you goddamn idiots!

Applause, that's nice but then the buzz starts up again and gets louder all the time and I get more tired, more and more and more. Thank God, at last it´s ten o´clock, it´s over.

What a flop, what a dark abyss; I am utterly exhausted.

Thursday, March 9, 1978

We're back in the Grosvenor Court Hotel in London. The crossing went well; I enjoyed the bus ride from Sheerness to London. The poet bought a suit, grey pinstripe, 1925 style; it looks divine on him. Well, he's a handsome devil.

Today we're catching a plane to New York if we can pull it off.

In the plane, TWA 707

Yes, we made it. I'm stoned as a beaver and full of expectations of America. The film I saw was alright, my grandfather was in it, playing God; the actor was a spitting image of him. We're a long time in the air already, four and a half hours I guess. I'm terribly excited, it seems like I'm dreaming. It's like a miracle. Instead of talking shit I should compose a song to celebrate my first trip to the States. Nobody knows that I'm on my way there.

Friday, March 11, 1978

I'm seated at a lovely desk in our room in Hotel Taft in New York. Wow! This is a nice hotel, large like the Hilton and Inter-Continental Hotels, naturally less sophisticated but first class anyhow. The room is large with blue flowered curtains and the same pattern on the quilts on the twin beds, thick light green carpet, television and we're on the eleventh floor. I just took a bath and feel invigorated. The poet went shopping. The hotel is near Broadway, Fifth Avenue and 42nd Street.

We walked around a bit this morning and I must say that this city made an overwhelming impression upon me; all those skyscrapers and ultra modern buildings, very impressive.

We arrived yesterday at seven twenty p.m. at Kennedy Airport. I was tired of the long flight and the food was abominable. Landing was magnificent because underneath you could see New York, a sea of lights through which the great stream of cars gyrated like a colorful ribbon, it was fantastic!

It's about 2 degrees Celsius so quite a bit colder than in England and in Holland. In some places there're still mountains of snow which hasn't melted yet after all those snow storms they had here.

Oh, how surprised mom, dad, Marjorie, Lil and Ben will be when they receive a card from me out of America!

I could've called Marjorie but somehow I didn't feel like it. And now I'm here, I really am!

We had a good breakfast this morning in a coffee shop on 44th street for only seven guilders fifty together. Prices are reasonable here, also of clothes. Amsterdam is ludicrously expensive compared to London and New York. You can spend a lot here of course, there's so much to do and to buy.

We just spoke to Ada and Bailey, sister and brother and good friends of Lee who consider him family. They're all so excited to hear we are in New York. Tonight we're meeting Bobby Reid and his tiny girlfriend Jane. We were at their house on Prince Street this afternoon but they were not home. Turner O'Brien, a friend of Lee from his time in Paris, is also in New York and this afternoon we'll meet another acquaintance of Lee in Greenwich Village.

I went to the Sheraton this afternoon, here on Seventh Avenue and spoke to the General Manager who told me they get all their entertainment through an agency of which he gave me the telephone number. To make an appointment proved to be very hard, the secretary said if the agent made appointments with everyone who calls him he would be doing interviews all day long. Heck, well, this is New York after all; I can't expect it to be easy.

Chapter 11

Life in the Big Apple

Saturday morning, March 12, 1978

New York is not only the exciting life, fun and having a good time, there´s another side to it of course.

The bell boy of this hotel told us several times already to lock the door while we´re in our room; two locks and a chain. There's a lot of crime.

Last night Bobby Fox visited us. We met him in Amsterdam two years ago; since then he keeps us abreast of the latest news in show business, the theater and cultural events by mailing us clippings from The New York Times, The Village Voice and other sources. He brought a bottle of wine and is so happy we're here. We went for drinks downstairs in the bar. He's gay and ever so sweet, entertaining and frank. He wants to take us to the hit Broadway Show the Wiz and dinner at the Top of the Sixes before. The Top of the Sixes is a building where you have a splendid view over the city.

We visited Bobby Reid and Jane after we said goodbye to Bobby Fox.
Bobby Reid is still the same; he drives a white Cadillac and boasted that
he has two. He also talked a lot about the high rate of crime in New York.
He took us to the jazz club Ali's Alley on 77th Green Street in the East
Village. There played a band for two hours uninterrupted, so good, so
together, and as creative as I have never heard and seen in Holland.
Unbelievable! What talent, what music!

As far as my own singing endeavors: I have addresses of two agents
whom I have to send publicity material and Mister Longes of the Holiday
Inn is on vacation, I can't reach him until the 20th.

It's lovely weather, Manhattan is full of color and gayety.

Tonight I'm meeting Ada and Bailey for the first time. She just called to
say we shouldn't eat too much today 'cause she's making a little
something for tonight.

'Are you comfortable over there, darling,' She said, 'I don't know why
you didn't come to me because you're welcome to stay at my place. I have
a room and beds, you know…'

On and on she went and I kept saying thank you. Lee doesn't want to
stay at people's houses, not enough privacy.

I agree with him and I love being in this hotel.

Sunday, March 12, 1978

Wow! Lee came home; he found money, just like that, three bills lying in the street, one of fifty, one of twenty and one of ten, eighty bucks! Cash! That man is so lucky; he always finds money, everywhere he goes. I've seen it happen.

He found money several times in Amsterdam but also in Paris, in Tehran, in Barcelona. And when he doesn't find money he gets it from people he never even met before like in Istanbul and Nigeria. In the Istanbul Hilton an Englishman emptied his wallet on the bar and gave the contents to Lee, a little over a hundred dollars. He told us he was retired and on a trip around the world and that he admired us for the people we are. 'An example of the fraternization between races and nations, 'He said.

In Nigeria Lee was also given quite a bit of money just like that by someone. Amazing, isn't it?

We're off to a cocktail party at five; I believe it's something important, intellectual and prestigious. Much depends on the contacts one makes in this exciting, fast town; for work I mean. We shall see; I'm fairly optimistic. Lee's changing money at the moment. I've mailed a lot of cards already. Perhaps something's on television. I didn't bring my guitar but I intend to buy another one here. First see if I can get my foot in the door.

Tuesday, March 14, 1978

No sun today but drizzle. Lee and I are trying to make contacts for work. I´ve sent my publicity material to four agencies and just got another name of an agent on Rhode Island. The procedure is that large hotels get their entertainment via booking agents and the ones I called so far want to look at my material before they want to set up an interview with me. It doesn´t go that fast of course, after all, we´re only four and a half days in New York City.

Thursday, March 16, 1978 (Happy Birthday, Michel)

It's snowing and so foggy that the view from Ada's and Bailey's apartment on the 20th floor is rather limited. We left the hotel last night and now we're staying here, quite comfortable I must say. It's all so classy and beautiful and elegant. I feel at home. I simply love the bathroom, all in soft yellow and the kitchen is spectacular with every luxury and comfort one could possibly want. Tuesday night Lee's friend Tom Bailey came by to see us in our hotel and later a friend of his came as well. She's a blues singer and brought her guitar. Her name is Mary Blithe and she's really nice; she's of Irish descent and I just love the way she talks, very melodic. She sang and I did too and we had a lovely night. Tom is such a funny character, we saw him last in Amsterdam, four years ago. He was with Helen then, the writer. We all went to Paris together where Helen fell in love with Omar.

Omar is back in the States since a few years and we never heard from him anymore. Tom Bailey is a great cook and used to be a seafaring man. Mary gave me the address of a club where I may be able to perform; they pay $50 a gig. I have to go there in the late afternoon, perhaps today after our visit to Dr. Harrington.

Two ladies just stopped by, one of them is also a singer and gave me a telephone number of a club in New Jersey. I called already; the man I need to talk to wasn't in. It's still snowing, fine as gossamer flakes descend in large numbers onto Manhattan. We're watching television; we had to postpone our appointment with Dr. Harrington. The weather conditions are too bad so we made it for tomorrow afternoon. I'll stop now; the movie is nice, with Humphrey Bogart.

Nighttime

Lee and Bailey are watching T.V. in Bailey's room, I'm watching in Ada's room and Ada is watching in the kitchen. There appears to be an energy crisis in the world today, if that is the case the Americans aren't bothered and go about their business. In this house alone more energy is being used than in three households in Holland. Unbelievable, this luxury, it's a completely different lifestyle. There are more than twenty-six channels, good programs, and many movies. The only irritating thing is all those commercials.

Tonight there are various movies again. This afternoon I saw The Magnificent Obsession. What a lazy little life these days with Ada and Bailey; I'm enjoying it very much. Another poem of Lee came out in The Negro History Bulletin in Washington D.C., with a photo of him this time. I'm so proud of my husband.

Friday, March 17, 1978

It's Saint Patrick's Day today, an Irish holiday. There's a big parade in town and I'm watching it now on television. I have to say that I've gained weight, especially my face is fuller. I noticed it myself yesterday and Lee said it too. On Ada's scale I'm 115 Lbs, that's far too much. I've got to get back to 50 kilograms, that's the ideal weight for me.

Saturday night, March 18, 1976

Last night Lee and I went to the 107th floor of The World Trade
Center. It was fantastic! It was as if you were in a plane right before
landing, so high! The Statue of Liberty was a little girl and the cars dinky
toys. Earlier in the afternoon we went to see Dr. Harrington who gave us a
booking for Palm Sunday at four p.m. Lee and I will give a show in The
Community Church on Park Avenue. Dr. Donald Harrington is an
important man, minister of the Community Church but also leader of the
Liberal Party of New York. He has worked a year with Doctor Albert
Schweitzer and there are photos in his study where he stands next to
President Jimmy Carter.

I bought a nice sweater yesterday, blue with stripes, to go with my grey
deux-piece. Friday it was nice and sunny but yesterday it was freezing
cold. Today we're taking Ada to hospital. She suffers from excruciating
pain in her back; she has to have surgery. She is so nervous and scared,
poor thing. I hope she recovers completely; she's such a sweet woman.
After we've taken her we go to Church and then we've been invited by
Bobby Fox.

March 23, 1978

After we took Ada to hospital we drove in Bailey's poison green big car back to the apartment. His daughter Celeste was with us also. We went to Church first though. Doctor Harrington's service was about Jesus, as a human being rather than an idealized saint. It was again fascinating and the choir consisting of four women and four men sang so beautifully that it almost brought tears to my eyes.

On Monday I went by a couple of music stores with Mary Blithe guitar hunting. One guitar pleased me very much, it has a warm, deep sound and costs hundred twenty five dollar; in another story, Manny's, I found a Yamaha, also good, for hundred and thirty dollar.

I was an idiot for not bringing my faithful old Oscar Teller but anyhow, I need another guitar.

Monday I had an appointment with a Mrs. Riotta on 138th Madison Avenue; she was nice and said she can help me get work. Here I can make about three hundred and fifty five dollar a week, in hotels, like I did in Amsterdam, Tehran and Kabul. The agency takes 10% or 15%. I hope I can get something soon. Our money is almost gone. After that interview Lee's friend Marion Brown picked me up and we drove to a friend of his in the Village. Afterwards Marion dropped us at No.2 Bond Street, the Life Loft Jazz Club where Bobby Reid invited us. It was an opening only for press and invited guests. It was much fun and excellent playing by a band with Slide Hampton and George Coleman. We bumped into acquaintances like Steve McCall (I met him in the Kroeg, a jazz café on the Marnixstraat in Amsterdam one night in July or August last year when Sonny from Istanbul was staying with us and so beastly annoying) and also James Newton whom we met at Ina's in the Kinkerstraat where Louis Armfield and Bobby Relax, the Canadian pianist were also. They're all jazz musicians. Lee met an actor here, Arthur Turner is his name.

There was plenty of everything: food, drinks and a relaxed atmosphere. Afterwards, Steve McCall and his girlfriend Bibi invited us for a drink in The Tin Palace, a nice restaurant/bar in the Village.

On Tuesday we went to Marion Brown's house in North Hampton. He and Lee are both form Thomasville, Georgia and Marion teaches musicology at Amherst University. Archie Shepp came by at night and gave Lee an address of someone in Massachusetts who can possibly do something for our poetry/music shows. We shall see.

Marion made chicken that was delicious. I must say he's a sweet man. I enjoyed the Amtrak train ride. The country side is breathtaking; mountains, forests, rivers, little streams and brooks, wooden houses in all colors of the rainbow; really beautiful. Most of the scenery is still covered with snow and the small lakes are frozen; a real winter wonderland.

Wednesday morning we went back to Manhattan. Ada has been operated on; she doesn't want phone calls or visits. Apparently she's in a lot of pain. Maybe we can see her today.

Nighttime

I have a guitar, hurrah! I believe I made a good deal, it has a lovely, warm sound. With sturdy case I paid a hundred and ten dollars, not bad. At any rate I'm delighted with it.

Mary Blithe just called me. Tom Bailey invited us to see a movie tomorrow night, The Fury, Maria is coming also. We went to see Ada, she looks good, still some pain of course but that's normal.

It appears to me that people here are generally speaking quite fucked up, aggressive and hysterical. It's the excessive criminality in this city I think. Nobody trusts his fellow human being. You can see it in the subway and the bus, all those tight faces, skittish moving eyes, the fast walking. Today Lee and I witnessed a cowardly outburst of aggression.

It happened in downtown Manhattan, on Broadway I believe. A rather old man received a few vicious blows on his head; his glasses went flying through the air. Fortunately another passerby took immediate action and kept the hothead in check. It went so fast. I heard the guy scream: 'Fuck you!'

It probably was something as trifling as two people bumping into each other accidently.

Saturday afternoon I went into deep Harlem for the first time with Lee. We saw Bailey who on Saturdays works in a barber shop (his old profession); he had forgotten his lunch box.

It was in the neighborhood of 145th street, Sugar Hill, so called because there the more affluent blacks used to live. It was alright there, clean streets, nice houses. But there's also a lot of shit in Harlem; heaps of rubble, broken down houses, mounds of garbage and throughout it all the blacks: children, hustlers, housewives, gangsters, and youths. I would be scared to walk here alone. Someone yelled 'Hey whitey!' at me.

The South Bronx is even worse. It was just on television and looks like a bombed city, awful!

The Americans I meet here all seem to be on the verge of hysterics; they shout instead of talking normal and it's all about them. New York seems fascinating yet intimidating and scary as well. There's so much life, lights and everything, it's hard to put into words. One has a sense of everyone being right here, everyone's on the move, busy, the city beats and bangs like a gargantuan heart in a monstrous beast. Something like that. I don't think I would want to live here, it isn't as relaxed as Amsterdam.

Sunday, March 25, 1978

Lee is working out the sequence of our program tomorrow afternoon at the Community Church. I will do eight or nine songs, mostly in English but also a couple of Dutch, one in French, one in Spanish and maybe one in Italian.

Last night John called, the Italian/American we met in Afghanistan and again later in Tehran and with whom we experienced wild scenes with the Turkish border authorities. I hit a customs clerk over the head with my fist. He was a little roly-poly man and I never forget the sight of the man's utterly amazed face when he turned around and saw that a woman had hit him. It took Lee a lot of talking, showing him our marriage book to convince the man to let me go. He said he had the power to have me locked up for six months for hitting a police officer. I laughed about it later but at the time we spent some tight moments. Lee told me to apologize to him and to do it in a subservient manner and I did.

After hours and hours of waiting at the Iranian side of the border the three customs officers closed the glass door right when we were about to step through. We, that were Lee and I, John and his girlfriend Maggie, the Palestinian, the Canadian and the German boy. John, a photographer, got so mad that he started cursing and banging his tripod against the window whereupon he was jerked inside. They shoved him into a little room where two men held him while the third gave him a couple of hard punches in the stomach. This is what he told us later. They wouldn't let him pass so he and Maggie traveled back to Tehran. The custom officials were kicking and throwing our luggage around and were very nasty to us. At one point I saw Lee with the little roly-poly and in my anger and confusion I thought I needed to come to Lee's rescue. I have to laugh writing about it. What a spectacle!

Anyway, John told Lee that he's going to catch our show.

Wednesday, March 29, 1978, Washington D.C.

We're at the house of another friend of Lee, Charles; he's a playwright, in Rockville, Maryland. The crickets are making a deafening racket.

Our first show in the Community Church went very well. I had an interview with Mister Morgan of the Sheraton Hotel today. He was very nice and said he will give me a booking soon. We've done so much; I don't know where to start, sightseeing too. And we're always meeting people, friends and friends of friends. Everyone wants to take us out and show us a good time it seems. Ada is coming out of hospital on Sunday.

Saturday morning, April 1, 1978, a quarter to twelve.

We're in Union Station in Washington D.C. I never saw such an elegant, imposing station hall.

It is a large dome, white with soft light blue and gold inscriptions and designs, statues and a kind of bridge on both sides with pillars underneath, large round pots with tropical plants and palm trees and everywhere crème colored carpet. And all the time you can hear the sound of lovely symphonic music. I am flabbergasted. I never saw anything like it. Now I hear a choir, holy Moses, how lovely; I close my eyes and listen.

Sunday, April 2, 1978

Yesterday was extremely hot, lots of wind but hot like Ibiza. The anchor man said it hasn't been this hot since 1906! I feel optimistic despite the fact that our finances are indeed quite meager now. We're back in the Apple. I did two auditions today and feel good about them.

Tuesday, April 4, 1978

Well, twelve days late with my period but today the fucking Umpire from Hades waved the red flag again. No baby for you, Miss! Shit! Why do I still believe it is possible? I felt so sure it was happening this time. I already saw myself performing with a big belly in a flimsy thin gown (like my grey one) and I had planned on telling Lee about it when my period hadn't come in three weeks. But no! I was moved to tears when we made love a few days ago and Lee said: 'This is our baby, love!'

I don't understand, after years of tests the doctors couldn't find anything wrong with me or Lee but why then can't I get pregnant?

Wednesday, April 5, 1978

We're in the Nassau Hotel on 59th Street between Park and Madison. We pay $104,20 a week, not bad. I've done two more auditions and the managers seemed to like my singing but no one has called me back yet.

I just took a bath, washed my hair, it has grown back and is quite long again.

Thursday, April 6, 1978

Today we're exactly four weeks in America. After all the walking we did today Lee went back to the cleaners because a stain didn't come out of his white jacket. First we went to the Bank of America on Wall Street and then to Federal Plaza no. 26 to extend my visa. That took a long time but we ate well there for very little money.

The lean days are here again! No prospects for work yet, at least not immediately. Anyway, we won't give up.

Monday, April 10, 1978

I just took a shower and am now watching a comedy on television. It's beautiful weather, I'm going to take a stroll.

Tom Bailey took us out to dinner the other day; it was delicious. Afterwards we visited Julius and his wife. I love their little girl, Sherida, she is three and cute as a cucumber. Saturday we saw Ada, she is recovering. Sunday we went to Church. There was a guest speaker, a Russian general who can't go back to Russia because he's against the regime. There was also a Polish woman speaker; the theme was human rights. Dr. Harrington wrote us a very nice letter thanking us for an excellent very professional performance. Ada was watching baseball and we stayed until the game was over. We then went to Mary Blithe. Tom was there too. Mary had been in the hospital, a few days earlier; she was drunk and fell down the stairs. Luckily she was not badly injured. She gave me a list of clubs where I can try to get work as a singer. I still didn't hear from the agent and from the two hotels in Washington. Patience, patience, dear!

Lee and I have a performance next week in a little theater on 72nd and 1st Avenue. We don't get paid but the owner invited agents and newspaper people. So…maybe something will come of it.

I'm going back to Amsterdam tomorrow. If all is well there are four payments waiting for me there. Officially I'm entitled to three weeks holiday pay. Lee wants me to also pick up a hundred of his books with Willem Klein, his publisher. And I'm supposed to bring back Nigerian bags as well; he intends to sell them here. So, I'll have plenty to do in just a few days. I want to be back here Saturday, Sunday at the latest.

Lee is taking me to the Airport tomorrow. I'll take a standby flight to London and from there by boat and train to Amsterdam.

I had a nice walk by Central Park over Fifth Avenue ten blocks up and via Lexington Avenue back to our hotel. This is an elegant neighborhood with many expensive hotels and lots of lovely boutiques. I'm watching young Steve McQueen in a Western now.

Tuesday, April 18, 1978

I was in Holland but will write about that later because right now I
don't see the point in this situation at all anymore.

Monday, April 24, 1978

We just arrived in Hotel Earl on Waverly Place in Greenwich
Village. This room costs us $64 a week. Our last 'home' was on Madison
and 33rd Street and cost us $94 a week so you see distinguished reader that
the price we pay for a roof over our head goes down. At least we have a
nice view here over 6th Avenue and the Village.

We manage and optimism reigns; we have good prospects for work in
the near future. We have an agent now; I don't know, he talks big but
perhaps he's full of shit.

My trip to Holland was a 'trip'; cold, rain, less money than I expected.
Anyway, Lee's friend Teddy in London was great. He took me out to
lunch and gave me money to fly to Holland. I didn't even ask him for it.
Thank God, there are nice people in this world!

I had seventy five cents in my pocket when I walked into my apartment.
Insane, isn't it?

Mom and dad were so happy to hear my voice over the phone but very disappointed, especially mommy, when I told them that I was going back to New York. They just took Lilly to the Airport; she's a tourist hostess on the Canary Islands, lucky girl!

I was in Hoppe's Café last Friday in Amsterdam. Jack and Ellen were there and old Arthur, the watchmaker who always asks Lee for a piece of hash and Lee thinks he chews on it, and Michael and Dick. It was lots of fun and nice being back in Amsterdam if only for a little while. I also spoke with Paul and Honey; they gave me Gregor's address in Virginia. Shouki wasn't home.

I spoke with Mister Muizenberg of the Dutch Consulate today, he was very nice. Perhaps I'll be singing next Monday, May 1st, at the reception to honor Queen Juliana who celebrates her birthday April 30th.

I've been so busy with auditions. I also visited Jack and Charles. Jack was in the Sweelinck Conservatory with me studying recorder and Charles, his boyfriend, is a great dress maker who made me some lovely dresses in Amsterdam. They live in a nice Loft on the Hudson River in the Village and they took me out to a fabulous dinner at a Chinese restaurant there.

~

Chapter 12

Our day will come

Wednesday, April 26, 1978

We are trying since Monday to reach the agent from Talents Unlimited. He was so enthusiastic and nice when we spoke to him but I think that he took on too much in his enthusiasm. He was supposed to have set up an interview with the United Nations where I could possibly get a job for a few hours a day as a translator.

It's frustrating to be here for seven weeks already and to not have accomplished anything. All the agents I wrote and called several times fail to come through; the two hotels in Washington D.C. who were so happy with my performance haven't called. I'm beginning to lose heart a little. We live day by day and it looks like we don't get one step further. It feels like we're living in a kind of vacuum.

Well, my horoscope says that movement is around the corner, starting April 25, yesterday. I hope so.

When I sat in the plane (after seeing Saturday Night Fever with John Travolta who reminded me of Michel) I dreamt of an island, beautiful and romantic like Cyprus, where I finally could come to myself, to write, to compose songs, to swim, to lie in the sun, to dance. My handsome, sweet Michel holding me in his arms…oh, when will I finally see you again, my darling Apollo? Our intense and pure romance on Cyprus, I will never forget it.

I want to get pregnant so much, to have a child of my own, to love, to play with, to teach, to learn from, to help….

It serves no purpose to fall back into melancholy, let it be.

Considering everything, I have nothing to complain about and I'm still young. Lilly is on the Canary Islands, we're all so far apart, like grains of sand spread out over the globe.

Tony, the agent, just called. He'll call me back in twenty minutes he said, about the United Nations.

Evening

What can you do when you feel as if you are watching powerless while powers stronger than yourself keep you in an invisible chain and your course of life passes as if in kaleidoscope by your eyes; you are only an onlooker in your own life story, in this carnival mirror, in this maze of reality.

When this feeling of powerless alignment to invisible powers struggles with the sober, only with logic facts fencing inner ego who somewhere deep within shakes its head and smiles, as if the solution to all these problems and even all the gigantic, unsurpassable world problems or even universally, is just for the taking – confusion reigns.

Poverty is a person's worst enemy, it tears your soul apart, having to cope with too much adversity, giving up, letting it all pass by or sit down and just cry or…stand up and shout, shout and shout and drink away the pain, realizing vanity or pride, or goodness, or whatever, it's all in vain.

Too much love goes down the drain, returning instead bitterness and hate, for some people the 'All aboard!' came too late or maybe they couldn't hear, beaten down too much or riddled by silly guilt and fear; so much injustice and stupidity, too many suffering in apathy.

Tranquility might be the answer, the key. Who knows?

Saturday, April 29, 1978

Well, one performance I have. On May 26th at a cocktail party in the Netherlands Club at Rockefeller Center. They only pay sixty dollars, not much but maybe I'll meet people there who may want to book me for a night. On ne sais jamais, n'est-ce-pas?

We met Jonathan Scott whom we didn't see for three years. He's gotten bigger than he was already. We visited him yesterday morning, drank coffee and whisky. He's got a lovely flat on Fifth Avenue not far from our hotel. It's great to meet old friends so unexpectedly and to meet new people too. Last night we visited two women, one of whom we met at Bill Hudson's (the painter who Lee knows from fifteen years back and whom we also bumped into in the street the day before yesterday), her name is Dorothy. They took us to a Senegalese movie in the Henry Street Theater in their neighborhood. It was called Ceddo and so beautiful and very interesting. Lee is invited to the Black Writers Convention in Washington D.C. so we go there next week. Tom Bailey had stomach surgery yesterday. Mary Blithe called to say that the doctor told her that the operation was a success. Thank God for that, we'll visit him tomorrow.

Where is Lee? What's taking him so long? We're supposed to go out to have coffee and breakfast.

May 1st, 1978

Every day one obtains something and every day one loses something. One gathers wisdom and one loses illusions.

All that big talk from this one and that one, bah! Hot air, that's all it is! As far as the actual situation is concerned it is as follows:

On May 26th I have a performance in the Netherlands Club at Rockefeller Center and on Monday June 8th I have an audition in Rusty's Restaurant on 75th Street and Columbus Avenue.

I have three dollars and some change to my name. The rent for the hotel is due tomorrow, that's sixty-four minus the deposit of twenty thus forty-four. If we want to go to the Black Writers Convention in Washington D.C. it will cost us at least $200.

The pawnshop has two rings of mine and a camera which will cost $60 to get back. We have some stuff from Nigeria to sell that is if we can manage it in such a limited amount of time. Lee is at Julius who says a friend of his wants to buy the crocodile bag. I hope and pray that this will happen. Everything is so speculative like me going by some clubs tonight. I haven't even mentioned our financial obligations in Holland: rent, gas, light, everything is due. The America trip is becoming very heavy. Nevertheless I keep my chin up.

I have a few discomforts: blood (since last year December) at irregular intervals from my behind, pain also irregular in my left arm and the chest area since about last November and four warts on my inner labia. I will have a total physical check-up when I'm back in Holland. I can't afford to worry too much about that now.

Wednesday, May 3, 1978

I have a performance Thursday, May 11th in a famous club, Trude Heller on 6th Avenue and 9th Street. I'll do a show of forty-five minutes. The way it goes is that I will sell the tickets of $3 a piece myself so the more people come the more money I make. The guy who owns Trude Heller is very nice, he reminds me of Manfred Langer of the Amstel Taveerne Club on the Amstel in Amsterdam.

His mother, Trude Heller, and Donna Wachtel (a friend of Austin Green who is a good friend of Tom Bailey and that's how I came to Trude Heller's) are friends for more than twenty years.

Lee wants to go to Washington tomorrow for the Black Writers Convention; me too, get away from Manhattan's hustle and bustle, set up my show for the eleventh....

I'm very excited about that, it's a great opportunity for me. Everyone knows Trude Heller's, many stars performed there.

I also have several auditions lined up this week and interviews with two agents.

Thursday, May 4, 1978

It's our wedding day today, I forgot all about it. We're married six years now. We don't have a nickel to celebrate. Lee forgot all about it also. He's so disappointed that he can't go to Washington today. He was supposed to do a radio interview there today, he didn't even tell me. But he told me today that he's sick and tired of doing things for free. He could've pawned his ring but that's about the last security we have left. So he decided not to go. Poor Lee, it's so unfair, he's a brilliant poet. He's visiting Tom Bailey in the hospital. He often says to me how lucky we are to be in good health because that's all the wealth in the world. Tom only has 30% of his stomach left.

We are so poor now, I'm mostly hungry. I mean I eat crackers, cheese, apples, now and then a salad and once every three days something warm. We drink juice too. It's meager but you get used to everything. It isn't easy to suppress a feeling of depression and despondency at times. I have never more than a dollar and a half in my pocket it seems.

You know what? I'm going to write something, a nice piece for Lee when he gets home, a surprise for the occasion of our anniversary. I have no money to send a Mother's Day card to my sweet mama. Perhaps she thinks I forgot it.

Okay, stop it, cheer up now, girl!

Later at night

We just saw King Kong, a great movie. Lee met another friend from Paris when he went out to get hamburgers for us. He took him to our hotel and Peter came by also. Everyone is very impressed with my upcoming show in Trude Heller. Today when I passed the club I saw a poster of Connie Francis who performed there last Wednesday.

Imagine my teenager idol!

Saturday, May 6, 1978

It's about ten thirty at night. Lee and I are in bed watching television, we switch from one movie to the next. I'm trying to decide on the sequence of my songs for the show. I like all my songs but I have favorites of course. I made a temporary selection of twenty numbers but that's still too many. My show is forty-five minutes so that means fourteen to fifteen songs. The sequence will also depend on how I feel and how the atmosphere will be.

I'm invited to The Community Church for breakfast tomorrow to be welcomed as a new member. Yes, I'm becoming a Unitarian!

Jesse (black American painter we know, Lee knows him a long time, I know him from Amsterdam) came by last night and bought a ticket for my Trude Heller Show. I sold six so far.

Monday, May 8, 1978

Lee and I have a performance on May 21st at the Poetry Festival which Charles Turner is organizing. Today Tony Williams paid us for the two Nigerian bags, well; he gave us $150 so he still owes us $110. He was busy with moving boxes and furniture in his new office. And he started up immediately again about all the great projects he's working on and all the fantastic things he has lined up for us. Strange guy but anyway, we were very glad with the money. I bought some supplies in the 69cents shop (everything there costs 69cents) like a pair of pink and blue and white socks. I'm wearing them now with my pink dress and striped blouse and gillet; I put my hair in braided rolls over my ears and look hip and cheery if I say so myself.

I'm watching the four o'clock movie. Where is Lee?

He just came home and went back out again. He's acting very mysterious and I'm starving. I ate well today but still…oh, look at that! What a delicious cake I got from Jesse! Lee bought chow.

Tuesday, May 9, 1978

I just read in the paper that Phil Greenwald booked Bill Cosby in the Concorde Hotel starting May 22nd. That's in the Catskills, a resort in the mountains. I'd love to sing there for a month or two. A few weeks ago I had an interview with Phil Greenwald, a fatso who seemed impressed with my publicity material but when I was getting ready to leave he leaped towards me like a giant toad, put his arms around me and pressed me tightly against him. I pulled loose and ran out of his office. Shit! These dirty old men!

I bought a nice Mother's Day card for Sietske, my sweet mommy.

Wednesday, May 10, 1978

It's almost Startrek time. I worked out my program. I also made a poster and the manager promised to put it in the window. I am so excited and longing. I'm going to wear my blue outfit that Charles designed and made for me and I want to buy a flower to put in my hair. If about twenty-five to thirty people show up I will be very content.

Thursday, May 11, 1978

I showered, took care of my body, washed my hair, did some gymnastics, some breathing and vocal exercises and went through a couple of the songs I intend to sing tonight. It's a wonderful, sparkling day. I hope some people will show up, that I have lots of success and that someone (agent or manager) discovers me and books me in Las Vegas with a big band and a dynamite backing vocal group or someone who offers me a record deal or someone who gives me a job to sing in a first class club or hotel. Dreams and expectations that I nourish since I was a child...still, there will come a time when my dreams will come true. I remember what an old man once said to me in the Inter-Conti in Tehran. He said: 'You're a very good singer with a warm and very flexible voice.

Don't give up, keep singing, one day somebody will come along and recognize your talent.'

Friday, May 12, 1978

Trude Heller was fine, there were about thirty people; I did well and they liked it, lots of applause and Bibi made photos.

Sunday, May 14th, 1978

Rain, rain, all day rain. Headache, hunger, broke, no cigarettes, not even a butt and rain, constantly leaden grey lines of rain. This is a miserable feeling, a feeling of emptiness, anger, depression; it's dreadful. How will we ever get out of this vicious circle of poverty? How can you ever accomplish something creative under the heavy pressure of keeping yourself alive? I am so tired. What a life!

Hunger, hunger…oh, a cup of soup, warm, steaming vegetable soup. Or sweet smelling potatoes, fresh salad, and a beefsteak….Stop! I'm making myself crazy.

Monday, May 15, 1978

Get up early, bus uptown, at a quarter to ten in the agent's office,
Tony; it looks quite imposing there already, he gave us $50 and a letter of
recommendation for me for a part time typing job. We walked back, had
breakfast and coffee somewhere, one dollar each. Lee is in turn gay and
elated then quiet and gloomy. We laugh; we look at people and walk on.
No mail for us at the Kenmore Hotel, from there to the hospital, too early
for visiting hour but we get permission to visit Tom anyhow. He is
surprised, says he's doing fine; he has to eat well to gain strength. He said
we can call Mary to ask her to use her telephone to call Gerard in Holland.
In the hospital Lee buys a bag of meringues for us to suck on 'cause we're
getting hungry again. We walk to Larry's house, quite a long haul but he's
not home, then back to our hotel. Manny, the manager is waiting for us
like a vulture but Lee is ahead of him, in a loud voice he tells him we'll
pay the rent this afternoon. We get the two Nigerian bags and go out
again.

It's cold outside, cutting wind, it seems like winter but fortunately it
doesn't rain. I'm wearing my summer coat, the Russian scarf around my
head and my green sunglasses and Lee is wearing the orange rain jacket
borrowed from Julius yesterday. We go to the mid-fifties and are both
nervous. When we get out of the bus Lee walks ahead and I follow at a
distance.

He found a spot, spreads out the rug and holds up the bags; I act as if I want to buy something and a few people stop but as soon as they hear the prices we ask for the bags they buzz off fast. I look in all directions for the police because to sell something in the street you need a peddler's license. They can confiscate everything if they want.

At first it's rather exciting, we don't stay in one place too long; a few times I say: 'Police' to Lee and we hurriedly pack it up and move. I have eyes everywhere.

A couple of hours pass that way; it's cold, folks are in a rush, nobody buys something. We even try on the posh 5th Avenue but no luck.

Back to Tony's office that's buzzing like a beehive. He doesn't have the $110 he still owes us. We take the subway back home, it's ten past six and Manny, the manager, has left, thank God.

We watch the last part of Startrek (good as always) and Lee decides to get us something to eat. I fall asleep. When he returns he tells me he found another dollar, yesterday too. His catch of the day is: a hamburger for me, half a chicken for him and macaroni salad for both of us, bread and orange juice. The food does us a world of good. What a day!

Tuesday, May 16, 1978

Another pissing rain day! The poet's ring is in the pawnshop; rent and television are paid for a week. It can't always be this tough; something has got to give one of these days.

Wednesday, May 17, 1978

I have good news! The sun beams benevolently and smiling into our room, Pan Am now has direct flights to Amsterdam for $170 and Ada has a letter for us (probably from mama) and Bill Hudson gave Lee an old but willing typewriter on which I'm typing Lee's poems that have to be mailed for a fellowship of the CAPS.

Thursday, May 18, 1978

Like a fish in a glass bowl I'm sitting, hollow and full, in the dirty rinsing water of the television. What misery!

Hopefully we can soon change this paltry hotel room for a nice little flat.

Last night Lee brought me a small bowl of frozen strawberry yogurt, delicious. Today we ate well: fish, corn on the cob, Cole slaw, barbeque spare ribs and chocolate cake. I just got another frozen yogurt, banana flavor but from the wrong store. Where Lee bought it yesterday was much more for less money. What trivial farce all this writing. We bought an electric cooker and a saucepan together for $4, 50. Smart, eh?

Sunday, May 28, 1978

It's lovely weather. I am twenty-nine today. Last night I went to Neri's Continental, a bar/restaurant where Mary Blithe worked as a waitress. I got a gig there for Tuesday coming up.

Lee hid a little present for me under my pillow. That dear, with the little money he has he did want to surprise me with a little something: a shower brush and a deodorant. I feel good and optimistic.

My performance in the Netherlands Club last Friday went well. I'll get a cheque for that for $60 on Wednesday.

Lee drives me nuts sometimes. I think we're too much together really and no matter how sweet he is most of the time, I've noticed that our marriage is beginning to show rut symptoms. It can't be avoided I guess.

Bibi's photos of me singing in Trude Heller's came out great.

Wednesday, May 31, 1978

Lee turns fifty-one today and is, in my opinion, the most handsome, sweetest, most intelligent and bravest man in the universe. We eat so well since we bought cooking utensils. Yesterday we had chopped meat with onions, tomatoes and cucumbers, beefsteak today. We also eat a lot of corn on the cob, a boiled egg now and then and we drink a lot of tea and coffee. We eat lots of fruit of course and we keep bread, peanut butter, jam, mayonnaise, pepper and salt in stock. We buy a cake now and then and often yogurt or frozen yogurt.

I sang at Neri's Continental on 37th Street and 3rd Avenue last night. I made forty dollars, thirty-five from the club and five dollars in tips. There were few people unfortunately but I can go back there next week. Fantastic! If I manage to get two or three nights in other restaurants everything will look a lot brighter.

I had planned to hit the clubs with my guitar in midtown Manhattan after Startrek but this terrible thunderstorm stops me in my tracks. I received a nice letter from Ellen de Thouars and her husband Jack Kröner yesterday. Jack translated my song Aarde (Earth) into English, that's so nice of him and he did a great job of it! I'm so happy!

Friday, June 2, 1978

I've got to make a lot of phone-calls. Yesterday I was hunting for singing jobs again. I've got an audition on Saturday, two on Monday, another one next Saturday and an interview on Wednesday with a Catskill agent.

It's so hot in New York; I walk around sopping wet constantly.

You often only much later realize the value of experiences that you have now, Ellen wrote in her letter to me; such a wise woman, my friend Ellen, the actress.

Tuesday, June 6, 1978

This morning I did an audition for The West Side Story that's going to be put on in Orlando, Florida, when I don't know. If they pick me I will be called at six o'clock tonight. There were about thirty singers, male and female.

Three papers are important in New York: Backstage, Variety & Billboard.

Tonight I'm singing in Neri's Continental again and tomorrow afternoon the interview with a Catskill agent. Lee wants to send me home.

I don't want to go back. I'm very sad. I tried so hard, day in day out auditions, interviews and now I'll come back a total failure.

Wednesday, June 7, 1978

I am taken completely by surprise as it were. A young man, Willem, whom I met at the Netherlands Club when I sang there, was very friendly and helpful. He called last week to give me some valuable information about what to do to get started here. He advised me to buy Backstage, Variety and Billboard and to call Joe Franklin at WOR TV.

I saw that show off and on, it's a kind of Willem Duys show in Holland, broadcasted early in the morning and repeated late at night. So I called yesterday. His secretary suggested that I try again later and talk to his assistant.

This afternoon I called and somebody there gave me Joe Franklin's phone number. I spoke to him, just like that!

He seemed very nice. It puzzles me that it was so easy to get connected through to him. He wanted to know all about me and said he'll try to put me on his show in three to four weeks. I can't believe it! Willem Duys thinks himself such a God that he throws fan mail unopened in his waste paper basket. His secretary told me so when I tried to get him to talk about our Charity Shows in his popular radio program Muziek Mozaïek. When I asked her to be connected through to him she laughed and said: 'Heavens, no!' and that it was absolutely out of the question, unthinkable even. What arrogance! I feel great now and full of new courage.

It was so nice in Neri's Continental yesterday, more people than last week and a lot of familiar faces from last week who brought others along.

~

Chapter 13

Perseverance and fortitude

It was an exciting time trying to get ahead as a singer in New York but very hard as well because although I managed to get gigs here and there, it didn't come easy and at times funds were so low that we walked around with our stomachs growling. That's when I found out what it is like when you don't have enough to eat; your mind centers around food all the time, one just can't help it; food is all you can think of.

Living in Manhattan together was great fun, also because I had Lee by my side all the time whereas in Amsterdam he left me alone a lot.

I don't exactly know how it happened, such things go gradually I think but Lee and I became more like brother and sister than lovers. We didn't have sex very much if at all and it didn't bother me in the least. I was totally focused on furthering my singing career and having him close at hand was enough for me.

However, as time went by it was unavoidable that the little lady would fall in love again. In retrospect I think that our so-called open marriage was beginning to take its toll; although I loved to fall in love at the drop of a hat, part of me didn't like it that my husband wasn't jealous and let me do whatever I felt like.

The lack of money most times began to wear me down quite a bit. Fortunately my hitting the pavements in search of singing gigs paid off eventually when I landed jobs in prestigious establishments like The Monsignore II and The Top of the Sixes.

If 1978 was the year of trying times, the next year, 1979 would turn out to become the year of departure and arrival; in May 1979 I met the father of my two adored sons.

~

June 11, 1978

What a drip I am! I'm so sick and tired of everything. Our sex life amounts to nothing anymore. Sometimes, like now, I wish it was all over with. Dead; I'm not happy anyway. It's as if my heart is bled empty and I am like a cactus that will never bloom again. What did I do wrong in my life?

Oh, well, it's just this rotten mood I'm in. I'm also homesick, I want to go home. I'm so very tired. Lee has been gone all day.

Monday, June 12, 1978

Lee's cold has cleared up, thank God. We bought a couple of chicken legs, powder milk, sugar, three oranges, one lemon and we just had a nice cup of soup. Lee just read a review in The New York Times about the show of Steve McCall's group Air and Marion Brown Saturday in the Public Theater. Lee and I were there and enjoyed it tremendously.

Sunday, June 18, 1978

Ah, I've been so sick, a bad cold. It's hard to sing in Neri's Continental but I managed. It's still not over and this fucking period won't stop either, seven days already. I kept up my auditions even though I was sick as a dog. We go to Church in a little while. Dr. Harrington gave us another booking, in October and he gave us $110.

I had such fun last night with Jim Verder, a tall American of Dutch descend; handsome face, grey curling hair and ever so nice. He's fifty-three he said but he looks younger, he's got a captivating personality and comes to Neri's regularly to listen to me sing. Yesterday he took me out to dinner in an intimate restaurant on 28th and 3rd avenue. It was fabulous! Afterwards he took me home in a taxi and said goodbye with a tender little kiss; he's a real gentleman and it was a perfect evening. I really like him; I think I've fallen in love a little. On to Church now! Monday, June 19, 1978

I just came back from the WOR-TV Studio; it was a total surprise of Joe Franklin.

Yesterday I called him and he asked me to come to his office. He gave me some addresses of clubs and an agent for commercials. He told me to call him at twelve noon today. When I did he asked me to come to his office at three o'clock. He said: 'Come along, sweetheart', so I did. I went to a building nearby his office on Broadway. Not until we walked in there did I realize that we were in the television studio. I thought how nice of him to take me along and show me how they tape the show. So I sat down and listened to the show and his guests talking when suddenly I hear Joe say: 'We'll be back, stay with us. We have some continental people in the next half hour of the program, so and so from Cyprus and a beautiful lady from Holland….' my mouth dropped and I froze in my chair. I had just enough time to put some lipstick on. It was glorious! I didn't sing but it was a great introduction and publicity. Fantastic!

It will be broadcasted Wednesday morning and again late at night. I'm elated and Lee is over the moon for me.

Joe asked me to call him at one o'clock tomorrow. I really think he wants to help me.

Sunday, June 25, 1978

It's mommy's birthday today, she's fifty-three now. I liked myself on the Joe Franklin Show, I did well. Ada also liked me and several people I don't know saw me and said to me: 'Didn't I see you on television?'

I made auditions every night this week, I even went to the famous Stork Club. I tried to get in at Catch a Rising Star also but I turned back on my heel; there were so many people waiting, the line went around the block and many had camping stools with them. They won't hire new acts until September it appears, at least that's what they told me.

I saw Frank Sinatra last week in Dangerfield's where I made an audition after my work in Neri's and Frank Sinatra Junior was performing there. Frank Senior with three bodyguards walked so close by me I could have kissed him smack on the lips. He is so handsome, those bright blue sparkling piercing eyes! I was stunned, speechless of course.

Sunny was with me, a really nice guy I met a week earlier in Neri's when Steve McCall came to hear me sing. Sunny had coke and Steve and I went to his house. I was quite tipsy later on, bad girl that I am.

A few days ago Sunny gave me a wonderful skirt; he's in the rag trade on Seventh Avenue. The cobalt blue skirt is made of a parachute that was used during the war for dropping medicines and food. Isn't that nice of him? I love the skirt; I've never had something so special and awesome.

Friday we saw Ada and picked up our mail. There was a card from Lilly, she's sitting under a palm tree in Barbados and wrote that she and her friend are trying to find a way to get to Curacao as cheap as possible. I'm so proud of my little sister, traveling all over the place, so independently. I guess she's fluent in Spanish by now.

Tuesday, June 27, 1982

Mister Blom of the Dutch Consulate just called me; four hundred and fifty guilders have been wired to me from Amsterdam. It's unemployment money still owed to me.

How wonderful for the poet and I because we are dead broke. The agent who promised me a commercial told me to be patient and call him on Thursday.

Wednesday, June 28, 1978

I just finished reading The Fifth Dimension and the Future of Mankind by Vera Stanley Adler. I've read this book several times already; it always gives me such a positive feeling, really a marvelous book! Last night was my last performance in Neri's Continental, the owner, Paul, is closing down for the summer, not enough business.

The poet intends to take the bus to Boston tomorrow and to hop a cheap flight with Pan Am to Amsterdam from there. I'm going to stay with Mary Blithe while he's gone. It's sticky hot today, need to shower again.

Wednesday, July 5, 1978

Lee is in all probability in Amsterdam by now. It had some doing; he went back and forth to Boston in vain because all seats on that Pan Am flight were booked solid. Everyone is on the move because of the Fourth of July celebrations.

Friday, July 7, 1978

No word from Lee yet. Perhaps he calls later tonight or tomorrow. I was broke yesterday but luckily Sunny gave me thirty dollar, so kind of him. I spoke with the assistant of the President of the American Federation of Musicians, Mister Fred Dreher this afternoon, what a nice gentleman.

I should've done this much sooner. It's better to become a member of this musicians union if I stay and want to work.

I'm in a jolly good mood, perhaps things are beginning to get going now. He also recommended a couple of bona fide agents. Ada called yesterday, there's a letter from my parents.

Nighttime

Joe Franklin came by to listen to me sing but he fell asleep, haha! He promised me that I will be singing in his show this week. His show is watched by two million people every day.

July 8, 1978

Lee managed to get a ticket last night and took off, that's what Tom told me because I just came back from Mount Airy Lodge in the Poconos, Pennsylvania where I gave a show; I sang twelve songs. It's so lovely there, great countryside. The owners are Dutch immigrants. They said they liked me but couldn't hire me for a long term engagement because I'm not a Union Member yet. Scheisse! What a pity!

Mary told me that Lee has made a pass at her and that she doesn't like that one bit. I find it hard to believe.

I wrote a lovely song yesterday and am feeling great!

July 9, 1978

Finally the poet called me. He's okay, thank God and said that he'll be coming back this weekend but wasn't sure yet. It's very cold, ugly weather in Holland he said.

Monday, July 10, 1978

I want to go home! I feel lousy! All men should be castrated; I hate all of them sexist idiots who all want to put their filthy paws on me. Shit! When do I meet a normal person here? I just spoke to Helen Leclerq, she's here with her dance group and they're staying in this hotel also. She feels the same way as I do about men in Manhattan. She said that she wouldn't be able to stand it for longer than six weeks. They're going back to Holland on Sunday and she advised me to do the same. God give me strength!

Tuesday, July 11, 1978

Today is a very busy day. First I'm off to the photographer Gene
Cogen recommended to me. Joe Franklin had sent me to Gene Cogen, he's
yet another agent but very nice, all business and no hanky-panky,
refreshing that.

The photographer, Bill Yoscary, was also very nice. He shot four rolls
of me, always in movement and different cloths. He's got a huge amount
of outfits and hats and boas and what have you. Joe also told me to call
Ada Einhorn who has work for me. I quickly went home (I'm staying with
Mary in her apartment on Lexington Avenue while Lee is in Holland) to
get my guitar after the photo shoot and found Mary demolishing her
kitchen; she wants to modernize it. She's strong as an ox and used to work
in a carpenter's workshop. I feel happy and am going to lend her a helping
hand.

Wednesday, July 12, 1978

Marjory's birthday, she turns thirty-one today. I miss my Lee very
much. I long for him to be by my side again. Friday night I'm in a show of
Joe Franklin in the Blue Hawaii Club, it's something at least.

I saw Tom and brought him two bags of ice-cubes for his cool-box. He
doesn't feel so good since he ate those biscuits at Austin's on Sunday.

Those biscuits were delicious and the spiced stuffed clams too. Austin gave me a leather bag which you can wear around your neck or over your hips, very in at the moment.

Mary, her friend Kate and I rchcarscd again this aftcrnoon (wc want to perform as a three girls singing group) but alas, it's not up to much yet I'm afraid. I have very little money at the moment, only twenty-six dollars but…I keep my chin up. Better times are a-coming.

Saturday July 15, 1978

I met a nice agent (for a change) through Joe. He asked me to accompany him to a show of his that's running in The Village Gate at the moment. It was a great spectacle and I thoroughly enjoyed it. Afterwards we had coffee and deserts in a coffee-shop in the Village. I was quite charmed by him and physically attracted, so much so that I went home with him without hesitation. We spent a great night together, smoked a couple of Jays. It was nice and I don't regret it for one moment. This is the first time I went to bed with someone else since I'm in America; four months now.

Tuesday, July 18, 1978

What a shit town New York is! I wish Lee would call me. I don't see any reason for him to come back here. I want to go home! There is nothing but rotten apples here. It's so discouraging.

Tom said to me when he came by this afternoon: 'You have to know the game. Walk in like a green tree and you're gonna walk out like a green tree.'

I don't see what's bad about that. I love trees. They're green in springtime, in full bloom in summer, red brown and yellow in the fall and icy white and virginal in winter. A tree has everything: often a long life, strength, health and a tree purifies everything, gives us oxygen.

Here in Manhattan one sits on top of a measureless shit pile; the stench, the noise, the pollution, the disintegration. It's just terrible. What in Heaven's name am I doing here?

Ellen, I miss you and I miss my parents and sisters. Lee, please come back soon! I feel so all alone and miserable.

Wednesday, August 2, 1978

How good it feels to be alive. How good it is to feel human again and to relax for just a little while. To forget for just one moment that could last a thousand light years in Universe, all the problems of trying to keep it together, the human struggle to survive.

Sometimes it seems impossible to bear all this drudgery, misery, ill fortune, tears, all this adversity but Lord, isn't it good to feel the sun shine on your face, your arms, and body; to walk, to see all the colors of life.

People, children, dogs and cats, the plants, the trees and flowers, the houses, the bridges, the rivers and full moons; all of it gives you such a good feeling. It's so nice to be able to talk to somebody, a person, someone on the bus or in the street. How friendly the smiles are and it is in my opinion true that every face looks like God when it smiles; like a flower opening up, like morning dew over the meadows.

How lovely life is if one can just stop to think for a moment, once and awhile and be in love with God's creation, our endless Universe.

August 4, 1978

I have three lovers now. Yes indeed-io! Sunny is my partner in fun, we first met in Neri's Continental. He's in garments, the rag-trade they call it here and he has already given me loads of unique clothing and nice little presents.

Bill is the photographer, a peach of a man and so sexually accomplished plus he makes great photos.

Elias is the Israeli theater agent, of the three he's the most handsome but also the hardest to sound out. Even so, I am not in love with anyone of them. I love my crazy husband Lee Bridges…well, now and then. My three friends help me out with money at times, no big bucks though, neither one of them is very rich. However, Elias, hopefully can really help me in my career.

Sunday, August 5 or 6?

Lee and I are off to Church in a minute. I got the cutest little bag from him, handmade in Hong Kong, with red and white beads on a dark-blue background, so sweet and lovely. On Thursday I collected the off-white pants suit with waistcoat. Lee saw it before he went to Holland two weeks ago for only twenty dollars. The material is polyester to be sure but the lapels and finishing is done in satin and it looks great on me.

I went out with Sunny Thursday night, delicious food in a restaurant called Roma, good music there too so we danced and danced. We also did plenty of coke, it was a magical night. Sunny used to be a professional dancer and I felt like a feather in his arms. He gave me a blue tuxedo shirt and a little white hat; the total picture is magnificent. He also gave me a beautiful Chinese jacket, silk brocade in soft blue and crème and Chinese baggy silk pants, the colors are soft lilac motives on a white surface. It's so nice of him and his partner David to give me such beautiful things especially the Chinese jacket is a showstopper.

I have a portfolio now with very good pictures that Bill made.

Thursday, August 10, 1978

Exactly five months in New York. It's sizzling hot every day, oppressive with excessive rain pouring last week.

I have so many agents already. Via Joe Franklin to Gene Cogen, Elias Dishi, Ada Einhorn, Arthur Miller. Via Eugene Cogen to Bill Yoscary (photographer) and Anthony Noller (Dutch producer who lives already twenty-four years in the US) and Rod McBrein (TV. commercials, jingles, etc.) and via Rod McBrein to Ray Gasman (tonight at a quarter to six, he's in the record and music publishing business). I'll contact Arthur Miller again next week, he also casts for commercials; at least I have my portfolio now with excellent pictures. I met about a dozen other figures active in whatever, obviously not worth mentioning. Elias is in Detroit for a couple of days which means I won't see him this week. Since we met I've been seeing him regularly, two or three times a week. I like him best of everyone I've met here. It surprises me because he's as stressed out as everyone else here but I don't know; he's got something I guess. He told me that one of his productions is up shit's creek.

I am so silly, damn stupid! I blew a chance to sing somewhere. Joe sent me to Mister Sol of the BonTon on Third Avenue. He wanted to hire me for thirty dollars a night and I turned it down because I thought it wasn't enough money. Can you believe it? Stupid cow that I am! There's practically no job available, not until Labor Day.

I tried all day yesterday to reach the man and tell him I would accept the job but…alas, no luck. Joe didn't understand how I could hesitate and was disappointed in me. My parents haven't written me for quite a while now. I want to know how they all are and also I would like to have new photos of my little nephews. They grow up without me. I wish I could've been part of their life more. Well, perhaps later.

August 14, 1978

The poet came home, thank God, after I almost took off for London. He had told me on the phone that he couldn't get a seat on the plane, everything was sold up. He said that he was going to send me money. I went to Joe Franklin Saturday afternoon to say goodbye. He gave me a handwritten reference letter.

That night Lee came home completely unexpected. Tom Bailey and I were at Mary's house for a surprise party for her friend Michelle who had her birthday and suddenly the phone rang; it was Lee and he was in New York. It was a wonderful reunion and a smashing night.

August 16, 1978

Someone is annoying the hell out of me playing worse than mediocre on his damn flute while I just got an idea for a new song. I'll be alright; at least I have something new to work on. Still no new prospects on the horizon but I stay active, positive and going forward, full of optimism. Obviously we are still broke. I pretty much have got my new song down pat. I need to cool off. I've got an appointment in a little while with someone from Cable Television.

Thursday, August 17, 1978

Elias promised to call me last night, we were supposed to have gone out to dinner but he never called. So apparently I was just a little toy for him, thrown away when the novelty wore off. What an adolescent I am! Why the hell did I have to fall in love with him?

Why doesn't mommy write to me anymore and Marjorie? Doesn't she know how I'd love to receive photos of the boys? Damn!

Monday, August 21, 1978

I did an audition on Saturday in a restaurant near Rockefeller Plaza, a beautiful place, Iranian/Indian. They're looking to hire for the next season that will start after Labor Day. Jesse's girlfriend Nancy, a very nice girl, gave me the Show Business paper where I found the advertisement of that restaurant. Nancy is an actress and helps me out a lot with tips and suggestions. I also saw an agent, Julius Epstein, who advised me to contact Stanley Brilliant from La Chansonette. However, the restaurant is still closed. I left my number. In a minute I have an audition at The Brass Rail on Seventh Avenue and 49th. And so I go on, perseverance and my love for music and singing keep me going.

Tuesday, August 22, 1978

Oh, it's so frustrating! No matter what I do, auditions, telephone calls, interviews with agents, appointments…everything is stagnated until September, after Labor Day. Jesus, if all the restaurants, clubs, film productions, television commercials, etcetera, indeed engage me in September I'll have so much work and offers that it won't be humanly possible for me to do it all. Is it possible? Will the near future really be as rosy for me as everyone would have me believe? Or is it all false hope, a Fata Morgana? Everybody who hears and sees me sing is convinced of my great success in the future.

'You're going to make it big; you're going to make it all the way. You've got everything. You've got what it takes.' That's what they tell me all the time. Meanwhile Lee and I are flat broke again but for a few lousy dollars.

Manhattan is burning up and I've accustomed my stomach to the intake of very little food. I can't eat those junk ham burgers anyway.

This is my daily menu: coffee in the morning, sometimes with a piece of cake that Lee buys when our meager funds allow it. Then, at lunchtime I buy a pizza slice on 6th Avenue at the famous Ray's Pizza Place that only costs 65 cents and is ever so delicious and filling. Then, late at night when I'm ravenous again I sometimes buy a taco or a frozen yogurt. We try to always keep fruit in the place like peaches, prunes, bananas, a head of lettuce, an onion and a couple of tomatoes. I drink loads of water during the day; we buy it bottled. Once or twice a week someone offers me dinner and then I consume a nice hot mail. Lee also buys chicken and bread regularly but I really eat very little and evidently I lost quite a bit of weight again; it doesn't matter.

We had such a nice, relaxed fun night at Ron Yoes place; he's a poet and very nice and funny. Jesse was there and Claire, a blond with legs that just went on and on and on and Leroy, a drummer just back from Holland where he played at the Laren Jazz Festival. We had wine, beer, cheese, bread, peanuts and tai-stick joints; the atmosphere was top!

I almost pied in my pants laughing when Jesse and Leroy sang a duet, they were so serious and it was so funny.

Jesse, thin and tall as he is, swaying with his arms, looking just like the figures he makes of wire, singing: 'Where do I start...' (A line from the song I love New York in June) and Leroy with a heavy bass voice: 'Holding hands in the afternoon.' I was ridiculously comical. I'm going to take a nap.

August 23, 1978

I took the broom to all paper shit I had already accumulated since Lee's return and everything is now neatly arranged in a colorful file. In other words: I'm ready to leave again. Yes sir! I'm ready for the next trip!

Ada told me there's a card from my sister Lilly from Mexico. However, still no word from anyone else.

Thursday, August 24, 1978

It's great to hear from Lilly, she's fine. She and her friend Mandy are on their way to Ecuador. She expects to be there half September and gave me an address to write to her in Quito. I hope I also get letters from mom

and dad, Marjorie and Ben, grandma and Ellen and Jack and Shouki. I
miss all of them so much, especially the children.

Saturday, August 26, 1978

My brochure is ready to be printed. I'm very happy with the result.
Why hasn't Marjorie sent me more photos of her boys?

Monday, August 28, 1978

Today I signed a contract for one year with William Lee Armstrong;
he is now my American agent. I met him through a lawyer friend of Lee
and I think he's sympathetic and all business, just what I need. He gets
20% of all my earnings. Lee thinks it's okay. We shall see what the future
holds in store. I'm going to play my guitar.

~

Chapter 14

Trial and Tribulation

September 1, 1978

Hurrah, September at last! I saw a physician today and feel so much better. The warts on my labia are innocent, she simply burnt them away and said that there's no reason why I shouldn't get pregnant, if necessary through artificial insemination. I feel happy and relieved, Lee too. He's always so sweet and concerned about me.

In a minute we'll go out to dinner with Adrian, that Celine-like character, always good for a couple of laughs. He's Jewish with a 'snozzle' from here to Tokio according to his own words, part of triplets and although very funny he's quite cruel in his observations of human conduct, saying that the Red Cross is an international vampire society for instance and 'they should've gassed them all' about the Holocaust victims. I abhor those remarks of his but at the same time he's so off the wall funny that you can't help but laugh.

Furthermore he's a terrific painter I think; we have one of his works. It looks like monks in some mysterious cave and depending from which angle you look at it you can see different figures, images, hiding as it were; a strange, haunting, rectangular lovely work of art.

When Adrian had his first art exhibition in café Eylders in Amsterdam a couple of years ago he had marked them with quite exuberant prices, saying in that cynical voice of his: 'The mothers have no inkling and aren't worth my blood, sweat and tears so they shall pay dearly.' He sold out on opening night which threw him into frenzy whereupon he took off for the South of France and blew all the money in no time, returning to Amsterdam flat broke again. He's mad as a hatter and only to take in minimum doses at a time, however, fun and harmless I think. We're off to Chinatown, yeah! I'm reading a marvelous book: The Greatest Story Ever Told, about the life of Jesus. My sweet Jesus!

September 5, 1978

Today I received a letter from Marjorie. She writes about their vacation in the South of France and about my darling nephews. At the end she wrote: 'I didn't read your letter to mama on purpose, I was so enthused to hear from you. We couldn't help you because we just bought the caravan. Because we were unable to help you now doesn't mean we would leave you stranded if you were in trouble! You know that!'

My mother wrote me an angry letter some time back saying that I shouldn't have asked Marjorie and Ben for financial assistance. I did that because the rent in Amsterdam was due and I was worried we were going to lose our house. But my mother was pretty mean to me and it upset me terribly.

But now all is well again and I quickly bought some postcards and mailed them to my parents, to Marjorie, to my dear friends Ellen and Jack and to grandma.

I had to go to the Emergency of Saint Vincent Hospital yesterday. My vagina is all swollen and painful since Saturday. Two doctors examined me and took a smear. I have to come back on Tuesday and take four to five hot baths daily.

Listen, great news! I'm singing in The Top of the Sixes, a fabulous rooftop restaurant in Midtown Manhattan, every Friday and Saturday night. I love it and am thrilled.

I'm studying on Send in the Clowns and You Are the Sunshine of My Life at the moment.

Adrian is taking over our apartment in Amsterdam for six months, great; that's a load of our backs.

September 11, 1978

My manager paid me today, thank God and my brochures are ready, they look wonderful.

I went out with a black girl Saturday night after my show at the Top of the Sixes. We first went to the Ibis on Lexington and 52nd and afterwards we went with two Italians to Harlem, to the Cotton Club. She told these guys to wait for us in the car while she and I took care of some business; when we came out of the Cotton Club an hour and a half later the two suckers were gone of course.

She said her name was Brandy and she reminded me a lot of Keita Leita, the Jamaican dancer I worked with in The Acheron Club in Berlin, in October 1976.

We went to several other places; I thought it real exciting to be immersed in the nightlife of black Harlem. Brandy was trying to score some coke without success however. At about five in the morning she and this cab driver friend of hers drove me back to my hotel in the Village and then they went uptown again.

She told me that she was very wealthy and from Guatemala, that she had traveled the world and that she was staying in the Waldorf Astoria Hotel. I don´t know whether I should believe that story for she kept saying she was broke because she lost five hundred dollars gambling in Kansas City and that she needed to pin down a guy for some serious dough.

It was an excellent opportunity for me to see Harlem by night I thought, however, my husband was not amused.

~

And so we lived from day to day, the poet and I, hanging on, hoping and praying; trying to make ends meet. I sang in this club or that restaurant, auditioned till the cows came home, did an occasional run-on in some cable television program but, all in all my career was though not entirely extinguished then certainly floundering in all directions.

The singing gig I landed at The Top Of The Sixes was a lucky break; however, only two nights a week it still didn't pay all the bills.

I never for one second gave in to gnawing feelings of inadequacy though, I kept positive and believed in myself and my talent even though I wasn't going anywhere fast. I simply kept on going with the continuous and unwavering support from my pal, my best friend, my husband.

My health was less than perfect though. I had pain in my abdomen, lumps in my breasts, periods that lasted up to seven or eight days and when I saw a breast specialist on Wednesday, the 20th of September I suddenly became convinced I had cancer. They did a Mammogram but the doctor didn't want to take more than two photos each because I was so young and the photos they took showed nothing because my breasts were too dense. Then my eyes started bothering me again, giving me splitting headaches and I couldn't keep my contacts in for more than two hours at a time. My gynecologist wanted me to see a dermatologist because I have so many beauty marks on my body.

~

Thursday, September 21, 1978

Dr. Bell thinks they're only cysts but I was shocked by his reaction when he found something under my left arm. He asked if I had infections but I don't. It's all so scary; I don't want to think about it anymore.

September 22, 1978

I'm quite sick, stayed in bed all day today, high fever, coughing, pain everywhere and especially my breasts. Now I feel a little better, the fever has dropped. Lee takes very good care of me. He brought me fruits, chocomel, orange juice and Excedrin.

My ring and gold chain are in the pawnshop, it's all very hard at the moment.

September 23, 1978

I'm feeling much better, thank God. Just called Bill Yoscary and I'll meet him in a little while in the Alvin Theater (that he has been running for many years) he said he'll give me some money. He's such a dear, my friend Bill. I am indeed very fond of him. Aside from being a superb photographer he's also a sculptor and has his studio in the Alvin Theater;

at the moment he's working on a head of one of the cast from the musical Annie.

Sunday, September 24, 1978

Manny, the German sausage hotel manager with his little pig's eyes, lies in wait for a couple of days now ready to jump us. We have nothing left, no money, nothing to pawn and the hotel rent is due, 18 dollars from last week and 75 for this week. He'll probably start threatening us that we have to leave our room, that fox terrier!

Well, I'm not well yet and am going to stay in bed all day today. Perhaps this is our last day here. Where we will go then I haven't got a clue but everything comes as it is supposed to I guess.

The day before yesterday I heard him give all the details about Barbra Streisand staying here to some new guests. That must have been a very long time ago and poor Barbra must have hated it as much as I do now, this horrible typhus din.

Lee is so sweet; he pampers me, out now to get food and some more pocket books for me. I almost finished Two Sisters by Gore Vidal. He is such a darling, what would I do without him? Lee I mean not Gore Vidal though I love the way he writes. My manager, well, I'm afraid I would've done better not to sign up with him; he hasn't come up with anything yet.

Monday, September 25, 1978

I'm so cold and hungry. Lee borrowed forty dollars from his lawyer,
Mister Monett. Dr. Harrington helped us out a couple of times already
also. My manager gave me twenty-five dollars the other day. Lee and I
had double hamburgers, so delicious and he bought two kilo apples of
which I ate two already. I finished an Agatha Christie novel last night and
started La Bartarde by Violette Leduc with an introduction by Simone de
Beauvoir today; I go back to that now.

Wednesday, September 26, 1978

We're packing. The big day is here at last. We're abandoning ship;
departing from the Earle Hotel on Waverly Place in the Village. I have to
pawn my guitar now.

Friday, September 28, 1978

A room smaller than the guestroom in our flat at the
Amstelveenseweg in Amsterdam, in Hotel Terminal (Lee and I had to
laugh at the fitting name to our circumstances) on Lexington close to 44th

Street, midtown, soft blue walls, pink drapes and a lovely white bedspread for eleven dollars a day.

There was a wonderful, sweet letter from mama at Ada's, I cried from happiness. She wrote about their vacation in Spain, how much grandma enjoyed it also. And they loved my brochure and she said they are so proud of me that I was on American Television and that very few Dutch singers have accomplished something like that. She also wrote that I look a bit skinny, my face especially.

That's no surprise to me, Lee and I eat sparingly, ha-ha!

Lee and I inscribed with an office for temporary work like giving out flyers in the streets, demonstrating articles in shops, hostessing at conventions, et cetera; they pay $5 an hour.

We were visiting Steve McCall last night. He just came back from a European tour with his group Air and had a bottle of Bols Jonge Jenever which the three of us polished off no problem. It was such a fun night, haven't relaxed like that in a long time. I got homesick for Holland though, Amsterdam, the friends, the coziness, Hoppe and Eylders café's. His girlfriend Bibi was across the street from their Loft shooting pictures of a Fashion Award evening. Margeaux Hemingway, Bianca Jagger and other famous folks were present.

She called us to come on over, there was champagne and a buffet but Lee, Steve and I were already too out of it, having smoked pot as well.

We saw Johnny Griffin, the saxophone player, Wednesday when we were just getting into a taxi with all our luggage.

Lee has put Johnny in contact with Steve; they're both from Chicago and know each other for years. Nice!

Johnny Griffin and Dexter Gordon had a concert this past Saturday in Carnegie Hall, Lee and I didn't go, no money but we heard it was great.

The reviews in the papers called it The Battle of the Horns; typical American of course, everything even something as universal as music is turned into a competition. Lee used to be very close friends with Dexter, in Paris and also in Copenhagen where Lee lived before he moved south. Johnny he also knows for ages, he introduced him to his wife Marianne who was Lee's girlfriend before. And he did time with Max Roach he once told me, ages ago of course. My darling has lived a whole life already before we even met.

Saturday, September 30, 1978

Bill gave me twenty dollars and Jesse gave twenty dollars to Lee. Jesse's little sculpture of Mohammed Ali has been sold to the Chemical Bank on Wall Street. That's so nice for Jesse.

Yesterday we visited with Ron Yoes, he's a poet and the most gentle, nice person I know, always poor like us. He said he'd been sitting in the house all day dreaming about a pot of beans and ham hog but he had no money to buy food. However, we ate delicious chicken wings that he prepared and later at Turner O'Neal's we had some white wine.

When we walked home we had no more than three dimes between us, a rotten situation. I hope one of us or both of us manage to get more work soon. I spoke with Mary Blithe the other day, she told me to go talk to Gina, manager of club/restaurant Café New York; she'd heard they're looking to hire a singer there. I saw her and have to audition on Monday so it's imperative that I retrieve my guitar out of the pawn shop.

Thursday, October 5, 1978

Dr. Harrington's service on Sunday was about the seven deadly sins according to Mahatma Gandhi.

It was quite a feat to get a guitar from someone for the audition on Monday but luckily at the last minute, Henry, a friend of Ron Yoes had a friend who had a guitar, a Yamaha folk guitar with only five strings but I do have extra strings of course.

The audition went well; Gina said she can probably book me for a couple of nights a week. Tomorrow she'll let me know for sure. I met Arthur Needle there, a business man and a friend of Mary's. She told me he lent her 1500 dollars a couple of months back when Lee was in Holland and I was staying with Mary.

He's very nice and offered me dinner which I, hungry as I was, accepted in gratitude.

On Tuesday when I went to the club to give Gina my brochure Arthur was there again. He said he was taking his daughters out to dinner and we agreed to see each other at nine o'clock for a drink in Café New York.

He came and asked if I was hungry, such an understanding soul. To not jeopardize my chances for singing in Café New York he said: 'Go on over to Brews and I'll meet you there in ten minutes.'

I ate a scrumptious meal: filet of sole, filled with crab meat, salad, rice, corn on the cob…it was delicious! I couldn't even eat it all which made me feel guilty, thinking of Lee of course. Luckily I could take it home in a 'doggie bag'. Arthur said he'd loan me a hundred dollars next week to get my guitar back and have some pocket money. I thanked him and asked if he could loan me ten now. He said he'd be happy to but that this was not a loan.

Lee loved the food and warm, satisfied and content we made love, something which we, because of our staggering difficulties, haven't done for quite awhile.

Wednesday our problems loomed large again; still no work, all day not more than one donut, rain, and cold, miserable. At last at night back in our hotel Lee decided to go see Hazel Scott, the famous pianist/singer. He knows her well from Paris when he used to supply her with hashish. She sings and plays in the Ali Baba club on First Avenue. She was very cold and arrogant to him but he did sell her a book of his poetry for ten dollars.

This morning I called Arthur Needle to ask if he could lend me the hundred dollars now instead of next week but before I even could say something he interrupted and said: 'I have the money for you. I felt bad about saying to you that I would give it to you next week while I have the money to give to you now.'

So, happy as a lark, I dashed over to his office to pick up the hundred bucks. I have my guitar back, my one ring with the little diamond; we ate well and put some money away for the hotel. So we can breathe a little again. And Arthur doesn't expect anything in return, he's just nice.

October 6, 1978

Congratulations, sweet daddy, with your 55th birthday. I went out to dinner again with Arthur, an Italian place this time and a drink afterwards in Once Upon A Stove.

He's a very nice man, gave me money again without me asking for it and just a little peck on the cheek to say goodnight. He said I should never be ashamed or too proud to ask him for money. 'I'm glad to help you,' he said.

Good news! Next Wednesday I'll be singing in Café New York. It pays only 35 dollars but perhaps I'll manage to get one or two other spots to perform.

Saturday, October 7, 1978

Cathy, Mary and I are rehearsing again. We made a list of twenty-five songs we want to do together and Cathy typed it in threefold.

Monday, October 9, 1978

I'm freezing my ass off in this little cubbyhole, wearing gloves, a couple of sweaters and a house coat.

Thursday, October 12, 1978

Mary Blithe is such a doll. I just came from her house and am writing in bed. Lee is reading the paper. She loaned me some song books. And she took me to a lovely bagel shop in her neighborhood, treated me to a bagel with tuna salad and a dish of carrot salad and ice cream to top it off. She also wouldn't let me pay for my cigarettes. I love her a lot, I always feel very at home with her; she's the motherly type.

~

~

My so-called manager kept carrots dangling in front of my nose like for instance a booking in California. He even had me talk to his partner over there who told me I'd be working in The Icehouse and The Troubadour in Los Angeles. I should have gone there with or without the certainty of work; the opportunity to sing in the famous Troubadour could have been the break I was waiting for, however, at the time I had no idea how important that club was for musicians. And being so devoted to my husband I doubt if I would have gone there on my own even if I had known about the importance of that famous place. I didn't do anything without Lee's blessing and although he always encouraged me, the advancement of my singing career was not foremost on his mind as he was mostly concerned about himself and his poetry.

Joe Franklin of WOR-TV kept me dangling as well but at least he put me on to some people through whom I sang now and then or did a shooting for a commercial occasionally.

We had friends and there were parties and home cooking but the continuous financial difficulties were beginning to take their toll.

My well doer in those days, Mister Arthur Needle, a perfect gentleman who never laid a hand on me, kept taking me out to the well known food spots and watering holes like Pen & Pencil for instance. I always left some food over to take home in a doggie bag for my husband.

Lee tried to get jobs and now and then he did some temporary work like interviewing folks for a survey for instance, however, as the months passed and our situation

didn't improve he too became fed up just like I did. We wanted to go home, back to Holland.

~

Chapter 15

Trotting Along

October 23, 1978

We're out of the 'hole'; we have a nice large room with wide windows on the tenth floor of the Warrington Hotel (we were here once before for a week I believe) with a view of the Empire State Building, on Madison Avenue. We have no bath but a shower yes and a new television set, lamps, cup boards, closets, desks, armoires…it's real cozy. We have seventy-five dollars in the bank. Lee has a job via Flight485; he makes four dollars an hour. It's easy, he has to go by stores who sell lottery tickets and write down names and addresses of those who want to sell the tickets next season.

Everything looks better and sunny again!

Wednesday, October 24, 1978

I'm restless and nervous. We got an angry letter from our landlord in Amsterdam. He wants us to pay up (1100 guilders) before November 1st.

He says that the present occupant pulled the wash table off the wall in our bedroom resulting in leakage and problems. Where the heck is Adrian? Anyway, I'm cooking spaghetti; my angel will be mighty pleased when he comes home from work. I also have work next week via Flight485; I have to pass out cigarettes in the street.

I'm going to post letters to my family today; Lilly is in Lima, Peru now. I'm thinking of visiting my dear friend Bill Yoscary also today.

Thursday, October 25, 1978

Adrian wrote us, he says he'll be here in ten days, great!

God, I'll be thirty next year, God willing, that's nearly middle aged!

I went back to St. Vincent's Hospital; I have some lumps in my breasts. The doctor (young and handsome) told me not to worry, they're only cysts.

My agent says he's made a flight reservation for me for Los Angeles but I think he's full of shit.

Oh, I forgot to tell, Arthur Needle gave me a pair of lovely expensive boots and a beautiful morning gown, dark blue with light blue stripes which my husband appropriated immediately. He looks like Lucy Ball in it, a black Lucy Ball!

I think that Arthur is in love with me, he has never tried anything yet but he's got his mind set on having me one of these days so…I've got to watch my step!

I'm looking forward to cynical crazy Adrian's arrival. He's really mental but that's why I love him. Lee is nuts also. Just look at him lying in my new duster on the bed watching that stupid football again.

I'm reading a good book, Blind Date by Kozinsky.

October 31, 1978

It's a godsend, aside from singing two nights a week I also have work as a waitress doing lunch now in Café New York off and on. Arthur still takes me out to dinner (I guess I have been inside most of the hot spots by now) and gives me money each time, thirty, twenty-five, forty, sometimes fifty bucks. It's easier these days. Lee works all the time now for Flight485. I received a nice letter from Marjorie.

It's Halloween and the top of the Empire State Building is illuminated beautifully in red, orange and yellow.

I stood in the street with cigarettes today and yesterday. The people are like vultures, some come by ten times. Others snatch two packs out of your hand. We're supposed to hand out one try-out packet a person. You get dizzy from all those people; all those hands seem like claws. Gimme, gimme, gimme...umpf, terrible!

I'm not going tomorrow, can't do this kind of work day after day. I'll go again for a few days next week.

We work from ten a.m. to two p.m. without a break. Now and then I put the box down to give my shoulders a rest. We stand in groups of two girls and one man who gives us new supplies all the time. We're wearing a stupid little hat with 'Golden Lights 100' written on it. Though we don't work for eight hours, we get paid for eight hours work a day.

I'm off to the Community Church in a bit; Dr. Harrington is doing a reading about Universalism; and still no sign of our illustrious friend Adrian.

Saturday, November 4, 1978

Adrian arrived yesterday and left for Baltimore today. He didn't pay the rent in Amsterdam and left the key with Jeroen of all people!

Arthur gave me a lovely plum colored hat. It looks great on me. He also gave me seventy dollars. He's very sweet but I'm absolutely not in love with him.

Lee and I are going to do another show in the Community Church on December 10.

November 5, 1978

Lee has promised me to go see a doctor about that burning sensation he keeps feeling lately in the chest area.

Monday, November 6, 1978

I auditioned for the Off-Broadway play The Diary of Anne Frank today. It was Equity (I cannot yet become a member, have to have my green card first) so I had to wait till the end, luckily there weren't hundreds of people as usual.

The producer seemed more than a little interested in me, he talked to me for quite awhile, said I had the right coloring. Oh boy, wouldn't it be just great if they picked me to play Anne! She's my childhood hero; I feel I really know her well. I went to United Artist Studios to meet with Richard Moses. He was in a screening, his secretary asked me to call him tomorrow at 9.30 a.m.; Eugene Cogen gave me Richard Moses's address.

This afternoon I saw Bill, he's such a sweetheart. We made love in his studio while sunbeams poured all over our naked bodies. I adore Bill and couldn't resist him. Lee is becoming more and more like an older brother to me. I love him forever of course but, well, I don't know, sexually we don't match anymore. It happened gradually I guess. Actually the poet has a low sexual appetite and I do suspect my libido is above average. So…there you have it.

Bill is an artist and a lover of women; he has a wife in his house with swimming pool in New Jersey somewhere where he spends the weekends and he shares an apartment with his girlfriend here in Manhattan.

His studio is huge and has a studio-apartment in it, very cozy. I like him very much.

November 8, 1978

I have to write. Everything seems so unreal. Lee is in the hospital on intensive care, coronary care. Oh God!

My sweetheart has had a heart attack! I can't write now. Oh dear God, help me, help him! I can't think straight, so nervous.

Thursday November 16, 1978

I have been going bananas with everything, Lee in hospital, all those problems awaiting us in Holland but it's over, I'm alright and, more important, Lee is fine, spic and span and healthy. We don't smoke anymore. It's easy; I don't even long for a cigarette.

I just finished typing his poem 'Afterthoughts of Kabul/The Afghans'. In my mind's eye I see us again in that desert country amidst the Afghans, friendly, melancholy people. This year, in March I believe, the Afghan government was ousted; Daoud, the president and twenty-five members of his family including children were murdered. There's a communist oriented regime now and I take it that things have changed there. In Iran there've been upheavals throughout the year which are getting worse and bloodier all the time. The Shah appointed a military government and martial law. People in Iran are totally fed up with the Shah and his American friends.

Last year we walked in those regions; how time flies and how quickly things can change.

I love Lee's poems; they're so beautiful, deep and true.

~

~

That was quite a shock indeed when I received a call while I was working lunch in Café New York from the manager of our hotel.

'Mrs. Bridges, your husband has been taken to New York Hospital; he's suffered a heart attack.' I stood there, speechless, trembling, almost buckling over.

A waitress, a tall buxom girl from Australia, quickly propped me up on a bar stool and made me drink a snifter of cognac. She offered to go with me to NYU. When we arrived there I told her I was alright and alone I walked into the room at cardiology intensive care and saw the love of my life sitting propped up in his bed reading the newspaper.

He looked over his glasses and smiled broadly when he saw me.

'I'm fine, puss,' he said, 'don't know why they want to keep me here.'

I was baffled and sat with him for awhile holding his hand. It turned out that he had some sort of heart rhythm problem, not a real attack but they wanted to keep him there for a few days to monitor his condition. After three days he was released, fine as a fiddle.

We stopped smoking, however, over time we both started up again; bad habits are hard to overcome apparently.

~

Thursday, November 23, 1978

I work so hard, auditions, waitressing and I did some translating for a German business man. I only stayed one afternoon there. I didn't like the man and the atmosphere in his office; dead animals all over the place, a lion, a panther, a tiger, a buffalo's sad head, a crocodile and in between a herd of smaller animals. It gave me the creeps and made me think the man was probably a Nazi.

Now I'm singing in a Japanese club since two nights but I don't like this job either. I only get to sing three or four songs (there are many girls who sing) and the rest of the evening you just sit there pouring drinks and lighting the Japanese business men's cigars and cigarettes like I am some goddamned geisha! It's too boring, the hours simply don't move. I hate this job!

Something awful happened, some guru, James Jones, lead eleven

hundred people, including children, into massive suicide in Jonestown,

Guyana. I cannot comprehend it! What is this world coming to, dear Lord?

Monday, November 27, 1978

How handsome my husband still is at fifty-two. I love his smooth

skin.

I want to buy presents for my cutie pie nephews at A.F. Schwartz now

that I have some money from all my hard laboring. I have never even been

inside there; it's on Fifth Avenue. It's snowing, how romantic. I don't like

the cold though. I would like to go to California; however, my stupid

agent is full of shit! I'm going to have a cup of tea now and watch the four

o'clock movie. I wish I was a mother; perhaps I will be one day.

Sunday, December 3, 1978

I did a singing gig again at Barbarann's, fifty bucks, piece of cake.

Lee is lying on bed watching Football again as usual; I don't know how he

can stand it! How do I stand it? Good looking hunk-a-dunks but I think

it's a silly sport.

Lee has written the program for our Show at the Community Church, we start rehearsing tomorrow.

On Thursday I received a stack of mail from my fans from all over the world, so nice. Lilly is having a good time in Peru, in and out of flaming fairy tale love affairs. She and her friend Mandy are true blue adventurers, girls after my heart.

Oh and there was the sweetest letter from Michel, he wrote me on the 9th of September but I only received it now.

He played with the Greek National Soccer team in Greece; they won with one to zero and Michel made the goal. The Greek team wants him, offering him a lot of money but his club in Cyprus refuses the transfer. How mean of those bastards! Michel is so handsome and a great athlete. He also asked if he could come here to live with me and if it's easy to get a work permit in America. We must live our life together, he wrote, to live in the same room and make love every night. How enticing it sounds! The way he talks to me in his letter; that he can't live without me. Ah, my sweet, darling Michel, my Apollo. I am still your Aphrodite, love, and I always will be.

Marjorie sent me lovely pictures of the boys and there was a sweet letter from mom and dad and a letter from my aunt Tjitske. And...there was also a letter from the Department of Justice, an ominous sign of course.

And sure enough, if I haven't left the United States before the 12th of December I will be arrested and deported.

Lee was rather upset about it. We went all the way downtown to the Free Legal Aid Office. When we finally got there he remembered our good friend Turner O'Neal, the lawyer. So, uptown again, luckily he was home and made a phone call; all is well again.

We now have to send in forms for me to obtain permanent residence and a green card, to be able to work legally.

Arthur Needle was in Bar None Friday night. He was angry with me for not calling him. I said: 'You never call me either.' 'Yes,' he said, 'but how can I when your husband is always there with you.'

I don't like it, who does he think he is to lay claims on me! I told him that I will call him next week which I won't.

Tuesday, December 5, 1978

I can put it down to my period; crying over nothing, depressed, etcetera. Last night I suddenly burst out crying because newlyweds in a movie had their first baby. I felt the missing of a child so acutely again.

Lee comforted me and said that when we're back in Holland, when things go better here and we'll have our own house we'll start tests again. He saw on television a new method to help women, who have problems conceiving, something other than artificial insemination. A minute ago I wailed because I thought Lee was angry with me. He wasn't angry with me but because I keep going on about getting my fur coat out of storage he said he wished he made money instead of me.

And I don't want that, particularly not that he feels guilty because I carry most of the financial burden. That's what makes him nervous and gives him that pain. I could bite my tongue at times for the things I say. Suddenly it has become an obsession for me to get my fur coat back. I'll get it of course and the weather has been so mild this week, I don't even need it yet. I'm so mad at myself for leaving my fur hat in Amsterdam when I was there this April. I'm scared to think of our dear house. Dear God, please help us.

What will the landlord do with our things? All my diaries, the songs I wrote, my clothes, books, records, my china and all my other possessions? And our lovely paintings! God, save our paintings!

Scheisse! Anyway I am going to rehearse my songs for the show on Sunday at the Community Church.

Friday, December 8, 1978

I've got my Fox back! Yeah! We're off to Washington next week.
Adrian called; he's going back to Holland tomorrow.

Tuesday, December 19, 1978

I washed my hair last night; put it in braids so now I've got curls up
the kazoo, Rita Hayworth like.

Washington was one big flop. Only about five or six spectators! We did
our show of course and that went well; the church itself is beautiful, such
resonance, superb!

But the assistant minister was a cold potato; he'd invited none of his
congregation, didn't announce us and went away before our show started.
Plus...he locked the door where our clothes and my guitar were. Luckily
the boy who took care of the sound system had a key.

Bailey's son in law was there with his girlfriend and they took us to a
cozy bar afterwards where we had cocktails. Later he took us on a tour of
Washington by night. What a lovely town it is with all those magnificent
buildings, large squares, so much green and lovely houses, awfully nice. It
was full moon and that, more often than not, is an ominous sign for

Gemini's. I suddenly got sick, we were just near Watergate; George stopped the car and I puked on Watergate! At Capitol Hill I had to throw up again.

The next day Adrian's friend, Serge, came by; we drove to the airport where we smoked about six pipes. All in all it was a flop trip. Lee went to such lengths to get us here and today, naturally, we're flat broke.

Friday, December 22, 1978

My agent is such a jerk, today it's all uncertain again whether my performance on the 24th is still on. My singing career is in still waters. Something's got to be done, a new project, a new goal. Lee and I have no money as usual and it's Christmas this weekend.

I visited Mary Blithe yesterday. She's built a neat workshop in her house and makes good money now making electronic parts for radios, recorders, and etcetera. I'm so happy for her, what a clever girl!

It's lovely weather, sunny and mild. I mailed my Christmas cards.

I passed a shop on Lexington between 59 and 60, when my eye caught a red dress priced down from sixty to twenty-nine dollars. Inside I went, tried on two dresses, the corn flower blue one looked best on me. It's wool, acryl and mohair, 42% wool; a lovely simple dress. But the lunacy, where do I get the money to buy that dress? I want it so badly. Mama used to have a dress like that when I was a little girl. It looked so good on her, she was so pretty, and she looked like Greta Garbo; now she's got many wrinkles and worry lines.

I keep seeing myself in that dress, silly idiot that I am! The poet would love to buy it for me for a Christmas present. I'm like a child who believes in miracles.

Ron Yoes is cook in a restaurant and through his mediation I talked to the owner, gave him my brochure. He says I can sing there three nights a week. It doesn't pay much, only twenty-five a night but something is better than nothing. At least I can invite people to come and hear me sing.

P.S. The poet and I haven't smoked for a month and a half. He's doing okay, thank God!

Saturday, December 30, 1978

I was in Mimi's Pub on 52ⁿᵈ Street last night. I had my guitar with me but couldn't play, it's a piano bar. Mary and her friend Richard were with me. I sang Body & Soul and Lover Man and I got 'carried away' like Tom Bailey always says about me. It was fabulous, I closed my eyes and just sang; it's the best thing there is in this world.

The audience went wild with enthusiasm, one man in the crowd called out to me to not waste my voice with amateurs 'because it's too beautiful.'

One day I will break through, yes, one day I will! I see green fields with thousands of flowers, a blue sky with here and there a white soft cloud and I see deer, squirrels and children roaring with laughter, playing and I see a troubadour who plays his flute, wondrous fairy tale like music and I hear angels sing so lovely, so clear and pure and then the sonorous warm tones of a men's choir. They are fishermen in their blue and green keels, their brown strong arms, weather-beaten faces, far away looking eyes. Toujours l'amour pour la vie magnifique!

Sunday, December 31, 1978

It is New Year's Eve in New York City, in the Warrington Hotel, on Madison Avenue on the tenth floor, room 1004; outside rain and the top of the Empire State Building hiding in grey, low hanging damp clouds. Inside the spacious yet somewhat shabby room a large king size bed domineers and the Daily News is spread out over the blue flowered bed cover and Lee with glasses is focused on the television set: football again! I hate those all afternoon sports events! Ah well, let it be!

Lee brought me a chocolate cake and that's very nice.

1978 is passé, over and done with. Over are the nostalgic, melancholic, passive, underhanded and aggressive seventies. But who knows, maybe a miracle will occur and we will not be doomed to live like in the book 1984 by George Orwell. I'm lazy, tender and sluggish. Perhaps we'll go for a stroll today that is if it stops raining. Still, all in all, I cast a hopeful and optimistic glance towards the future. That feeling is indestructible notwithstanding the problems and sometimes hopelessness especially on the last day of the year. I miss home but not so much that I want to throw in the towel and forget about making it here. We aren't here that long after all, not even ten months yet.

~

Chapter 16

A New Dawn

New Year's Day, January 1, 1979

It's still raining but warm, 56 degrees Fahrenheit. We celebrated the changing of years so nicely! We went to the Community Church on Park Avenue. Dr. Harrington, his wife Vilma and about twenty-five mostly elderly people.

There was punch with and without wine, cookies and a record-player with dance music. Dr. Harrington asked if I brought my guitar and Lee his poetry books. He was going to recite some poems himself as well. So, Lee and I went back to the hotel. We did a nice little show; Dr. Harrington read a couple of poems and Vilma told some jokes. An old man (85) who often plays the piano after service on Sundays was dancing up a storm and played the piano of course and a frail old grey haired lady sang soprano old melodies. We even did the 'Zevensprong', an Old Dutch child's folksong and dance. Dr. Harrington studied in Leiden years ago and still remembers some Dutch and old games and songs. He is such a wonderful inspiring man! Yesterday there was an article in the Daily News about who had been praised too much the past year. The journalist thought that Dr. Harrington, that religious man, had been praised far too much. Donald Harrington is head of the Liberal Party in New York and on speaking terms with lots of prominent people, heads of states, President Jimmy Carter one of them.

In my opinion he can't be praised enough because here he was, on New Year's Eve, choosing to be with the lonely and elderly instead of family and friends or expensive parties. Those there were plenty of last night. The Waldorf Astoria party was three hundred bucks a couple and in the Palace even six hundred dollars for two people.

At eleven o'clock we went upstairs; Dr. Harrington put on his official black and red robes to give the Night Watch Sermon. He spoke beautifully, about the old year, the disappointments, the terrible excesses, the fear, the riots in Iran, et cetera but also about the good things and the coming year. There were some thirty-five large white candles illuminating the altar in a fairy tale like way. At twelve o'clock Mr. Franz, the organist, rang a pure sounding little bell.

Outside I was surprised not to hear the cacophonic crackling noise of fireworks like in Holland. I had thought that in a big city like New York all hell would break loose at twelve o'clock on New Year's Eve. That was a bit disappointing. In thought I embraced all my loved ones and wished them a very happy new year: mama, papa, Marjorie, Lilly, my little nephews, Ben, grandma, Ellen and Jack.

And now it's 1979. We shall put our best leg forward. To do the best you can is what you can do for the best.

January 6, 1979

I can long so much for an ordinary life at times; a nice job, a lovely house, one or two children…hopefully it will come still.

Sunday morning, January 7, 1979

I dreamt of Michel. He was so close to me and sweet. Naturally the dream was weird. He was performing with the Rolling Stones, I was backstage and after a fantastic show (Michel lifted me off my feet and swayed me 'round and 'round center stage till I got dizzy) there was a parade although there was nothing to be seen. We sat on the steps of a white building, some sort of palace, there was a brass band and someone informed us over the loudspeaker that the Shah of Iran and Farah Diba had laid out a lovely flower-bed, however, we couldn't see it.

And then, suddenly, there was water at the bottom of the steps and a boat. I tried to get aboard but the boat keeled over. Grandpa was there and

Marjorie. That was a peculiar twist in my dream and I can't remember very well what happened next. I awoke with a strong longing for Michel. Then I lay awake thinking of ways to have and Lee and Michel forever close to me, however, the solution of that thought kept me hanging in a void. Michel obviously is still deep inside my heart even after two and a half years.

I really love him but I also love Lee and I would never be able to leave my Lee.

It's snowing, yesterday also. Today football again of course and tomorrow afternoon I'm going to do an audition in the Village Gate. I hope to receive a letter from Michel again soon.

Sunday, January 28, 1979

I have a terrible cold. Tomorrow afternoon I have two appointments and today at five the poet and I are going to a party of the Gotham Book mart; it's a reception/opening of an exhibition. Bill Yoscary told me about it. He will introduce Lee to publishers and writers he knows. Everybody comes there, he said, it's a yearly event. Perhaps I'll run into Tennessee Williams, the playwright. Tuesday I have another two appointments for work. No one can say that I get discouraged by rejections. Still…I haven't heard a thing from the audition that went so well two weeks ago. Staying alive!

Saturday, February 4, 1979

Lee and I just came back from the Tin Palace where Steve McCall performs now; nice to be out for a change. I wrote a story for my two darling nephews. I put photographs of Manhattan with it and will send it to Marjorie so she can read it to them. In the story my two nephews have fun adventures in New York City. I also translated my Dutch song Mooie Ogen into English: Something in Your Eyes.

I have to make a cassette recording for someone I met and who knows two producers who want to back a good artist for a recording deal but, alas, the batteries won't hold out long enough! Scheisse!

Monday I have an audition again for a restaurant, wait and see. Something is better than nothing; it's a chance at least. My spirit is well and I am full of courage and optimism.

Saturday, February 10, 1979

I sang Monday and Tuesday in Chances, a bar/restaurant on 58th between Madison and Fifth. I met a nice guy there; his name is Daniel

Ziti, an Italian American, a cutie with black curls and hazelnut colored eyes. He's athletic and sexy but…attention, he's a Scorpio! I spent two nights in a row with him and am a bit in a daze. He calls me every day and I catch myself thinking of him a lot.

I am sending my brochures out all over the place. This morning I mailed five: three to California, one to Guatemala and one to Mexico City. And hopefully I can start sending out my 8 by 10 glossy's that Bill made with resume on the back soon also, that is when I've got the money to pick them up from the lab. I haven't seen Bill in two weeks but am going to visit him on Monday. He's such a good friend. My new infatuation, Daniel, reminds me a bit of Michel.

I wonder how the kids like my story about them in New York.

Wednesday, February 15, 1979

All roads seem to open up suddenly, not all the way but more like a lifting fog, as if chances and opportunities are just for the taking. I have a very strong feeling this time.

Today someone called from Hershey Park, Hershey, Pa; about an audition I did for them a couple of weeks ago. That was for a musical and they were having auditions for two weeks straight every afternoon in the Nola Studios on Broadway.

There were so many people; I sang only one song with piano accompaniment. The man who called said that they want to see me for a second audition on March 4th in Hershey, PA, and that he will send me a letter about it today. This show will run for ten weeks and the salary is $250 a week. That's not bad and quite encouraging for me considering that about a thousand people applied for the job. Lee got forms for us to fill out for a CETA job; this is a sponsored program for work (35 hours a week) for artists in all categories. Bob Anthony called Monday night. He said that he lost my phone number and that he called my mother in Holland. I have to sing in a club in the Village. I didn't understand it at all but he said he was going to pick me up in a taxi which he did promptly arriving a half hour later.

I sang there but hell, I still don't know what all the commotion was about. He never called me before for something and now suddenly he seems very interested in my career. Well, we'll see, it looks promising I guess. This afternoon I called Stanley Flato (a booking agent), I sang a song for him and he said that he was very impressed. 'I will book you for sure!' he said. Time will tell.

I spent the afternoon with dear Bill, in bed, cognac and cigarettes within arm's length. My God, it was such fun and so cozy! He's such a sweet man! He let me call my parents. They were so surprised to hear my voice.

Mama asked when we finally come home again, having been gone so long. Bob

Anthony didn't call her she said. I suspect that he called my friend Ellen de Thouars and thought she was my mother. Oh dear, poor Ellen, to be called in the middle of the night by a crazy American who demands to know where I am.

'She's in New York!' I can hear her say it, flabbergasted.

Bob looked at me sternly, 'Why don't you give your mother your phone number? 'He wanted to know.

March 20, 1979

Richard Moses' (RCA) secretary told me he'll be back in two weeks. I'm so curious to find out how he likes my treatment for a film script. It's about my adventures in Cyprus, September 1976, my mythology-like love affair with Michel and my run-in with macho Greek-Cypriot Mafiosi types. There's much to be grateful for, I will continue to try and do my very best.

Tuesday, April 10, 1979

Last Saturday I sang in the Concord Hotel in the Catskills, it was great! I was there with Peter List, a nice man I met in the Mardi Gra on Broadway where I dance. That's what I do since a week and a half, dancing topless, I am a go-go dancer, that's what it's called. My name is Rusty and I make $60 a day plus tips and commission (from the champagne). Eight hours working days in several clubs where I'm being sent by the Go-Go Agency, a half hour dancing, a half hour pause. It is okay and I bring home some decent money at last so that we can climb out of debt, out of the hole we're in. I want to save enough money for Lee and me to go back to Holland for a couple of months. Friday night I sang in Newark, New Jersey. That was via Stanley Flato and Ada Einhorn. I made seventy five dollars and I made a hundred bucks in the Concord Hotel. The manager there asked me if I am free this summer. The audience really liked me; I hope they'll ask me back soon.

Thursday, April 19, 1979

I don't work today, taking it easy. I just finished typing the treatment of my Aphrodite-Apollo story. The poet will read it, edit and critique it. Richard Moses of RCA is in Japan, coming back in a week. I am still working as a go-go dancer, hopefully not for too long anymore. God, how I wish I could sing steadily somewhere; keep faith, girl!

I received such a nice card from Lilly of a cute little Indian girl. She and Mandy are living in Brazil, Rio de Janeiro now at a stone's throw distance from the famous Copa Cabana beach.

Saturday, April 28, 1979

Not writing much lately; my work as a go-go dancer is rather heavy of course. You're there for eight hours and dance every half hour, so in total that's four hours dancing. With tips and commission from the champagne I make between $62 and $75 a day on average. Sometimes I have outstanding days and make $90 or $100. Not bad, eh?

I work four to five days a week, often in the Mardi Gra on Broadway. That's a large, beautiful new club. Most times I work from 1.30 p.m. to 9 p.m. Now and then I work a night which runs for instance from 8 p.m. till 4 a.m. or from 5 p.m. to 1 a.m.; obviously it's a dumb little job but it pays well and I exercise my muscles. I even meet nice men occasionally. Anyway, hopefully I'll be singing on a regular basis again soon. I have two performances coming up, in Westbury, L.I. the 12th and 13th of May, via Ada Einhorn.

The poet read my story; form and grammar leaves much to be desired but he's helping me now to get it right. He also ordered books for me about creative writing. I'm saving money and I hope the poet and I can go on holiday the end of May, the beginning of June, to Holland.

Lilly and Mandy are in Bolivia now; they're going into the jungle, those brave girls. I wish I was traveling with Lilly.

May 3rd, 1979

Lee can make me so mad at times! Tomorrow we'll be married six years, that's quite a long time when you think about it. I sometimes don't know what to do with him!

Something so stupid! He with his so-called clever ideas! This time he agreed that I was right but it doesn't change the fact that I'm left with the damages.

Saturday, May 15, 1979

Tonight Lee and I are performing at Brookdale Medical Center, in Brooklyn. It's a charity affair so we don't get paid but perhaps the publicity will help and anyway, I love doing shows with him.

I now have saved enough money for one return trip to Europe. Now I need contact lenses; I've been without since January and my eyes are gradually getting worse. What pleasure it will be to finally see clearly again! Everything is out of the pawn shop, hurrah! The rent is paid; all thanks to my go-go dancing.

Friday, May 11, 1979

We're right smack in the middle of a heat-wave since five days, temperatures up to 95 degrees Fahrenheit. I received a letter from the Jakarta Hilton, Indonesia. They are interested and want to know my conditions; Lee wrote them a letter back immediately.

May 27, 1979

Friday, May 18th I met him for the first time, in the Broadway Pub where I was dancing. And now I am head over heels. He is a Gemini, brown wavy hair, mustache, beautiful, 5.11" tall, athletic, brown/green eyes and the same sparkling smile as Michel. His name is Josh Moore and he's Jewish. He's much younger than I, only twenty-three. I am totally in love with him. His smile reminds me of Michel and his voice too. I will write more about him sometime because just like that I have a feeling that he and I are going to love each other for a very long time even if it's only as friends.

We're going to Holland, Lee and I; you'll be hearing from me. So long!

~

~

When I took a waitress job in a club in midtown Manhattan, the Broadway
Pub, a go-go dancer there said to me that I was being silly waitressing
because I could make three to four times more money if I danced.

The life Lee and I were leading, living in dingy hotels, never knowing
from one day to the next where the money would come from, auditioning
my ass off, getting gigs here and there but nothing long term, I had
become so tired of it all. And, I was becoming more and more homesick, I
wanted to go back home. I thought about what that dancer said to me and
figured she was right. Working as a go-go dancer I could finally make
some money and save up for our return to Amsterdam. The agency for the
dancers was right next to my agent Ada Einhorn's office and I was a bit
embarrassed when she was surprised that I was a topless dancer now,
however, she didn't put me down for it and kept booking me for posh
parties on Long Island that always paid good money, three hundred dollars
usually. The unfortunate thing was that they were in and far between.
Furthermore, even when I was called back for second auditions I couldn't
manage to get a steady singing gig so I was forced to waitress. All my
hard work didn't bring in enough money. So, being a topless dancer was
at least a chance for me to get out of the hole we were in.

I told myself that I would've made enough money if I held out for six
weeks. And so it happened. I met Josh Moore carrying a large package

with him around noon time. During my break he said to me: 'What are

you doing here? Are you from South-America also? '

Most of the dancers were exotic dark haired girls. I laughed and told him I

was from Holland. We hit it off right away.

I said I knew what was in the package. I didn't of course but as luck, or

faith, had it, I guessed right.

'It's a saxophone player and very colorful.' I said looking like the

Cheshire cat of Alice in Wonderland. His mouth dropped, he couldn't

believe it because that's exactly what the painting showed.

He told me he was on his lunch break, that he worked in his father's firm,

something to do with fire prevention and sprinklers and he asked if I

would have dinner with him when my shift was over.

'Yes, okay!' I said. He left and came back a few hours later. We took a

taxi and began kissing passionately. I told him I wasn't that hungry and

'Let's go to your place!'

He shared a lovely house in Westbury, Long Island, with a friend who

wasn't home when we got there; Josh made a salad and baked two steaks.

We spent the night together and in the morning he dropped me off at my

hotel. I had told him right away that I was married; I always did when I

went out with other men.

From that day on we saw each other every day for two weeks straight; he'd pick me up in the morning when he had driven from the firm in Mineola, L.I., and we'd have breakfast together. At about six or seven p.m. we met and had dinner in restaurants in Manhattan and occasionally we went out to a club or discotheque. Lee knew about my latest infatuation because I was always honest and told him everything. It never occurred to me that my philandering about could be very hurtful to him; he said he didn't mind what I did as long as I looked after myself and always come home to 'daddy'.

Josh said that if we were going to see each other he didn't like it if I continued as a topless dancer.

That was no problem for me as I wanted to stick to my decision not to do this kind of work longer than six weeks.

On my 30th birthday I danced in the Mardi Gra and made a lot of extra tips from the men there. I must say that I never had any problem with men bothering me. On the contrary, I was always treated with respect. I had also told myself not to go out with any men I met in the clubs. Only three times I broke that promise to myself. Once I had lunch with a Brazilian boxer, Peter List took me to the Catskills (I didn't go to bed with him, we had separate rooms) and on May 18th, I went home with Josh.

My thirtieth birthday was the saddest birthday ever but it was also my last day as a topless dancer. I now had enough money saved up to go back to Holland.

We knew by now that our house on the Oosterpark was a lost case. Adrian, that nut, had let a vague friend of Lee, Jeroen, into the apartment who, as it turned out, was dealing drugs from our house and the police found out and arrested him there. Adrian had never paid a penny of the rent as he had promised us. That's why I was so angry with Lee, because of his stupidity we had now lost our lovely home on the Oosterpark in Amsterdam; I could've strangled him.

However, I never could stay mad at Lee for long, I loved him too much.

Josh Moore begged me not to go back to Holland; he said he would give me money to stay longer.

'I have a husband, 'I said, 'you know that. And I have to go back home, I just have to.'

And so it happened; two weeks after I had met the future father of my children, Lee and I boarded a KLM plane back home.

~

Chapter 17

Back in Amsterdam

Alkmaar, June 9, 1979

I'm sitting on the bed in the front room of my parent's house. The family was so happy to see us again. We are staying here now. On Wednesday we visited Ben and Marjorie; it was so wonderful to see my darling little nephews again. They talk so much and have grown a lot. We brought them a Sesame Street game; they love it!

Miracle of miracles, our things are still in our apartment in Amsterdam. The lawyer of the landlord told us however that we have to be out this weekend because the process server is coming next week to have it cleared.

Lee and I took two suitcases with clothes out yesterday. My guitar is gone as well as some jewelry. I especially am sad that the gold Indonesian ring Ellen gave me is missing.

Tomorrow my family will help us to clear all our stuff out. Lee is in Amsterdam today, he's trying to find someone to take over our house. I hope he succeeds. With the money we then could go to Spain, to Formentera, to the house of our friend Alain Camus. I would love to spend some time in the sun there, work at my songs, another film script maybe. We'll see.

I miss my lover. Josh I mean. I was so crazy about him. I think of him all the time, such a fun loving, handsome young man and, witty as hell.

Oh, here comes mama. Later!

Amsterdam, Thursday, June 28, 1979

We are living in the attic of a large four floors house on the Prins Hendrikkade in Amsterdam. It's okay.

One room in the back with a few old arm chairs, a round coffee table with crème colored tablecloth, two one person beds, positioned one behind the other, like in boats and trains. Do you get the picture?

I just cooked spaghetti for myself. I'm home alone. John (the Englishman who's so kind to let us stay here for free) is hardly ever home. I guess Lee will be back soon. I tried to call Josh from the American hotel, collect, but no one answered the phone. He's probably just gone to work. Two weeks ago Josh called me in Alkmaar. It was wonderful to hear his voice again. 'Hello Beautiful!' he said.

I'm reading a good book: Looking for Mr. Goodbar, but it depresses me a bit because I recognize myself in Theresa now and then. However, I never want to become bitter, old and ugly. I want to keep believing in the true, the beautiful, and the good.

Oh, Josh, I miss you, and you too, Michel, although we haven't seen each other in almost three years.

I met Josh two weeks before Lee and I went back to Holland. I have really fallen in love with him and our romance is wonderful. Just like with Michel. He has a lot to do with this also. They resemble each other.

The same delightful laugh, the same melodic voices, well-built both of them, beautiful thick curly hair and both of them are athletic. Michel a bit more so than Josh; he's a professional soccer player after all but nevertheless Josh is very well proportioned. I adore him, really.

I wrote a fantastic new song almost immediately after arrival here, it was such an inspiration. It's called Amsterdam's Magic. But now I'm not singing much these days, however, the other day a melody came to me and I managed to make a great song using a little poem Josh wrote for me in it. He told me he wrote it one day after we met and that he never before wrote a poem in all his life. Wow! It's really lovely and I am quite elated about the compliment.

Wild as the animals that run free in the breeze

Beautiful as the fruits that grow on the trees

Sweet as the flowers that grow on the land

Loving as the bodies that roll in the sand

You are as special as you can be

For you are you and I am me.

I'm longing for him, his body, the sex, the fun and laughter we had. I laugh a lot with Lee too of course, always but…oh well, I just can't help it, and I'm in love with Josh Moore. He's a Gemini like me. Lee is a Gemini also. Weird, isn't it?

Tuesday, July 3, 1979

I'm so taken with my thin silk outfit; it feels so nice, so frivolous. Lee's tailor, Tjerk Kok, made it for me. I love it!

I just saw the Woody Allen movie Annie Hall, great film! I also spent two hours at the American Consulate to be told that I won't be issued with a visa! Why the fuck not?

Tomorrow is the fourth of July and Lee is furious.

Yesterday when I walked by Hoppe Café on the Spui, old man Arthur, former watchmaker, called me. Two women were with him and one of them, Cecile, asked me about Lee, said she would love to see him because they knew each other on Ibiza. She lived with him for awhile, she said.

Lee saw her this afternoon and tonight, he, she, her friend and I go out on the town. She is Swedish. I think she's very attractive; tall with classic features, long wavy auburn hair and very beautiful green eyes. A striking beauty! Naturally I'm a bit jealous and Lee loves that, the swine!

July, 6, 1979

Scheisse! Because I asked for residence papers in   America I can't get a visitor's visa now. Lee and I are finished I believe. Our relationship has deteriorated since we're back. I don't know what's happening. And Josh far away and out of reach in New York. The poet and I had a big fight over that Swedish woman. They went out to dinner together. Lee didn't even ask me if I wanted to come along. He left me sitting on the terrace of the American Hotel just like that. After more than two hours they came back; she wanted to go dancing so we all went to a disco where I had to sit and watch her being all over my husband. All the time I kept a brave front but on the way home he began to verbally abuse me. That I have no class, that I ruined the evening, that I'm a bourgeois silly cow, et cetera. I'm so mad at him. Who does he think he is?

Saturday, July 7, 1979

I made a new song and therefore I feel so much better. However, I'm going to leave this place. I have to go; it can't go on like this. I don't know the solution yet.

Monday, July 9, 1979

I can go to Marseille, I have enough money for the trip and some extra but I'm scared. Will I find work? Lee is doing a modeling job at Schiphol airport. I wonder when he comes back; he's been gone for hours already. I don't see much of him anymore anyway. And we don't have sex since we fought over that Swedish bitch. I don't know what the future holds in store for me; I'm nervous. Don't cry, girl! You'll find work; don't be afraid to be alone. You're beautiful, intelligent, talented, thirty, you'll be alright, don't be afraid!

Leeuwarden, Tuesday, July 12, 1979

My sister Marjorie is thirty-two today, congratulations, sis!

I am staying with grandma. It's quiet here; grandma is very sweet and I have all the privacy I could wish for.

Lee called last night. He lost his voice, very hoarse. He lives with his friend Liam and Liam's girlfriend Tonia; they have a huge apartment at the Amstel River. Lee has his own floor with shower, toilet and his own kitchen. That sounds perfect.

I'm worried though because it looks to me we're really separated now. We need to get another house together. There's a letter from Alain Camus, waiting for me in Alkmaar. I'm so curious. Mommy forwarded it here the day before yesterday but it hasn't arrived yet. He was such a nice man, often brought me a joint when I sang in the Inter-Continental in Tehran. We visited his brother, Lee and I, who was a correspondent for Le Soir newspaper. He lived in a lovely villa in Tehran and Alain took many photos of Lee and me for the interview that was published in Le Soir, however, we never saw it unfortunately.

Leeuwarden, Friday, July 13, 1979

Life with grandma is very relaxed. I feel good and rested. I work on my songs every day and have four new ones already; great! I wrote to Josh, asking him to come see me in Holland because it'll be quite a while before I can go back to the States. I really miss him. And I keep seeing Michel before my mind's eye; the two images blend and I don't know whom I am missing, him or Josh. I also wrote to Michel. The idea to be alone with Josh or Michel…I dream about that all the time.

Alain's letter was very sweet. He's still in Tehran but visited our house on the Oosterpark in February. The old lady, our only neighbor there, told him that we were in America. He said family members are in the house in Formentera now but after September 12th, we are welcome to stay there as long as we like. That sounds fabulous! He also writes that he would love to meet with us in Paris before we would be going to Formentera.

Thursday, July 9, 1979

Lilly hasn't returned to Alkmaar yet. She's been gone for more than two years. Lee sent me money and a letter in which he expresses his hope to take me to Spain in August. He also sent other mail for me; a letter from Josh, so sweet! He wrote among other things that I am welcome to stay with him when I return to America. Oh, Josh, I love you!

Saturday, July 21, 1979

I couldn't fall asleep again last night. I miss Lee and I feel he doesn't miss me at all. He didn't call yesterday or today. Grandma is making vegetable soup, nice. Well, what can I do? I'll just be cool I guess and hope for better times. Lilly told me that there's mail for me in Alkmaar. She's is back and I wanted to go see her right away but she told me not to because she was taking off again the same night to join mom and dad, Marjorie and Ben and the children who are on holiday in Austria. It was a slap in my face. I cry myself to sleep every night. I am so sad; Lee told me to stay where I am. What is this? Is he divorcing me? I'm so hurt and lonely. I wish I was lying in Michel's arms or Josh'.

It's afternoon, napping time again. My life slides by, quite sluggishly, regimented and silently these days. Grandma is so sweet and not happy about the way my parents went on vacation, leaving the key to their house with a neighbor instead of me while knowing full well I don´t have a house anymore. ´That´s not right, ´ Grandma says.

I don´t understand why Lee hasn´t called yet.

Though I´m comfortable here I´m beginning to feel secluded now after almost two weeks. I have nowhere else to go and it doesn't look like Lee is missing me much either. He says Liam and Tonia are great to him. Oh, well, of course…wonderful!

I have to go see a dentist because one of my molars is killing me; I'm living on aspirins. Everything is uncertain and I am depressed. Lee says he's trying to make enough money for us to move to Spain. I'd like that.

I can't stay here forever. My grandmother says I can stay as long as I like, she's so kind.

I used to be a romantic girl who believed in the prince of her dreams. How different life was woven for me, my ship was taken in a turbulent stream.

Sunday, July 22, 1979

I can't sleep at all anymore. I need valium desperately. And to see a dentist, I can't take this pain anymore. The dream I had this morning was peculiar; I awoke singing. I was in an army tent that kept falling apart. There were a lot of children, dressed in rags; we tried to light an old stove for we were freezing but we had no oil or coal. Suddenly I was grown-up and walking over a deserted platform. I sang Angelitos Negroes; then a dark skinned man came and followed me while softly singing along with me, very beautiful.

Lilly left immediately for Austria; she wouldn't wait one day so that I could come to Alkmaar. We didn't see each other for more than two years. I'm so sad.

Saturday, July 28, 1979

It's so hot, I've been lying on the grassland in front of grandma's senior citizen house but now I'm in the shade under the trees near the canal.

Well…Lee is gone! He left for Spain without me. I received an envelope with fifty guilders on Friday and a scribble that he probably would leave on Friday and that he will call me on Tuesday.

I called Josh and asked him for money, he said he would send me two hundred dollars right away. He also said that he would like to come to Europe to see me in August.

I'm already missing Lee's company so much. Last Sunday we slept together in Alkmaar for the first time in the twelve days that we live separated. I was so lonely and upset in my parents' house that I called him, crying. He came over right away. Thank God, I saw my dentist in Amsterdam on Monday.

I wrote another song, it simply came to me, out of the blue; it's about my separation from Lee which I'm trying very hard to view in a positive way. But it's hard because I miss him, his bodily presence and most of all his sparkling, clear, original spirit. We were quite happy and content in New York, in that hotel room in the very heart of Manhattan. Lee, my darling husband, I need you and I miss you so much.

I stayed with Tess Monday night. Her little daughter has just turned five and I brought her a nice plastic bag with a comb, a mirror, a hair brush and a nail file. She looked very pleased with it. I gave Tess a giant bunch of lovely smelling flowers. I also passed by Shouki's, her husband came later on with Chinese food. Tess was so kind to say to me that I can always call her if I need help even if it's in the middle of the night and that I can always stay at her place when I need shelter. If things go well I'll try to get a flight to Ibiza from Amsterdam.

Monday, July 30, 1979

A terrible thunderstorm last night, it woke us both up so I crawled into grandma's bed with her, cozy. I hope that she stays with us for a very long time still. What a jerk Lee is, to take off and leaving me here! I have altogether one hundred and ninety guilders; that's not going to get me very far.

Nighttime

Lee called me from Ibiza; he said that he sent me seventy-five dollars yesterday. Perhaps, if all goes well, I'm there too this weekend. He said that the weather is lovely. I long for him, I want to hug and hold him. I also long for Josh but that's different. I hardly know Josh and my bond with Lee is so strong, we've been through so much together.

If the sex between Lee and me would've been in sync, I would've had a perfect marriage I think because we are on the same wave length. I also think that Josh doesn't want to commit himself to one woman yet, he's still so young. I can have fun and romance with him but nothing serious I believe.

Wednesday, August 1, 1979

How can I put it? I feel guilty and excited simultaneously. Josh is arriving on the 11th on Schiphol and then he and I will go on vacation for eight days to the South of France. Wow! I didn't really believe he was going to come here and take me on a trip to the sun! The coming reunion with him makes me all giddy and excited. I can't deny that my meeting him two weeks before Lee and I left the States was very special indeed. We met in that cockshy place on 45th Street where I was a go-go dancer. What a comical encounter that was!

Yes, I am very much looking forward to seeing my handsome lover again. Quite remarkable: grandma thinks it all great and encourages me, as if to say to me to enjoy my life as long as I can and to not let myself be taken for granted by 'husband dearest' whoever that may be. She likes Lee, calls him a doll but naturally she's unhappy about him taking off to Spain by himself without saying a word.

Grandma (my mother's mother) is really a very nice, funny woman and far more with it and enlightened than any of her daughters, my mother included.

Mama would get a complete nervous breakdown from something like this and think me very bad if she knew that I, as a married woman, went on vacation with another man.

At about six o'clock the postman rang and gave me a money-order (one hundred and forty-six guilders), at the same time Lee called. I told him I wasn't coming right away, that I first am going to Tess in Amsterdam.

'Why?' He barked.

'Do you have enough money?' I asked.

'I've got enough money, why are you going to Amsterdam?'

'I'm not coming.'

'What? Why not?' He sounded quite angry. I told him in one breath that I'm not coming because Josh is coming here and we will go on holiday together for eight days. For a few moments there was a painful silence.

'Is that what you want?' He asked at last in a gruff voice.

'Yes.' I said after which we talked reasonably with each other for awhile.
I gave him Alain Camus' phone number and told him that I would write to
him. That's what I did and I'll mail it special delivery tomorrow; an
honest, open letter full of true meant love. I will always love Lee, forever
and ever. He understands my soul and he will always stay in my heart.

Half past two, nighttime

I can't sleep again, just drank some warm milk and read an interview
with Jane Fonda in the Viva. I think she's great. She says she hopes that
her husband, Tom Hayden, will make it to president of the United States
one day. Imagine: Jane Fonda as First Lady!

Thursday, August 2, 1979

Grandma and I went to the Frisian Museum this morning. This is
Friesland after all, Leeuwarden, the capital of the province where my
sisters and I were born and more than four hundred years of ancestors lie
buried. It was very interesting. She is resting now and I'm going through
some songs of mine.

Saturday, August 4, 1979

Recapitulation: Thursday afternoon I all of a sudden decided to go to Ibiza. I felt guilty and the longing for Lee got the better of me.

So, on the phone I was to collect all necessary travel information. Friday the train left at five to eleven in the morning, I would arrive at Gare Du Nord, Paris, at five p.m. and then a train would leave at nine p.m. from Gare Austerlitz to Barcelona. I then could catch the boat to Ibiza the next night and arrive in Ibiza Sunday morning. I calculated that I had enough money to get there with forty guilders left to eat. So I took the bus to Alkmaar on Thursday night.

However, sitting in the bus I changed my mind again. The way Lee has been treating me over the last month and a half puzzles me because, you know, he didn't even want to come to spend time with me in Alkmaar the other day. 'I'll see you at the train station,' he said whereupon I bust out in hysterical sobs and he finally told me he would come to me. And when we were still living on the Prins Hendrikkade in his friend John's house, he kept saying things like: 'I'd better send you to Spain', and, 'What a pity you can't stay with your mother.'

What is this? He seemed so relieved when I decided to go stay with grandma. Next thing I know he's left for Spain without telling me about it first and goes and sends me only fifty guilders. I feel like he sees me as a minor who waits patiently for what father decides is best for her.

Besides, what was I doing? I had already agreed to meet Josh at Schiphol on the eleventh. If I went to Spain I would've made myself dependent of Lee again. So…I decided not to go to Ibiza also because I shrank from that awesome long journey to get there.

When I came into my parent's house in Alkmaar there was a letter from my bank and it turns out that there was four hundred and fifty guilders booked over to my account two weeks ago! It's almost inconceivable that I forgot about that but…there it is! What incredible luck!

I could've been in Spain two weeks ago, fancy that!

Then, as I'm sitting there on the couch smiling from ear to ear with the bank statement in my hand, the phone rings. It's grandma and she asks if I'm coming back; there's a letter from Josh.

'Yes, grandma, yes,' I almost screamed with joy, 'I'm coming back!'

I first went to Amsterdam yesterday morning to withdraw some money and I arrived back here in Leeuwarden last night.

I wonder if and when Lee will call me. Is he fed up with me?

I spoke with Ellen while in Amsterdam; she said that perhaps it would've been better if I hadn't told Lee about my plans to go on holiday with Josh.

Well, I don't know how all of this will end, however, I do know that the poet has neglected me lately and I don't like that. He didn't try to keep me with him, at least not hard enough in my opinion. What will happen? I have no idea but I do know that I love Lee and always will. I'm suffering, it's too complicated. I can't unravel my own feelings anymore. Diary of a lunatic!

Will I ever amount to something?

Lee called just now to give me the telephone number of the hotel he's staying in. He sounded cheery, said I should enjoy myself in the South of France. Thank God, that's my little bear! How wonderful it will be when we finally have our own home again; I really love him, I like so much having him around.

Amsterdam, Thursday, August 9, 1979

I'm here with Tess and her little daughter Carla since Monday. My insomnia is gone, I feel much better. Monday-night Shouki and I went out on the town; we had a ball, I came home at two-thirty a.m.

Tuesday afternoon at Hoppe's Café it was like old times; Ellen and Jack invited me over for dinner. It was good; spinach, potatoes and steak.

Jack said that I am a bitch on wheels for going on holiday with a lover while Lee is probably staring sorrowful *ins Blaue hinein* in his hotel room. What bullshit! Lee is not one for staring in despondency. But Jack wouldn't let up even though Ellen kept telling him to mind his own business. At last he urged me to call Lee right there and then; I did but the receptionist told me there was no one under the name Bridges staying in the hotel. What a disappointment. Where is he then?

Well…there were two special delivery letters from Josh. He arrives Saturday morning at half past eleven so I'll have to get up at the crack of dawn to meet him at the Airport.

I went to the hairdresser yesterday; it's shorter now, cut in layers so that I have more volume. It looks very nice if I say so myself. I can't deny that I'm looking forward with great anticipation to the reunion with Josh.

Jack gave me a hundred guilders the day after his verbal abuse of me and that I think was very kind of him.

It's Tuesday-morning, August 14, 1979, Golfe Juan, South of France.

I'm so happy! He's still sleeping. It's early, nine o'clock and we didn't sleep before four last night. I am so intensely happy. Everything is so wonderful and fantastic. I can't even write it down. This time here with

Josh suffices me for the rest of my life if it stops now. He is just great!
Now I go back to sleep.

Monday, August 19, 1979

Josh flew back to New York today. I can't begin to tell how splendid
it was. I feel like another person, as if I was born again. He is so
wonderful! I'm terribly, irrevocably in love. I'm sitting in the Twee
Heiligen Café on the Prinsengracht opposite the Westerkerk. It's cozy
here.

Sunday evening, August 26, 79

Last week Josh missed his plane because he had in his head that the
plane would leave at twelve noon but it left at ten a.m. How we laughed!

We had so much fun together; sometimes I almost pied in my pants from
laughing. He's a regular riot. That time when we sat at the bar near the
pool of our hotel Jasmine and Josh said we should really take a swim.
Without a moment's hesitation I took off my dress and, in my flimsy
underpants, I jumped in the pool. Josh was limp with laughter, he could
barely take his pants off but he did and joined me. We didn't give a hoot
about the people there. It was like that the whole time, as if he and I were

on a pink cloud of bliss and all the people knew we were in love and smiled indulgently. Paradise! We touched paradise together there on the Riviera. We went to Nice, Cannes, Juan Les Pins and our hotel in Golfe Juan was so lovely. What a glorious time! Naturally I miss him terribly.

I'm working afternoons at an office for a temporary agency. I work with a computer, something new for me.

~

Chapter 18

Troubles in Paradise

The eight days vacation with my new lover Josh was indeed a smash hit and I will treasure it till my dying day.

However, soon enough it was back to the grindstone for me.

Riddled as I was with doubt and guilt and insecurity I had to make some money because I felt it was time for me to go back to the States, with or without my husband.

The fact that Lee and I had lost our nice apartment on the Oosterpark was one of the main reasons I think that our relationship was falling apart.

Had I considered my love for Josh at first as just another infatuation, a fling like so many before, after that holiday in the South of France something had changed. I now couldn't imagine myself living my life without ever seeing him again anymore. I had indeed fallen totally and irrevocably for the young and dashing Josh Moore.

~

Rotterdam, Saturday, September 1, 1979

It's about a quarter to five Sunday morning. I just came home, a nice room for twenty-five guilders a day in Pension Oud Holland; the only setback is that the owner, a grubby little woman, keeps a cock as a pet and I have to be careful each time I walk into the kitchen not to be pecked at by that ferocious beast.

I sing in a nightclub here, a Polish band accompanies me. I have a contract for one month and I make a hundred and sixty guilders a day.

I called Josh on Wednesday from my office job. It was great to hear his sweet, melodic voice again; we talked for almost an hour. I think he really loves me. I long for him so much. I guess I was born with a bad streak in me; how can you love two men simultaneously?

Sunday night, September 2, 1979

This is crazy, I keep thinking of Lee and of Josh. I feel like I'm caught between two loves. However, I haven't heard from Lee and I haven't got a clue where he is. I'm so worried about him and I feel terribly guilty too.

I called Liam but he told me that he hasn't stayed with them for quite awhile. 'He's staying with a friend,' he said but he wouldn't tell me who. He said that he doesn't know but I don't believe him.

I've got a hammering headache.

I spent one night with Lee last week. First he took me out to dinner. He was very sweet to me.

When I lay beside him I realized how much I had missed him, his physical presence. He told me the next morning that he understands; that I am so much younger than he is and that he can't give me enough sexual satisfaction. It hurts but what can I do? I feel very attracted to him still, that hasn't changed. He still is a handsome, slim man with his fifty-two years. I love his sweet, reliable face.

I can't understand myself. How can it be that I truly love my husband and still also be madly in love with Josh? It's almost as if Michel was given back to me. He didn't write to me anymore for a long time. I also feel guilty towards him because if I really cared for him that much why did I abandon him and never came back to him? Perhaps it's better this way so he can put me out of his mind. I know Michel loved me. And now Josh loves me too. And so does Lee. And I love all three of them, in three different ways. But Lee remains the central magnet. For him I left Michel and for him I cry when I'm sick and lonely. My mind doesn't function properly; I long for my new love while I can't say goodbye to my old love. What will happen?

Monday, September 3, 1979

I'm singing with this combo, Old Friends they call themselves, and it's going great! They are fun guys also and the audience adores me. I get so many compliments about my voice. How nice!

I bought a thick silver bracelet from Tess, she and Carla lived in Sierra Leone, Africa, for a couple of months and she brought back a lot of things which she sells here, lovely stuff really. I still owe her the money. I didn't get paid here yet and I'm almost broke again. It's a present for Josh. I spoke with him the day before yesterday.

Every night I get flowers from people in the club, roses mostly and consequently my room looks like a flower-shop and it smells so wonderful. I am content.

Early morning,

I can't sleep, I'm too wound up. I saw Shouki yesterday in Amsterdam; she loaned me two gowns to perform in, fabulous evening gear. Tess also loaned me a couple of dresses.

I get by with a little help from my friends. Lee left again for Ibiza yesterday. I hope he's okay.

I'm sitting on the beach in Scheveningen, it's lovely weather and I'm enjoying the sun warming my white body.

Saturday morning, September 8, 1979

I wonder how things will be with Josh and me in New York. I also wonder how it is going with Lee. I miss him. I have to get more clothes from Alkmaar.

Wednesday, September 12, 1979

I don't eat well, have got no appetite. I'm a bit lonely here in Rotterdam. I miss my husband. No matter how infatuated I am with Josh I need my little bear. I hope he calls soon.

Friday, September 14, 1979

Just ate some spaghetti but my appetite is very low. It's because I live alone. I like being alone now and then but living all by myself depresses me.

If the poet hadn't thought it imperative to take off for Spain he could've lived here with me, much cozier. Eating together, laughing together but alas, it was not to be.

Lee, oh Lee, if you only knew how much I really need you. Without you all my days are grey and lonesome.

It seems so long ago already, my romantic holiday with Josh on the Côte d'Azur.

I do long for him but I don't know about living with him in the States, it leaves me indifferent. I do intend to go to him. God, it's all so complicated, I can't pin down my own feelings. What do I really feel for him? I think I love him, we have fun together. I am very attracted to him and he seems a bit mysterious to me as well. Don't know why but hell, I'm just going to play it by ear, what the heck! Between Lee and me things will not turn back to normal as long as we don't live under the same roof. I feel sad because I can't shake the feeling that he prefers it this way. Being separated is not the result of my umpteenth unfaithfulness but because he's rather fed up with me. It's an intuitive feeling but very persistent so…there you have it. I have felt this way since we returned to Holland.

Saturday, September 15, 1979

I wasn't smart last night. Frederick, a regular visitor of the club (he gave me a bunch of red roses once) was there and Karin, a hostess, sat with him. Later on she asked me if I wanted a glass from her bottle Dom Perignon (two hundred and twenty-five guilders a bottle), it was almost closing time.

Then he gave Marian, the barmaid, a hundred guilders and a little later a hundred to Karin as well. If I had used my brain I could've got a hundred from him as well. However, I couldn't do it. I knew he expected me to ask him for money as well but I didn't want to. It was beneath me at that moment but today I think, silly cow, money is money and you could've got it so easily. I am not crafty at all.

And those boring stiff asses don't interest me in the least. Anyway, I only have to hold on for two more weeks and this job will be over and done with. I have more than a hundred roses in my room; the fragrance is so delightful.

Tuesday, September 18, 1979

I was in Amsterdam again. Josh called me; we talked for over an hour. He's climbing the walls with longing for me, the sweetheart, me too.

I spoke to Mister Basilar today; he says they're still waiting for the police report and the petition from New York. There was also a letter from the lawyer, Mister Bonder. He wrote a letter to the Immigration Service in New York on September 10th and asked them to send my application to the Consulate in Rotterdam; furthermore he wrote that he will write to us as soon as he has an answer from them.

Lee called me Sunday morning; I hope he comes back soon, I didn't ask it, I hoped he would say so but no. I'm not going to beg of course.

Shouki told me Liam called her and said that he and Lee are living together. Liam is such a sly fox and I do hope Lee doesn't get into trouble by association with him. Please God, safeguard my little bear. I worry about him constantly.

September 19, 1979

Today Lech, the piano player, was with me. He's such a nice guy, forty-one, married with two daughters of eleven and six; he showed me pictures of them. I am glad that Lech is my friend; it feels less lonely this way. I'm going to call Ellen now.

September 22, 1979

I just ate Chinese. Lech and I went to town today; he wanted to buy papers because he needs another car. Afterwards we went to my room. He gave me a terrific body massage and then he made love to me, ever so tenderly. Lech is a sweet man, soft and passionate. All members of the band are nice guys actually. I brought them a bottle of Smirnoff Vodka the other day; they polished it off in no time.

In Amsterdam I went to the joint exhibition of Tess and Shouki

in Café Eylders. It was a lot of fun until Liam walked in. He told me that Lee and he have a lovely apartment in Santa Eulalia and that Lee is not coming back soon. Naturally I am shocked and tried calling my husband but he's never in it seems. I want to hear from his mouth what his plans are. Don't I have a right to know? I got two hundred and fifty guilders from two Dutch men last night; they have a hotel in South West Ireland and offered me a job singing there for two weeks next summer. Nice but that's still far away.

Saturday, September 23, 1979

Last night a Norwegian Government official gave me a hundred guilders.

I have become crafty after three weeks in this nightclub by saying things like: 'I'm glad you like my singing so much, perhaps you want to reward it with a tip, you see, the salary isn't so high here.'

If I'd been smart from the start I would've made a bundle already.

I spoke to Lee, he said Liam doesn't know what he's talking about and that he's coming back to Amsterdam soon.

I have a performance this Sunday in The Face of Folk in Amsterdam; nice.

Thursday, September 27, 1979

There was an Englishman in the club last night who told me he was in love with me and would pay twice my week's salary if I went home with him. Ha! No Sir, thank you very much! If I start doing that the end is not in sight. My self-worth is more important to me than money, besides, I make more than enough here and I am definitely not a hooker.

Josh called me today and told me he enlisted the aid of a lawyer to get me to America as quickly as possible.

September 29, 1979

What a theater! Last night we had company from The Hague underworld. Now and then there's plenty to laugh in this club but I am not cut out for this kind of work. I've got medication from a doctor here; I have anemia and lost quite a bit of weight. I am not allowed to drink which I don't since a few nights and I must say I feel better already.

My appetite is back. The trick of the trade is to throw away most of the champagne when the men aren't looking; the carpet is saturated with it. Lee sent me such a sweet letter, I keep reading it and each time it brings tears to my eyes.

I also have a lovely letter from Josh and a nice card from Vilma and Donald Harrington.

Lech and I spent a nice afternoon.

It's a good thing my mother doesn't know about my carrying on as I do but without Lech's friendship I couldn't have lasted the month I'm afraid. Nightlife is tough and not good for my constitution.

Saturday, October 13, 1979

It's over between the poet and me. What I sensed for months is true; he wants to be single again. I bought a bus ticket to Barcelona but he told me he'd rather not have me come to Spain. It hurts so much. But there's nothing I can do. I have to go on living and start a new life. It will be made easier, thank God, because Josh loves me.

I guess I have to be philosophical about it, play it by ear so to speak. No telling how things will go with Josh and me once we're living together. I have myself, my music, my feelings, and my life!

I'm going to start all over, yes I will!

On Monday, October 22nd, I will fly to Montreal. Josh will pick me up there and we will drive in his car to America. If it goes wrong for some reason, if they send me back...well, bad luck! I'll move with the tide and put my faith in God.

~

The experience as a singer in a Rotterdam nightclub was valuable in the sense that you learn a lot about the nature of men. However, after a month I was very happy it was over. I had made a nice bundle of money and when to my great disappointment my husband didn't want me to join him in Ibiza I decided to take my chances and go back to the States. Since I had been told by Lee's lawyer that I couldn't travel back and forth between Europe and America while my green card was being considered, Josh and I developed a plan that we thought was solid. We were going to meet each other in Montreal; he would purchase an airplane ticket in my name and our story if we were stopped at the border would be that we had met in a bar in Montreal and that he had invited me to drive to New York with him instead of flying there.

It was of course great seeing each other again and, full of confidence that our plan couldn't fail, we drove down to the American border. And there all went very wrong; the patrol man didn't believe my story that I didn't have my passport with me and that I was of Dutch origin and had lived many years in California. I don't know why I came up with that ludicrous tale because when the man asked for the name of my High school I was dumbstruck of course.

We both had to step out of the car and were lead away. The car was checked inside out and they did find some marihuana crumbs.

The official who interrogated me tried to trick me into admitting that Josh and I had known each other before and not just met in a bar in Montreal. I stuck to my story and eventually I was let go.

There I was in the middle of nowhere with not a clue or idea what had happened to Josh. I hitched a ride back to Montreal with a truck driver who let me out close to the hotel where Josh and I had stayed before we took off on our adventure.

I walked straight into the bar and ordered a stiff drink from the bartender.

'Can I buy you that drink? 'I heard an unmistakable voice next to me say; I turned around and looked into my lover's face. We laughed and shrugged the whole experience off. We had at least given it our best. The next day Josh had to go back to New York, to his work but he told me he'd back within a day or two. I wrote the song *Crossing The Border* in the hotel room while waiting for his return.

That song later appeared on my first LP Going Places and many more years later also on my album All of Me.

Josh came back as he had promised and we spent another three days in beautiful Montreal before I flew back to Amsterdam.

The irony of that whole affair was that when back in Amsterdam I found out that Lee's lawyer hadn't filed for my green card yet and consequently I could've traveled to the States on a tourist visa, without a problem.

That's life; nothing ever quite turns out as you think it will

Back in Amsterdam I worked as a secretary via a temporary agency for a few weeks before flying back to New York.

Lee was still living in Ibiza and I got no indication from him when he would come back nor if he wanted to find a flat to live together again. It was therefore clear to me that waiting for him was pointless and that I needed to take my fate into my own hands.

On with the show!

Chapter 19

Caught Between Two Lovers

New York, Wednesday, November 29, 1979

I'm back in America since last Thursday, Thanksgiving. I live in Westbury, Long Island, with Josh. His best friend Bob and his girlfriend Lucy live here too but the apartment is big with two large bedrooms and two bathrooms. Josh furnished his bedroom very nice with a sturdy oak wood Swedish bed, night tables and an armoire. I like it. Unfortunately he strained his neck playing football Sunday and he's in a lot of pain, poor boy.

New York is great, lovely weather and it's wonderful to be back. Still, I miss Lee and I don't know how it will go between Josh and me. So far I think his attitude towards me disappointing, condescending, and sarcastic even. Not nice at all but we did have a good talk last night so, we shall see.

I'm on my way to Mineola, Long Island, by train; he's going to pick me up there.

The sex between us is great; the first few days were indeed terrific. Perhaps he's short with me because of the pain in his neck. Time will tell what's in store for us.

I saw Bibi and Steve and my good friend Bill of course and I visited Ada who is in a lot of pain again. I had brought her some perfume which she loved, however, she asked me to bring her some pot next time. Ha-ha! Straight, square, seventy plus Ada! I will though because I'm sure it will alleviate her pain somewhat.

Unfortunately Mary Blithe has gone back to California a few days ago; we just missed each other. Her neighbor told me and she didn't know anything about my parachute skirt (a gift from Sunny) and that lovely jacket Lee gave me that I had left with Mary when Lee and I left.

'Tell Sunny you aren't flying that high that you need a parachute to come down,' Lee said when we were packing and there wasn't enough room in the suitcase. I had to laugh. Lee always makes me laugh. But that parachute skirt (cobalt blue) was so unique and stunning; I'm really quite sad that I lost it now plus the gorgeous purple jacket. Scheisse!

Thursday, November 30, 1979

Yes, I really don´t know what will be; I feel happy and cast down alternately and it has me rattled, unnerved; what to do?

Tuesday, December 4, 1979

I was in Manhattan yesterday and today. I slept at Bibi's place; Steve is on a twelve day tour with his group Air in Italy. Josh is sweeter now; the pain in his neck is much less.

I'm reading Fear of Flying by Erica Jong.

I received a letter from the poet, ever so sweet. I'm longing to be with him again; to live with him on Ibiza. I feel alright though.

Thursday, December 8, 1979

I'm going to the Emergency at Saint Vincent Hospital today. I have a very heavy period for eight days already and the pain in my back is killing me. I hope it's nothing serious.

Josh will drive me into town. I'm having breakfast now; he'll pick me up in a little while. Our relationship is getting better.

But still…I keep longing for the poet, too much so.

However, I'm not going to show up in Ibiza, broke and with my tail between my legs, no way, José!

God! What day is it? Middle of December, the 14th I believe, don't know and don't care either. I had a period from the 29th of November till the 11th of December for the second consecutive time two weeks too early. Today, it's the 13th by the way and, there's blood on the flagpole again! Gene Cogen told me to use his physician.

Josh claims me too much; I hardly have time for myself while at the same time he acts as if he doesn't give a shit about what I do. I did a shoot with Bill; an hour's work and seventy-five dollars in the till. Yes!

Ada Einhorn booked me on the 20th in West Orange, New Jersey, for a party, it pays a hundred and fifty bucks. I have done better paying parties but still, it's not bad for a forty-five minute little show.

There's still no word from Lee. Right now I'm sitting here watching Josh play tennis with a friend; I didn't know it goes on for so long, they're at it for more than two hours already.

Bibi and I talked about relationships and living together with a man last night. We agreed that it is very time consuming for which you've got little to show for. I for one feel that I usually put far more of myself into the relationship than the other. And more and more I think the company of one of my friends, Ellen, Shouki, Bibi, Mary, Tess, far more rewarding and worthwhile than the claptrap with men.

Josh works very hard and all in all it's a sorry spectacle if you ask me. He took me dancing; we went to a luxurious disco on the island and we've seen a couple of movies. Last Saturday afternoon we went to the Broadway musical *Strider* but that was only because I was auditioning for a substitute role in that show. I didn't even get the part, damn it! He still didn't take me to his lawyer like he said he would. On Sunday evenings he plays poker with his friends.

We are very different. The fun has worn off to be honest, most of the time it's disappointing. If he doesn't do something original soon it won't last I think. I already have that passé feeling now and then, that sad c'est la vie feeling. I'm planning to go and stay in Bill's studio for a week. It's almost Christmas, I suspect Josh will work right through.

Actually I'm hoping to be called upon to sing in the Inter-Continental Hotel in Bali for a month or two.

Lord, why couldn't I get that role in the musical *Strider*? Why do they never pick me, that's what I'd like to know!

Ah, Josh looks very cute in his tennis enthusiasm. One time he ran so fast to play back a ball that he had to jump over the net so as not to fall and once he fell flat on his face, poor dear. I do love him, that's for sure.

Monday, December 17, 1979

I am in Lucy's square box apartment in Manhattan; blind walls all around. She'll be back on Thursday and until then I can stay here.

Josh bought me a pair of hip boots on Saturday. Today he told me that his best friend Paul, the nicest as far I'm concerned, has invited him for a week in Florida. Nice yes, to invite Josh but not me. Josh says he's not going. If he does I'm out of here, I didn't tell him that but I will leave if he takes off without me. I'm so mad about Josh; I love him more each day.

There's still no word from Lee. I feel I've done him great injustice. But why did he never ask me to come back to him?

His pride I guess.

I did two auditions in restaurants on Long Island.

Wednesday, December 19, 1979

There's a thick blanket of snow and I've got to sing in New Jersey tomorrow night. I'm home alone in Westbury. I'm doing all I can to have a gig with Christmas. Flato said he'll probably have something for me on New Year's Eve.

I'm tired of hunting down agents and doing auditions. I think I'm going to try to get a temporary office job, if it's only for half days. It's very boring here with Josh gone to work all day. And I need to make more money so that I'm independent of him.

Friday, December 21, 1979

I've got a letter from the poet. He feels much better, thank God. He asks me to join him the beginning of next year. I would like to see how he lives there in Ibiza but how I'm going to explain it to Josh I don't know yet.

The performance in West Orange last night was fun, plenty of food and drink too and Josh had a good time. The owners of the club (Iranians) recognized me from the Inter-Continental Hotel in Tehran where I sang in 1977 and offered me a job singing every night in the Cabana Club. I have ears to that, it's a beautiful club, it's a pity though that it's all the way in New Jersey. Josh is so sweet; we're having a great romance but I still don't know how it will end, anyway, what we had so far is lovely already.

December 31, 1979

All is well. I got another sweet letter from Lee.

~

~

All is well I wrote on the last day of 1979; little did I know that the New Year, 1980, would leave me shattered, heartbroken and sadder than ever before in my life.

My love affair with Josh Moore had its ups and downs; we were both Gemini and in that respect we were a lot alike yet we were from totally different backgrounds.

Josh was accustomed to a life of affluence in the posh Jewish community of Great Neck, Long Island. His father bought him a Porsche sports car for his 18th birthday for instance; he and his four year older brother had been made partners in the family sprinkler and pipe industry business and consequently he pocketed a fat paycheck every month aside from his share in the company's profits.

He and his many friends, almost all Jewish, were quite spoiled and childish in my opinion; didn't I realize that they were all a lot younger than I was?

I felt outcast by the girls in the group; they often laughed at my accent and sometimes when they thought I didn't know what they were talking about I caught the word goyim. The only one who was normal to me was Jill; with her I could be myself and we had fun together.

Later on we went to a comedy course at the New School in downtown Manhattan; what fun we had there. Unfortunately Jill died about fifteen years ago of cancer. I will never forget her.

What also made things difficult for me was the fact that Josh' mother was rather cold towards me. I felt her disapproval acutely and although I tried not to take notice, it hurt me nonetheless.

However, be that as it may, what really made our relationship a troublesome one was the fact that I couldn't let go of my loyalty to my husband.

Whatever had happened between us I kept on loving him and I missed him more than I had ever realized.

Yet going back to him, even though I thought about it from time to time, was no option either. I knew that it could never be like it was before, too much had happened.

And although Josh and I had our quarrels and problems I loved him very much and thought that in time everything would turn out alright. It did eventually but, oh boy, it certainly took some doing.

Wednesday, January 2, 1980

I appeared in the Joe Franklin Show, it went very well; Joe said that he was very proud of me. I am proud of me too!

I don't know but it is not going so well between Josh and me.

Why can't he understand what I'm trying to do here? I want to make it as a singer! Damn! At least the poet left me free to do what I want and to pursue my singing career. Oh well, que sera sera!

Thursday, January 10, 1980

Gene Cogen read my film script *Bittersweet* and said that it was damn good; I only need to elaborate, more scenery, dialogue and so on. 'I'm surprised', he said, 'you've got a lot of expression.'

I've got to be disciplined enough to rewrite it and work on it every day for a couple of hours. I'm glad I showed it to Gene. Richard Moses and his secretary Chris Laney, of RCA, liked it a lot also only not blockbuster enough for a motion picture.

Thursday, January 17, 1980

So much has happened since last Friday. A great party in Manhattan but the tension that's been building up in me exploded when Josh and I were lying in bed. I can't remember what exactly triggered it; something he said and unfortunately I lost all control. I went completely berserk and cut myself in the wrist with a razor blade! What the fuck is wrong with me?

Josh rushed me to the hospital, it wasn't serious, only a few scratches. I felt so ashamed and still.

The next day, on Saturday, I had to sing at a house party where I left two hours before I should have on account that I didn't like the hostess, she was unkind to me. I haven't got paid yet; I hope I get paid at least for the time that I sang. On Monday I packed my bags and went to Bill's studio where I am now. Josh and I have spent Tuesday night together in Westbury. I am so crazy about him but there are all kinds of things wrong with our relationship. He doesn't want to give me too much money at once because he's afraid I'll leave and never come back. I've cried my heart out over all this but now I'm okay again.

Monday, January 21, 1980

Friday night Josh spent the night with me in Bill's studio. We went to a party that was a rather stiff affair so his friends Henry and Dave and Josh and I went to the disco New York New York. We had a great time. Josh and I are madly in love again. All these storms between us seem to strengthen rather than weaken our relationship. I went to Rosland yesterday afternoon. I drive Josh' car (the newest BMW, beige) regularly now; it goes better all the time. He bought me a beautiful silk blouse, dark green. I'm staying in Westbury today. I'm not well; I threw up a couple of times last night and the bleeding started again, another period and a very heavy one. I hope it's over soon.

Tuesday, January 22, 1980

Yesterday Josh came in unexpectedly and surprised me with a bunch of red roses. At night he was so sweet and funny and gave me another present; a beautiful gold necklace with a tiny heart with little diamonds. I'm very glad with it.

However, this morning Josh had changed completely again and treated me to a sermon about that I should get myself a secretarial job. Is he nuts? That's not why I came to America! I believe that since he met Bill he doesn't want me to stay in the studio anymore, alone in Manhattan. I think he's very jealous, he needn't be; Bill is my friend and no more than that.

March 10, 1980

On Sunday, March 2nd, Josh and I came back from our little vacation. We were five days on the island Maui in Hawaii and stayed in the lovely Inter-Continental Hotel there. It was so wonderful and then we flew to San Francisco where we spent six days. Hawaii was such a treat, what a fairy tale place, so lush and beautiful; we ate oysters on the half shell near the pool every afternoon and once we rented a jeep. What fun we had! His brother Fred and his wife Suzy were with us but that didn't bother me too much.

We went to San Francisco without them and there we stayed with a friend of Josh from the University in Boulder, Colorado where Josh got his Masters in Small Business Management and his girlfriend Rebecca. His friend Brett works for Francis Ford Coppola, the movie director of American Graffiti, Godfather I and II and Apocalypse Now. One night we were in Copolla's gigantic house where we saw a parody of Apocalypse Now called Pork Lips Now in the screening room; it was quite an experience.

San Francisco is a fantastic city and we had terrific weather. We also took the ferry across the bay to Sausalito, a charming village. All in all it was a lovely wonderful smashing little holiday and I enjoyed all of it tremendously.

I'm saving money to get my own place, so far I have a little over seven hundred dollars. I have been singing in a Super Club for two weeks every night; it's called The Monsignore II, a restaurant right next to the famous Friar's Club on 55th street between Park Avenue and Madison. That was before our trip to Hawaii and San Francisco.

It was funny how I got the job because I walked in one day, on an impulse, with my guitar and as luck had it the place was empty but the owner was there; it was about two o'clock in the afternoon and I asked if I could audition for him. I sang two songs and he loved it.

'We have our regular singer,' he said, 'but he's on his two weeks'
vacation now.' It was a great job I must say, I got paid very well and
made even more money on tips. I worked during the daytime as well for a
temporary agency, for Newsweek Magazine. It was very tiring getting up
each morning at six to catch the train into Manhattan, first a taxi from the
house to the train station, work all day, dash over to the Monsignore II at
six and sing there till one o'clock in the night. The owner (a nice,
handsome middle age man) is such a sweetheart; the first thing he does
when I get there is ask me how I am and 'what do you want, some angel
hair pasta? And some vegetables, a nice steak? Tell me, sweetheart,
whatever you like.' They were all very nice to me there, the waiters, the
chef, and the kitchen help and bus boys…everyone. The chef and his
helpers always popped their heads 'round the door to hear and see me
sing. They especially liked the Italian songs I learned: Torni El Sorrento,
Mala Femina, Paloma and so on. The cloak-room attendant was ever so
nice also; she often talked about Prince Bernard, Queen Juliana's husband,
Bernardo as she called him, 'the kindest, sweetest man, so charming and
handsome, a real ladies man!'

I changed into an evening gown there, taking a different outfit and shoes
with me in a big bag each day, then singing till one o'clock, strolling
around with my guitar, and then into a taxi to Grand Central Station to
take the train to Westbury. Often I was so exhausted that I fell asleep in
the train and missed my station which meant catching another train back,

another taxi home where I'd fall asleep at three, three thirty, four o'clock. Then up again at six in the morning…

But what a great singing gig it was, only very wealthy people came there, mostly sports men and women and their agents and managers. Once I stood next to the famous fighter

Rocky Graciano; he farted and didn't blink an eye. Quite awful actually because he stood right next to me at the bar talking to his manager, Mister Goldman, who always gave me a handsome tip.

Once I sang my song *Something In Your Eyes* and one roly poly man with a large group loved it so much that he asked me to sing it again and then he put a note in my hand. Later I saw that he had given me a hundred dollar bill. Imagine that!

Now I'm more independent of Josh at least, that was of the utmost importance to me. The owner of Monsignore II has told me that I am most welcome to come back when their regular singer goes away on vacation again. I wish he'd fire him and hire me as their regular singer.

I'm planning to stay in Bill's studio for the rest of this week.

It's ideal rather and very convenient not to have to pay rent. I'm spending very little on myself, thank God. I gave Bill a kimono, bought it in Chinatown, in San Francisco; Josh has got one too.

I realize that I have to spend more time on my work and ideals and less time and energy on my unstable relationship with Josh.

Life with Lee was far more exciting and adventurous or am I romanticizing the past too much now? Oh God, I do love Josh but we are so different and we quarrel far too much. I want some peace! All those loud boisterous friends of his! They're always there and I wish I could spend more time with Josh without all those wild idiots!

~

Chapter 20

Romance Disrupted

It's Tuesday night, March 11, 1980

What now? I'm sitting in the little room in Bill's studio; I fed Siegfried the Iguana some lettuce. He belongs to Bill's son who's on vacation and Bill promised to look after this prehistoric amiable coldblooded animal. At first I was a bit scared but he's a vegetarian and not dangerous at all. I have a glass of white wine by my side and the Beatles on the radio.

I'm thinking of how it started last year between Josh and me.

I was a topless dancer and had kept it up for four weeks already.

Why was I dancing topless?

Lee and I lived in a spacious room in a flophouse hotel on Madison Avenue; we didn't even have our own bathroom there, a real drag! We had a one pit burner on which Lee, no matter how poor we were, cooked many a delicious meal. I was at the end of my rope trying to make ends meet as a singer and made whatever money I could above and beyond as a waitress in different restaurants. Lee had the odd job off and on, he did what he could but still we were broke most of the time. One day I saw an ad in the New York Post of a bar looking for a waitress. It was the Broadway Pub, here on 45th street, a few blocks from Bill's studio. Two women were dancing topless behind the bar on a thin strip and every half hour two other girls took their place. The bar was covered on all sides with mirrors, even the ceiling. The waitresses, I also, wore leotards, mine was pink; Bill gave it to me. My salary was two dollars an hour, the same as in other bars and restaurants but I hardly made any tips because all the men sat down at the bar. On my second day there one of the dancers said to me: 'Why don't you dance? You've got a good figure and you can make between seventy and a hundred dollars a day!'

She gave me the address of the agency where I inscribed the next day. That's how I became a topless dancer. Most of the other dancers were would-be artists like me and students. Lee didn't like it at all but I didn't care what he thought about it because I had my fill of poverty and I was homesick for Holland. I made a deal with myself namely that I would quit after six weeks because I figured I would've made enough money to pay our debts and get the poet and myself safe and sound back home. The other vow I made to myself was that I would never date any men I'd meet in those clubs. I said to myself: 'Men who frequent these kinds of bars must have sexual hang-ups, why else would they go there?' Actually I talked to some real nice men in those clubs, regulars among whom a retired English British Airways pilot and a NBC camera man.

My last day was on my 30th birthday last year, the saddest birthday ever.

The agency, right next door to my singing agent Ada Einhorn's office,

sent me to different clubs. I danced in the Mardi Gra, The Pink Poodle,

The Golden Dollar and others of which I forgot the names and of course

the Broadway Pub. That's where I met Josh. I had just done my dance

routine and came from the bathroom when a dark haired handsome young

man with mustache stopped me and laughingly asked where I came from,

Brazil? Many dancers were exotic types from Latin American countries.

At first I was irritated. *Another male chauvinist,* I thought, *a misogynist*

who can't accomplish a thing without a woman, making fun of us.

'No,' I said, 'why do you think that?'

'Aren't you all from South-America?' he said and I noticed his gorgeous

smile. 'No,' I said, 'she's American, she's from Germany', pointing

towards the two dancers who were dancing up a storm on loud disco

music.

'What are **you** doing here? 'He asked, more serious now.

'I'm from Amsterdam', I said and we got to talking. The barmaid came to

ask him whether he would buy me a drink.

He was not inclined to at first; the dancers only drink champagne, there is

just one club in the Wall Street district where the girls are served soft

drinks or tea and where you consequently can't make extra commission off the drinks. A glass of champagne costs five dollars and it costs ten or twenty dollars for a little bottle, a so-called piccolo.

However, soon enough Josh ordered a glass of champagne and another one after that, I thought he was nice and it struck me right off how much he reminded me of my Greek-Cypriot lover Michel especially when he smiled.

Then it was my turn to dance again.

'Are you a good dancer?' he asked.

'No', I said, 'but I've got a great body!'

He doubled up with laughter and the resemblance with Michel was striking. I gave him plenty of attention while dancing and he lapped it up, couldn't tear his eyes away from me and that dynamite body of mine. I was having fun and no intention whatsoever to let him get the better or me.

At one point while I was still dancing, he suddenly got up and left the place. He returned a little later and sat down at a table. He immediately ordered a piccolo for me when my dancing turn was over. He had a large parcel with him covered in brown wrapping paper; it looked like it might be a painting.

'Oh, how nice of you,' I said, deadpan, 'you bought me a present, that's so sweet of you.'

He thought my remark very funny and his beautiful smile reeled me in. I also told him that I thought it was a painting with something brown in it and many colors: pink, lilac, blue, orange, yellow and green. His mouth dropped. Much later, at his place, he tore the paper off the parcel; it was a very colorful poster of a black saxophone player at the New Orleans Jazz Festival.

In the Broadway Pub he was now coming on to me without restraint.

'You are so beautiful, such an interesting face, such lovely hair and magnificent eyes. And you do have a great body.'

I lapped it up and felt more and more attracted to him.

Hours passed and many piccolos later I succumbed to his charms and let go off my up to then tight rule of never going anywhere with a customer; Josh was the exception, the only one in six weeks. We took a taxi to Penn Station and the train to Westbury where he lived.

He wanted to take me out to dinner first but I suggested he prepare something himself. I thought he'd be a great lay for the night and I didn't feel like wasting another hour or more in some stuffy, stuck-up Long Island restaurant. I called Lee from his house to tell him I was alright and would be home the next day. I had told Josh right off that I was married. I always did that and never ever seriously considered leaving my husband for one of my numerous flings, not even for my darling Michel. But this time tings went differently.

Josh wanted to know all about me and my life up to then. I've always been a chatterbox and frank and open about myself and my unusual, bohemian artist's life. Josh seemed fascinated with me. We went to bed and made love with total abandon and utter delight. The next day he drove me into Manhattan after we had breakfast in a diner and dropped me off at my hotel. From then on he called me four, five times a day and we spent every night together. Lee was a bit annoyed I'm sure but didn't let on, being Mister Cool as usual.

It was not hard to figure out that Josh was completely smitten with me and although I was very attracted to him as well not for one second did I consider not going back home with Lee two weeks later.

Josh begged me to stay in New York, he even offered me money. I was very flattered of course but I kept my resolve and told him no.

'I'm going home with my husband, Josh,' I said, 'I will come back in a few months, really, don't worry.'

Nevertheless I knew without realizing it at the time that this man was not just another infatuation. It seemed to me as if I, by some inexplicable miracle, got my sweet Apollo back.

Back to today...I think it's all over now. He doesn't even call me. Why?
Why doesn't Josh love me anymore? I guess the novelty wore off. It
makes me so sad but...we are too different, he is six years younger than I
and he can't make a move without all those friends of his. It drives me
crazy!

Wednesday, March 12, 1980

I started work today at Newsweek Magazine, as secretary of the
Chief Personnel. Josh just called me, smooth as molasses. And I long so
much for him; I don't know...it's an addiction I think.

I had lunch today with Mister Vincent McDonnell (Vinnie to his friends)
in The 21 Club, one of the most renowned restaurants in New York City.
A few days ago Princess Margaret had lunch there with some friends I
learned from the New York Post. The food is exquisite; I've been there
several times already with Vincent. I met him in the Xenon Discotheque at
the I Love New York Awards Festival. Joe Franklin sent me there with
some idiot whom I left to himself the minute I set foot in the place. I like
Vincent. He's of Irish descent, middle aged, funny, intelligent, well-read
and cultured. He used to be police commissioner of New York under
Mayor Lindsey. Not so long ago he took me to a party at Gracie's
Mansion, the Mayor's residence. I was introduced to Mayor Koch, who's

gay and ever so nice. Everyone there was very friendly towards me. A lot of photographs were taken. Quite exciting to mingle with the big shots of the Apple, political figures and all, I loved it!

I'm going to play my guitar now.

11.30 p.m.

I've made other lyrics about our Hawaiian experience to the melody of my very first song, Tree Of Memory; my music teacher in Deventer, Daan Poelder, was so thrilled about that song way back when and arranged it for his sixteen piece orchestra, violins and all, for the great Show of the Jubilee of the Deventer hospitals where I sang it and was met with a standing ovation of the audience in the large auditorium of the Buitensoos Auditorium. I never forget that wonderful night and the first thrill of success.

Anyway, I was so pleased with myself and happy with the new lyrics that I called my lover on an impulse. Wrong! Very bad idea! My call woke him up and he was very grumpy towards me.

Oh, well, what the heck! There's a letter from grandma in Westbury. Tomorrow I've got an appointment with Dr. Harrington and I'm going out to lunch with Bianca, Lucy's sister.

Thursday, March 13, 1980

It's terrible outside, a snow storm. I went to see Ada after work, Celeste (Bailey's daughter) was there. I immediately was served a delicious hot meal prepared by Bailey with ice-cream for desert. They are such warm people.

What a difference with Josh's parents! I wouldn't care if I never saw them again; they're cold as ice especially his mother. They never invite me or ask how I'm doing. They're such snobs!

It might have been different had I been Jewish. To hell with them!

March 17, 1980

I used my lunch hour to buy something for myself, an ocean green deux-pièce at Plymouth. It was on sale, very cute and it looks great on me if I say so myself. It's fitting as well because it's Saint Patrick's Day today.

I went to Westbury Friday after work. Josh and I had a long talk. He got tears in his eyes when he saw me; he was so happy, me too. I can't help myself, I really love him and I believe that he loves me too.

We've got to try to make it work. We had a great weekend, a nice party at Bob and Alice's, a movie, Being There with Peter Sellers and Shirley McLean and dinner in Roslyn. It was blissful and I realized how much I missed him.

Josh saw a box of matches from The 21 Club lying on the table yesterday.

'Who's been in The 21 Club?' he said.

'Me.' I said.

'With whom?' he asked and I noticed sharpness in his tone of voice. I laughed; 'that's none of your business, darling,' I said, 'we aren't married, are we?'

I can be such a bitch sometimes. He didn't let on but anyway, I've got to keep him on his toes, as well it should be for a bit of mystery keeps the flame going under the pot of romance. God, how I love him! I think Josh is terrific and I am sure that his feelings for me are genuine.

Tuesday, March 18, 1980

We had such fun with a large group celebrating Paul's birthday yesterday with champagne, the works! The only sour note for me was this one girl who couldn't keep her hands off of Josh, no class whatsoever! Anyway, tonight Josh asked whether I was going out to dinner to The 21 Club again and with whom.

'With an elderly gentleman who wants to show me off to his buddies, I've had lunch there a couple of times, yes, but that's all. You have no reason to be jealous, Josh, I love you!' I said.

'I'm not jealous,' he said, and: 'Does Bill see you naked often?'

'No, of course not!' was my indignant answer. This is a blatant lie; Bill has seen me naked often enough, he even made nude photographs of me, very artistic and beautiful. However, it's my conviction that a woman has to keep some things to herself. I never told Lee about it either. I only slept once with Bill since I'm back here and I will not do it again.

From now on the only one for me is my sweet, darling Josh.

March 21, 1980

Springtime, hurrah! I got such a sweet letter from the poet again. Every time I get word from him I almost weep for joy. I really hope he's coming soon. Although once he's here I don't quite know how to handle the situation. I don't feel like living in a fleabag hotel with him again and I haven't got enough money saved up yet for my own apartment. Thank God, dear Bill lets me stay here in his studio on Seventh Avenue.

Lee wrote that Archie Shepp invited him out to Massachusetts. He will do a poetry reading for students there. Lee I mean of course, Archie is famous saxophone player. What will happen? If Lee and I start living together again can I still be Josh's girlfriend? I love both of them, for different reasons obviously. Is that so strange? It must be a deficiency in my brain or something but what can I do? Oh well, time will provide the answers to everything I think and I will keep a positive outlook.

People who say it's immoral don't know a thing about emotions, love, loyalty, passion, friendship and spiritual growth.

Friday, March 28, 1980

Good news at last! I have a chance, a good chance to obtain my very own studio-apartment! It's on 46th Street between 6th and 7th avenue; one large room, a kitchenette, a bathroom (with an art nouveau tub on cute little legs!) and furnished ever so nice. The owner is a friend of Bill's and is willing to rent it to me for only $350 a month, a real bargain!

There are two more letters from Lee, he writes that he's broke but that he wants to come here. I better send him some money. I long to see him again but at the same time I worry.

To be honest I have no desire to play the married woman again and to support him all the time. I know he means well and does the best he can but still, I know myself, I would never leave him stranded anywhere.

What can I say? I love him.

I'm working for CBS publishing, for a German woman, she's alright. I have two auditions to sing in restaurants on Long Island tomorrow.

Monday, March 31, 1980

Well, the shit hit the fan alright, Lord Jesus, what a kooky weekend, what a nightmare! Josh was like a devil, humiliating me, hurting me. Horrible things he said to me. I don't know whether I love you, I don't want to lead you on; this is not my kind of relationship, etcetera. It was so hurtful, like being in a dark tunnel.

This morning he said: 'We'll do something nice next weekend.'

As if nothing had happened, Lord, I am so fucked up about it all.

Lee called this morning. He could tell something was wrong with me. I kept saying No, no, no, I'm fine, really.

I sent him two hundred and twenty dollars on Thursday. It's all so weird, I wrote a song last week which so unnerved me that I tore it up. It began like this:

> No more crying over you
> You go your way
> I go mine
> No more relying on you
> Our story is over
> Our time was due
> So we part with no hard feelings
> Thinking just how lucky we were
> To meet the way we did

And all is fine
And all is fine.
That's the way it goes with feelings
Once here and then they're just gone
It's like a song, just like this song

I played my guitar for over an hour and I feel much better. It always helps
to sing.

Saturday, April 5, 1980

Josh took me out to dinner and spent the night with me here
in my lovely studio-apartment. We talked. Hell, I don't know, I love him
and I hate him. He's such a child. But his playfulness attracted me to him
in the first place. Basta! Only time will tell. My studio is great, I love it
here and I am so glad that I have my own place again at last!

Thursday, April 17, 1980

Lee has come. It was great seeing him again. We both had so much
to tell each other. He's gone to Massachusetts on Tuesday; he's doing a
poetry reading tomorrow at the University of Amherst.

It's not easy at all to live together with Lee again. It's been so long. I still love him of course but I'm not in love with him anymore. My heart belongs to Josh.

Naturally Lee's been cooking up a storm. We made love once but my heart is not in it anymore so now we live like friends. Josh was very upset when I told him Lee was coming. We've spent time together in Westbury and here but Josh can't handle the fact that I let Lee stay here. I understand and I don't want to lose Josh.

Bibi spent the night with me last night. She was totally out of it because Steve has an affair, with a Japanese woman. He's staying with her in a hotel. He even took that woman over to their Loft; very tactless and insensitive of him I think. Bah!

Josh is taking me to the Copacabana tomorrow, hurrah!

Wednesday, April 23, 1980

Lee came back Sunday night; his reading was a big success he said. Josh, Paul, his friend Ann and I spent Sunday in South Hampton and Josh was such a peach! Monday night I went out to the island to see him. We talked. He said he can understand that I don't want to send Lee out into the street but that it is hard for him too. I told him that Lee and I don't have sex anymore.

Lee is ever so nice to me, he does everything, cooking, shopping, and trying to find work. But I don't want to lose Josh.

May 9, 1980

Lee's friend Marion Brown (they're both from Thomasville, Georgia) has a record company with a friend. They already produced six albums, Sweet Earth Sound it's called. Lee talked to him and now he has promised to make an album with me. He will be the musical director and organize the musicians, Steve McCall on drums. Wow! I'm so excited!

He says he can get it done for between 2500 and 3000 dollars. I have to come up with that.

I've asked Josh but he's very negative about it. So, I'm trying to raise money elsewhere. I talked about it with Joe Franklin and with Vincent McDonnell. I was in Mike Manuchi's with him the other day, he gave me the pictures of the party at Gracie's Mansion, and they came out real nice.

God, I want so much for it to happen this time. Imagine, my very own album, with my songs, accompanied by great jazz musicians. It would be like a dream come true. Unfortunately Josh is not at all interested.

I sang in the Monsignore II this Monday. There was a woman, Joan St James, very nice. She loved my performance and asked me to send her my picture/resume. This fall she starts a new hotel in New York City.

Last weekend was great. Parties and fun in South Hampton and I rode a horse for the first time in my life. We drove out to Montauk. It was wonderful and I'd love to do that again some time. Josh was fantastic! I wish it could always be like that between us.

Saturday, June 7, 1980

Lee is helping me, teaching me how to write stories. I sang a lot lately. My record? Well, money is the problem as usual.

Lee has a job. He interviews people for the Census. With Josh and me it's still the same: on-off, on-off. It's on at the moment.

June 17, 1980

Mama is in the hospital, for the first time in her life. I called them from my office job yesterday. First I got grandma on the line. I mailed a card to her immediately. I moved in with Josh again. For how long it will last.

Monday, June 23, 1980

Mama is still in the hospital. I call Marjorie every day. She said they
don't know whether it's gallstones or something else. They took photos of
her kidneys and did all kinds of tests. Marjorie said that they will call me
as soon as they know what ails her. Mama ill; I wish I was there. I keep
thinking about her all the time. I worry but hopefully she'll be out of the
hospital soon and all better again. It's her birthday on Wednesday. She'll
be fifty-five.

I'm singing tomorrow and Wednesday in The Beanstalk on the Avenue of
the Americas.

My short story is going well. I see very little of Lee these days. I think I
either have to break it up with Josh or marry him. It can't go on like this or
I'll go stark raving mad.

I would like to take off, go to Holland, and be with mommy. I'm worried
sick about her. I'm smoking like a fiend. But I went through so much
trouble to get my green card and if I leave now it will all have been for
naught.

June 25, 1980

I'm having lunch with Lucy. It's mama's birthday today. I send you
lots of love, dear mommy and I hope you'll be well again soon and that
you have no pain.

Josh is way too heavy; he should lose some weight, at least 20 pounds. I
am so tired. Summer is here and it's scorching hot. I'm singing tonight
again in The Beanstalk and tomorrow in The Estoril.

Monday, June 30, 1980

I can't live in Westbury anymore. My short story is not going well, I
féel blocked. I was trying to tape some songs but the cassette recorder
doesn't function well.

Josh wants to take me to a bungalow in Vermont for four days. That
sounds good to me. My singing jobs in The Estoril and The Beanstalk are
steady so three nights a week I'm singing. However, today Josh was
yelling at me that I should go back to work for the temporary agency as
well. They told me that they have nothing for me at the moment.

I've also been asked back for one week in The Monsignore II.

Josh says he's moving to the city when Lucy moves in with Bob. But he doesn't want to live together with me. What is wrong with him? I wish he would grow up at last.

I don't think it will ever turn into something with us.

I met someone in the train two weeks ago. He was in Japan on vacation and had interesting stories to tell. He's ever so handsome; tall, dark, well-built, about thirty-five I guess and very nice to talk to. He's an Italian/American.

Since I still don't know which way the wind is blowing with Josh...And all that squabbling and fighting we go through. Oh, here he is now.

~

Chapter 21

Via Brussels to Athens

Josh and I had a tempestuous relationship going from fierce quarrels to blissful happiness and back again to outright war.

It nearly drove me insane yet I couldn't let go of him and apparently he not of me either. We vowed never to see one another again but every time we broke that vow we cried from sheer joy to be together again.

My studio apartment was situated on 46th Street a few brownstone houses away from the New York High School for the Performing Arts; I could hear the teenagers singing and carrying on which made me happy and feeling like I was in the heart of all that mattered theater wise, so to speak.

Later a movie was made of that High School and a very popular television series called Fame.

The studio apartment was smartly furnished with a purple leather couch, some orange colored wooden chairs and a large rectangular oak table where Lee had scattered his papers within no time, making me feel a bit sad because I felt he had completely taken over my place. It had a cute kitchenette, a luxurious bathroom and a king size bed in an alcove. Bill Yoscary's friend who rented it to me for a friendly price had a business together with his mother of theater cloths and paraphernalia like wigs and masks; he and his mother were small, almost midgets I would say but they were ever so nice and forthcoming. Perhaps I should talk a bit more about Bill Yoscary. There was a time when I thought the best man for me was Bill and if he had asked me I would've married him without blinking an eye.

Nonsense of course because he was married already (and I also for that matter) with a wife in his house with swimming pool in New Jersey and a girlfriend in his apartment in New York. His studio, a huge Loft on Seventh Avenue right smack in the middle of the rag trade companies - my good friend Sunny and his partner had their business there too - was where he photographed young pretty women like me who wanted to be models or singers or dancers or actresses. He had a whole array of cloths available to choose from and he took a lot of excellent photos of me in beautiful outfits.

Bette Midler started her first steps on the big star career ladder there where she sat and talked with Bill for hours on end I imagine just like me and where he put together her portfolio for her. He told me that her first singing gig was in a homo club in Manhattan. He had lots of fascinating tales to tell. As he was in charge of the Alvin Alley Theater for many years he knew a lot of stars personally. Jerry Lewis was a prick he said who sent out a guy each night when he did shows to pick out a girl from the crowd and bring her to his dressing room and he always played practical jokes and pranks on musicians, stagehands, what have you. Bill knew Liz Taylor and Richard Burton and told me how the two of them had cursing bouts that were legendary. He was also present when Elizabeth's husband Mike Todd threw a party for her in Madison Square Garden for her fortieth birthday. And he was Melanie Mercouri's lover during the time of the Colonel Regime in Greece and told me how they were once chased by Greek hoodlums while in her limousine in the streets of Manhattan.

I loved Bill, he was such a dear friend and throughout the years we remained very close. Later I also met his girlfriend Madelyn and stayed in touch with her as well. I remember he once showed me a lovely ring with little diamonds and a good size ruby that he had bought for her birthday.

He was also an accomplished sculptor and last but not least wildly attractive. He told me that his parents were acrobats who made their living performing in a circus in Italy. He had one brother who died of cancer when I knew Bill in New York. He was heartbroken about it and stopped smoking cold turkey; an astonishing feat because Bill was a chain smoker in those days.

Sadly Bill passed away in

July, 2004, at the age of seventy-four. I still miss him.

My new friend, Vincent McDonnell, was a very nice gentleman; he never

tried anything with me, not more than a peck on the cheek when we said

goodbye passed between us. I told him about my husband the Afro-

American poet and also about my boyfriend and the problems we had. He

in turn never stopped talking about Brigitte, his ex-girlfriend from

Sweden.

'She goes and shacks up with this Swedish guy,' he used to say full of

bitterness and hurt.

The man must have loved that woman like crazy and I think he never got

over it because although I liked him, hearing him talk about her all the

time became a bit tiresome. Once when we were in The 21 Club where we

often went and met with buddies of his, he suddenly broke out in a cold

sweat and quickly ordered a shot of gin, gulping it down while shaking

like a leaf. He had just spotted his ex-girlfriend standing in a corner

chatting it up with some guy. I felt so sorry for him.

I invited him to our big wedding party in 1982 when Josh had rented out

the Zipper Disco on Union Square. Vincent had a lovely lady with him

then and when I went to talk with him he introduced me to her and said:

'She knows about Brigitte, I told her about it.' The woman smiled and I felt for her because I knew he would bend her ear about that lost love like he had done with me.

'I'll put your name in big letters on the billboards all over town, sweetheart,' Vincent used to say to me. I didn't take it seriously and more importantly I was not in love with him and had no intention whatsoever to use him to further my career. I have never done that; maybe I should have.

He did take me to all the fancy restaurants and clubs though; once I sang in The Big Apple Club, somewhere on First Avenue if I remember correctly. I sang a song in a key that was too low for my voice and Vincent was quite upset with me.

'Why did you sing it like that?' He said in a rather gruff tone of voice, 'It was way too low!'

He was right. Somehow or other I sometimes sang songs in the wrong key for me. I have never had a manager, agents yes but a manager who would have steered me right…it would have been a great help but alas….

Vincent told all his friends that I was a great singer and feisty to boot and then he went on to tell them about my knocking over a table where a three card Monty game was in progress.

That happened on a Saturday when Josh had promised to pick me up to take me out but as I was sitting dressed up to the nines he called and said that he and his friends were going to gamble in Atlantic City, sorry.

I was heartbroken, hurt and very sad. Lee wasn't in at the time and I began drinking away my sorrow downing a whole bottle of port whereupon I ran out into the street where I saw a three card Monty game in progress. Although I knew damn well that it is a hustlers' trick I fell for it and within no time I was out a hundred dollars plus the golden ring with tiny diamond that my first boyfriend Johnny had given me when we became engaged.

Suddenly I realized what had happened to me and in my anger and frustration I started screaming and kicked over the cartoon box with the cards on it; everything went flying and apparently the hustlers were taken completely by surprise while I dashed off and disappeared into the crowd.

In the year 1980 it became known that a new mysterious illness was sweeping the world: AIDS.

Shouki and I talked about it and were quite worried because it was said that this illness affected homos especially and we had a number of great fun loving and off the wall homo friends.

Gone were the days of carefree sex frolicking without protection. We, the so called baby boom generation (folks born in the first ten years after the war) had the birth control pill and venereal diseases let alone aids were not the issue.

Sometimes, in retrospect, I think that part of my promiscuity was that I couldn't conceive with Lee and maybe I thought and even hoped I would get pregnant by someone else.

On the day Lee and I got married I stopped using the pill and I never used contraceptives again in my life.

I didn't wear a brassiere for ten years either. Oh, those good old days of sexual liberty, freedom of expression and glorious hopes for a better world.

The year 1980 would shake me though, turn my world upside down and cause me more pain than I had ever felt in my life.

Right! On with my story!

~

July 10, 1980

I'm back home, my studio on 46th Street I mean. I took all my clothes and belongings with me. The holiday in Vermont was so lovely. The bungalow was gorgeous, fire-place, everything just perfect. It was as if we had just met, like it was in the South of France and Montreal, Canada. The way he carried me through the streets in Amsterdam; all the outrageous fun we used to have then. Vermont was like that, magical! However, each time the bubble breaks and we're at each other's throats again. What happened this time? Already during the seven hours trip up to Vermont we argued a couple of times. He got mad at me for my wrong pronunciation of a word, I don't even remember what it was and when I wanted to open the car window he exploded because the air-conditioning was on and how could I be so stupid. How silly can two people get I ask you!

Anyway, on Tuesday the man whom I met on the train a few weeks ago came to the Beanstalk to hear me sing. He's nice and I like him especially since Josh and I argue so much. When I was done singing Jim asked me to accompany him to a jazz club on the Eastside. It was very nice. He told me he's twenty-nine, divorced, no children, got his own company, he's a small business consultant. He's got a house in Huntington, Long Island. He plays violin and guitar, loves the theater, ballet and skiing. He brought me home to Westbury where I found Josh, Bob, Lucy and a bunch of friends, drunk and stoned as beavers.

They had coke and naturally I joined in. But at some point Lucy started making fun of me, of the way I talk; Josh and all the others joined in. I felt such an outsider.

I have nothing in common with Josh's so called friends. They're spoiled rich kids, the lot of them. After they were all gone Josh started in on me, that I don't know how to act, et cetera.

I was enraged and began to yell. At some point he slapped me in my face.

I gave him the keys to his house this morning, packed my bag and wanted to call a cab but he was full of regret and insisted on driving me to the studio. We were both crying while we drove up here.

Lee was surprised to see me. A little later the doorbell rang, it was Josh; his car wouldn't start. Lee was very nice, he told Josh to sit down while he made a pot of tea.

He said: 'I don't know what it is with you two. Perhaps you should go and have a quiet lunch together. I don't know what to say. It seems to me, Josh, from what Stella tells me that things are okay when you're together, like you had a nice holiday but it's not going so well with so many of your friends around all the time, which by the way is entirely your affair of course....' Josh looked stricken. 'Yes,' he said, 'perhaps...but we can't be alone all the time....'

He was so nervous, called a garage, went downstairs and came back a few minutes later saying that his car started again. Later Lee laughed and said: 'Here I am giving advice to my wife and her lover! I must be mad!' I feel rotten even though the poet is very sweet and understanding.

Sunday, July 12, 1980. Happy Birthday, Marjorie!

I had a nice day yesterday with Lucy. We had lunch with her mother on Fifth Avenue and 57th. Her mother has raven black hair and the greenest eyes I ever saw on anyone, uncanny and hard to tear away from. Lucy is my friend, not Josh's roommate Bob's; I met her a while ago while singing in
Estoril. She's Italian/American and I like her a lot. I also like her mother Nina, she reminds me of Michel's mother, warm and sweet. I sent Michel's mother a letter a few days ago and asked how Michel is doing. I haven't heard from him for a long time.

After lunch we went to a gallery in SoHo where Bibi has an exhibition of her photos, two are shots of me she made last year in her Loft when she was doing a series on light and shadows. On one I sit with my head down near the kitchen sink full of dirty cups and plates, forks, spoons, knifes and on the other I look upwards, rather saintly.

Afterwards we went to The Tin Palace where Art Taylor played. He's a good friend of Lee, been over to our house on the Amstelveenseweg in Amsterdam many times. He was also one of the performers in our Charity Shows in the Concertgebouw in Amsterdam and the Doelen in Rotterdam. He's a nice man. We drank a lot of red wine and I was home at three o'clock in the morning.

I'm going to Floral Park in a little while to Daphne and Dwight. She is Dutch; they met in Holland when Dwight was studying sound engineering in Utrecht I believe. They got married and are living here four years now. I met her when I sang at the Old Westbury Gardens Estate. I was supposed to go there today with Josh but I told Daphne that we broke up. It even hurts writing it down. Dwight is sound producer at the Radio City Music Hall Sound Studios here in Manhattan. On Thursday he is going to tape six songs with me there and then he'll mix them to four and a half minutes for a demo record. It will cost about three hundred dollars for five hundred copies. I can use them to promote myself. I would like to set up a College tour.

Tuesday, July 15, 1980

Josh called yesterday. He said he wanted to see me. I told him I'm not coming to Long Island. In the end I agreed to let him pick me up here at four to let him take me out to dinner. We first had a drink at the Top of the Sixes. We talked. I told him I don't want to be treated like a yo-yo, I love you, and I don't love you. He said that wasn't true. Anyway, we walked to Central Park and then he surprised me by taking me for a ride through the park in one of those horse-drawn carriages. We then ate in Nirvana, an Indian restaurant with a spectacular view over Central Park.

Naturally he was horny as hell, telling me all the naughty things he wanted to do with me. He had an enormous hard-on the whole time and my underpants got wet. What can I say? No one turns me on like he does. I'm mad about the man. We had drinks in The Rose on 52nd Street and, wouldn't you know? I went home with him and spent the night. I don't know. I can't give him up. And I know he can't either. Maybe we'll even marry one day.

Saturday, July 19, 1980

I agreed to have dinner with Jim. He's been coming to the Beanstalk each time I sing there. I have gone out to lunch with him a couple of times. Since Josh is either wonderful or horrible to me and I'm getting annoyed with Lee also…I need a break!

This is my studio and he has taken over already. His books and papers and shit all over the place. I wish he would leave. I can't imagine why I ever asked him to join me here. I'm so stupid!

I want to be on my own, for once in my life, please!

Anyway, Jim said to me that he thinks we shouldn't meet anymore for awhile because I'm too involved with Josh and he wants more than friendship. I think he has fallen in love with me. He said that I can move in with him if I want to and that he would love to help me, to write down my music for instance. He has played in symphonic orchestras. He's really very nice I think.

I forgot to mention - shame on me - but the very good news is that mama is out of hospital. They haven't found out yet what is ailing her and that puzzles me. She feels better though and she and papa are going on vacation to Austria. I pray that she'll be her strong healthy self again soon.

When I came home Lee told me that Josh called from Atlantic City. He has gone to gamble there with his friends, same as last weekend. They blow a lot of money, drop Quaaludes…Bah!

What children they are! Josh has refused to give me the three hundred dollars I need for my demo records. No problem, I'll pay for it myself. I'm sick and tired of him and the childish games he plays.

I hate it that he needs those asshole friends of his so much. I think it's very stupid and it annoys the hell out of me.

Wednesday, July 23, 1980

Josh is driving me crazy. He's such an idiot! I'm seriously thinking about moving in with Jim for awhile. I like him more and more. Josh has never come to the Beanstalk to hear me sing, not once! I've asked him several times. He's always too busy with work but he's never too busy to hang out with those friends of his. Jim is very attractive and very nice.

Thursday, July 24, 1980

I went to a hotel with Jim when I was done singing. And I can't stand myself because once we were in the room I felt guilty, like I was betraying Josh. So, I told Jim that I had a migraine attack and asked him to take me home. Oh God, why am I such a crazy woman! Josh gives me nothing but pain.

He only needs me when he's horny, he doesn't want to lift a finger to help me further my career!

Jim took it so well. I respect him for that. He was very kind and took me home in his beautiful white Cadillac. He has given me flowers in the club when I sing many times.

He's mature, nice and cultured. I don't think Josh has ever read a book in his life. Why do I love him? I give up. I must be mad.

Saturday, July 26, 1980

Josh has given me two hundred and fifty dollars towards the cost of the demo records. At last but I'm very grateful nonetheless.

Peter Sellers died of a heart attack. What else?

It's hot, hot, hot and sticky every day. Tonight is my last performance at The Beanstalk. Tomorrow Josh will take me to the beach, at least he promised but that doesn't mean much with him.

I've been asked back in the Beanstalk the last week of August.

Next week I'll sing all week in the Monsignore II. Yes!

Bibi and Steve are trying to work out their problems. Lee and I visited them yesterday. Bibi's photo of me, published in Where Magazine, brought her luck. They gave her an assignment to photograph shopping people in Bloomingdale.

Lee still works for the Census and he finished a new poetry manuscript, I typed it for him. He makes good money now, cooks every day and is very sweet to me. Josh is very good to me these days also. All is well for the time being.

Sunday morning, August 2, 1980

Nowadays I don't find it hard at all to divide my time between Josh and Lee, on the contrary: I love it! It's the best of two worlds for me. When I was alone here, with Josh but without Lee, I wasn't so happy. Josh can't give me all that I need, mentally, creatively. But Lee can't give me all that I need either, physically, spontaneously, playfully. Now that I have both of them it is practically ideal. It couldn't be better!

I wouldn't mind it though if Lee went away for a little while, two months or so but no longer than that. Anyway, how it stands now the situation is rather perfect for me.

Apparently it's fine for my two men because neither one of them complains. They can't live without me, neither one and that's alright with me. I told Josh to call the lawyer on Monday, there's no movement at all in the case. No news on the horizon.

August 3, 1980

For some mysterious reason I feel attracted to Mister Jimmy, the owner of the Monsignore II. He's not unattractive but really, Stella! The man is in his fifties; corpulent, grey...I wonder...it seems I always fall in love with men who don't even try to conquer me. As if the hunter's game is my department instead of the other way around.

I do know he likes me though, the way he fusses over me when I come in; he always sits with me while I'm eating, inquiring how I like the food after he's gone out of his way to tell me what's the special that day and how the chef will prepare it for me. The food in the Monsignore II is out of this world, that's true. It is such a fancy restaurant. Mister Jimmy is married to a much younger, attractive woman and they have a sweet little girl called Jessica of about eight years old.

Monday, August 11, 1980

The Democratic Convention started today. The town is filled with democrats from all over the place and it's so oppressive outside. I have no energy left.

August 15, 1980

It's over, for good. No fight, I broke it off. I am absolutely fed up with his indecisiveness, his childish and irresponsible behavior. I'm sure I'll never see him again. I cursed him, called him every dirty name. I shouldn't have but I've been so frustrated for so long with him. He's driving me crazy.

I am studying Italian again, haven't done that since my years at the Sweelinck Conservatory. I have an audition tomorrow and on Sunday.

Oh God, I'll never hear his sweet voice calling me *Bonbon* again, I'll never feel his beautiful muscular body against mine. I am so sad but at the same time I feel as if a whole new life will open up for me. I will be better soon. It takes time for sorrow to die, rot and fade before new buds can blossom.

Never ever have I loved like this before, but is all over now.

August 16, 1980

I manage in the daytime but it's harder at night. Today an audition for Chapter Two, a Neil Simon play and tomorrow an audition as singer in a Las Vegas Show band. I'm studying my Italian with an almost demented zeal. I need to occupy every second in order to forget. Oh, Josh!

August 18, 1980

What's next? Michel, that's what's next! I received a wonderful letter from him. He's a professional soccer player now, he's got his own place, a car and….he's waiting for me.

He wants me to come to him and what do you know? I'm going!

Josh and I had a row again four days ago and he still hasn't called me. I can't stand it anymore. He's driving me insane! I do need a change I think; a change of atmosphere and everything. I'm planning to leave this weekend.

Afternoon,

I intend to take a standby flight to Brussels and from there a charter flight to Athens. I sent an express letter to Michel.

I am so excited, I can't wait to leave. New York has lost its magic spell for me at the moment. I'll probably come back here in about three to four months, on a new tourist visa. Perhaps Michel will come with me then…he could play for the Cosmos soccer team, who knows? Oh, my darling, handsome athlete, my one and only Apollo!

Lee says he's happy for me but he looks rather sad. Well, it can't be helped, I must go, there's no other option because I need a break from everything desperately. And anyway, Lee and I will always remain friends and probably see each other again in a couple of months…in Athens or Ibiza or Amsterdam.

I'm going to play it by ear, that's the best remedy for me at this point I think.

Life is wonderful and full of adventure!

By the way, my demo recording project is on its way; I gave Dwight the money and in four to five weeks the five hundred records will arrive here. Lee will send some to me and will take the rest with him since he plans to return to the Continent at the end of September.

I want to write a long, honest letter to Josh before I leave. I don't want us to be enemies, I couldn't bear that. It was so unique what we had…we could've had it all but…oh well, no use crying over spilt milk. We are at different mental levels I think…I don't know really. I need a change, that's what I do know and I'm longing to see darling Michel again after four years. It is the third time he asks me to come to him, living together and

~

Chapter 22

A twist of fate

And here it ends, in mid sentence. Why? What happened? My notebook was full I guess and I couldn't be bothered.

I have kept diaries throughout my life but there are hiatus of months or some years even. Writing down my thoughts has always been a relief to me; a way to create some order in my thoughts and to try and make sense of life's vicissitudes. I think it has helped me, instead of talking to a psychologist I talk to myself and save a lot of money that way.

However, it is much harder now to know exactly how I felt, what I was up to and to remember the sequence of events.

I will give it my best; here we go!

I thought that I hadn't told anyone that I planned to go to Cyprus but apparently I did tell Lee. He gave me some money, about a hundred bucks; Bill gave me a hundred dollars also and Vincent chipped in as well.

Josh gave me two hundred dollars when I said I was homesick and needed
to go see my parents.

He seemed relieved and thought it a splendid idea that I went back to
Holland for awhile.

Perhaps my first intention was indeed to go home, it might have been
but what I clearly remember is that when I arrived in Brussels it was very
overcast and raining and, on an impulse I decided not to take the train to
Amsterdam but to travel on to Athens and catch a flight there the next
morning. I walked around the airport for awhile, ate a hamburger, read a
book and later I made myself as comfortable as possible on a bench and
fell asleep. The next morning I booked the first flight out and was on my
way to Greece.

In Athens the weather was lovely, I took a taxi to the center of town
and managed to find a hostel near the Plaka from where you can see the
Acropolis. I remember that I felt wonderful and free as a bird.

It seems hard to imagine but I completely forgot about New York, Josh
and Lee...I was in another world now and just wanted to enjoy myself. I
thought I could land myself a singing gig in one of the luxury hotels and
would set out the very next day.

Life is full of surprises; when I sat down for lunch on the terrace of an Italian restaurant close to my hotel, a strikingly beautiful middle aged woman caught my attention. She was sitting there with a much younger attractive man and I immediately deducted that he must be her toy boy lover.

The woman smiled at me and started up a conversation. The young man was not her lover but her son; they were British and lived in Athens where she worked as a nanny/housekeeper for a rich Greek family. She was a sculptor she said and continued to talk at some length and with unconcealed pride about her porcelain figurines in the Albert & Victoria Museum in London.

I was drawn in - not by her chatter about the heel of a husband who left her without a penny, her adorable grandson William, her beautiful daughter with the red hair, Priscilla, her Greek tycoon boss and his prissy stuck up wife, the unruly children she taught English - but by the amazingly beautiful sparkling bright blue eyes that twinkled like diamonds. She had an oval even face with dimples in her cheeks while she talked, a full sensuous mouth covered in pink lipstick and a wild mop of blond short cut curls.

Her son, a lanky young man of about twenty I guessed, with brown eyes, good looking with thick curly brown hair to his shoulders, didn't say much. He had just finished Junior College and before going to University to study architecture, he was here visiting his mom.

It was nice to make contact with new people so quickly. I told them that I was a singer, that I had just come from New York and that I intended to find work here in one of the luxury clubs or hotels. I also told them I was still married but had fallen in love a year earlier and had lived with my new lover in New York but that I now needed a break to find out what it was that I wanted; going back to my husband, giving it another try with this new man or going to Cyprus to meet up with another lover whom I had known and loved four years ago.

Needless to say that the woman and I hit it off splendidly; within a couple of hours we put away a bottle of red wine between the two of us (her son drank beer) and when we finally said our goodbyes I agreed to meet them later that day in the square to listen to some good music.

I returned to my room in the hostel and slept for an hour or so. When I woke up I showered, got dressed and passed by two major hotels nearby.

Unfortunately I didn't manage to get to see the food & beverage managers nor could I make an appointment. They had no need for an entertainer.

I was not disheartened because one cannot expect to be successful in just a day.

Ruth and her son Patrick and I saw each other again in the square. I had eaten a hamburger and fries in a restaurant on the Plaka and had just finished when I saw them walking hand in hand towards me.

We went to a bar where a blues group played. Friends of theirs joined us and the atmosphere was lively and much fun. At about one o'clock I felt tired and sleepy and took my leave of them.

Mulling over the day and my encounter with new people, thoughts of Josh entered my head and pretty soon images of him, Lee and Michel all got tangled up. I felt utterly confused about what I should do. Finally I dozed off in a deep blissful sleep.

The next day I didn't feel in a rush to hop on a boat to Cyprus right away.

It was so nice to meet this woman and her son and what's the hurry, I thought. I figured I needed some time for myself, time to put everything into focus.

The next couple of days I wandered around Athens and met up with Ruth and Patrick every afternoon on the Plaka. Patrick and I visited the Acropolis which utterly fascinated and amazed me; Ruth usually caught up with us later when she was done with her job for the day.

Pretty soon other friends of theirs joined us and before too long I was part of a lively group of artists, musicians, loafers, students and what have you. I had a whale of a time and was not at all in a rush to travel on to Cyprus. In fact I was not so sure anymore that going back there was such a splendid idea.

The first day I had called my husband to tell him where I was and that I was going to stay in Athens for awhile.

I also called Josh who was very annoyed when I told him that I was in Athens.

'What are you doing there?' He yelled, 'you were supposed to go home.'

'Yes,' I said, 'but it was raining in Belgium and I needed a vacation.'

Josh was clearly not amused. When I called him again a few days later his roommate told me that he had gone on holiday to Club Med on the Bahamas.

It was as if I was hit in the face with a two by four!

However, I didn't let it get me down; Ruth, her son and the other people and I met each day on the Plaka. We had so much fun together especially with Theo, a Turkish friend of Ruth, who was indeed a regular riot. He had us in stitches continuously doing wonderful interpretations of movie stars, singers and political figures. He was no taller than 5 feet with tiny hands and a head that seemed way too big for his body.

When after two or three days I called Michel I was told that he was playing soccer and the next time I rang he was practicing with the team and then he had just left the building and so it went.

Each time I left the hostel and came back I was informed that there had been a call for me from Cyprus.

It was too crazy for words but finally I got through to him. His voice was just as soft and beautifully melodic as I remembered but his attitude was far from welcoming.

He started off by saying that he could put me up for three weeks maximum. I was baffled. This was a far cry from the

romantic, loving letter that I had received in New York. Rather crestfallen I said goodbye to him and wondered if I really should go and visit him in Cyprus.

Meanwhile my money was beginning to dwindle and I thought that perhaps it was a wise idea to head on to Amsterdam. I had gone to several first class hotels and super clubs but was turned down each step of the way.

'Why don't you come and stay with us?' Ruth said after about a week and a half since it became obvious that I was running out of money. I accepted her offer and moved in with them in their two bedroom apartment in a four story building near the center of town; I slept on the huge sofa in the living room. Ruth whipped up an excellent dinner each day and I had nothing to complain about.

Our daily routine of having lunch on the Plaka and hanging out till the wee hours with this lively group of people continued.

I decided to call Michel one more time to establish once and for all if he really wanted to see me again.

Again it proved very difficult to get him on the phone but when I finally got hold of him he gave me the impression that he was happy and indeed wanted to see me so… I immediately dashed over to a booking agency and bought a ticket by boat to Cyprus.

Then I called Lee and told him about my plan and purchase.

Lee exploded. I was dumfounded because he never ever had stopped me from going on a trip by myself.

'Are you crazy?' He screamed, 'Have you lost your mind? I forbid you to go to that island, do you hear?'

'I already bought my ticket,' I said, feebly.

'Return it!' Lee barked. And, believe it or not, that's exactly what I did. I went straight to the travel agency again and managed to return the ticket and get my money back.

To this day I have no idea why I listened to my husband; I had always done exactly as I pleased and Lee had never stopped me before.

After some more days in Athens I began to get restless. What was I doing there? Sure, Ruth and her son and the others were great fun to spend time with but I also felt that it was escapism.

How long was I going to keep this up? Besides although I didn't have to pay for a room in a hotel anymore I knew that getting a singing gig somewhere was wishful thinking on my part; it was not going to happen and, I was rapidly running out of money. I also started thinking about my mother a lot.

How was it going with her and wasn't it about time that I returned home?

I called my parents and said that I was in Athens but wanted to come home. My father and mother were very surprised to find out that I was in Greece, as far as they knew I was with my husband in New York.

'Oh, I just wanted to have a little holiday before coming to Amsterdam,' I said and would they send me three hundred guilders for the trip, please?

After three weeks frolicking about in Athens I arrived at Schiphol Airport where I took the train to Alkmaar.

My parents were very pleased to see me but upset with me as well especially my mother.

'When will you finally grow up?' She said, 'Daddy and I worry about you all the time. What about your husband? Why is he still in New York?'

'He is coming back in a week or so I think,' I said.

I apologized and hugged both of them, promising to slow down and stay put for awhile.

'Here,' my mother said and handed me three thick envelopes. They were letters from Josh.

I knew that she and my father didn't approve of my bohemian life style and were not at all happy that I was involved with another man while I was still married.

Who can blame them?

However, I always felt that my life was mine and nobody's business but mine; they just had to accept me the way I was.

To their credit I must say that they did even though it probably was not an easy thing to do, especially not for my overprotective mother.

I noticed right off that she had lost quite some weight. I wanted to know what had the doctors said and how was she feeling.

The good news was that they had been on vacation together to Austria and that during that time my mother hardly had any pain but now the pain had come back.

I also saw that she ate almost nothing; she played around with her food and when I asked her about it, she shrugged it off. I didn't like what I saw and began to worry about her very much.

Josh his letters were full of love and longing. He wanted to come and visit me. Wow! What good news! I decided to call him immediately, collect of course. It felt so good to hear his sweet melodic voice again.

Suddenly I had no idea what had gotten into me wanting to go and take off for Cyprus and I thanked Lee from the bottom of my heart that he had stopped me.

'Yes, yes, yes!' I jubilated, 'I have missed you too, darling, please come as quickly as you can!'

I went to work immediately, got a job as secretary for a lawyer with the firm Stibbe on the Rokin in Amsterdam. My sister Lilly was working there also; little did we know that some years later she would find her husband to be there.

I paid the three hundred guilders my parents had sent me in Athens back and waited full of anticipation for the arrival of Josh.

He came and I moved in with him in Hotel De Doelen in Amsterdam, very luxurious. We went to visit my sister Marjorie and Ben and the children in their house in the country. The boys (six and five at the time) loved Josh. He threw them up in the air and was very playful with them. I had already found out how much Josh loves children because when we flew to the South of France together in 1979 I noticed how easy he made contact with little critters on the plane; another aspect of his character that endeared him to me.

We also rented a fire engine red Saab and drove up to Leeuwarden where my cousin Ate got married to his Donna. That's when my father and mother met Josh and with them the whole family. Everybody was impressed; such a handsome young man and very wealthy to boot, cousin Stella had done well for herself!

'He is very attractive,' my mother said to me, and that he reminded her of the then very popular ice skating champion Eric Hayden.

Although my parents liked Josh, I knew that especially my mother didn't approve. One doesn't carry on with another man while still married was her firm conviction.

Josh didn't stay long, after about five days he flew back to the States extracting the promise from me that I would join him shortly.

'Yes,' I said, 'I will come back to you but only if you rent an apartment in Manhattan where we can live together without roommates. That's my condition, Josh, I mean it.'

I received a letter from Lee; he was in Ibiza. I felt a pang of sadness because that meant that I now no longer had the darling studio in Manhattan. *C'est la vie,* I thought and, as the trooper that I am, carried on.

My mother had an appointment at the hospital where they were going to do some more tests and take blood samples.

How can I continue? My mother was diagnosed with cancer. For my father, my sisters, my brother-in-law Ben and me it was as if the sky came tumbling down. Cancer? Why hadn't they discovered anything before?

In the spring she had been hospitalized for three weeks and then she had been sent home!

My mother had cancer of the pancreas. It couldn't be operated because it had already spread to her liver as well.

My father, sisters and brother-in-law were shocked. Who could have imagined this to happen? My mother had never been hospitalized in her entire life; she was always active and full of energy. How could this be?

In the winter of 1979 she and my father and Ben and Marjorie and the kids had gone skating and my mother on that occasion had fallen flat on her back; since that time she had suffered from rather severe back pain.

Her doctor didn't take her seriously, said that her complaints were psychosomatic, the idiot! Finally, after two or three months he decided to send her to an internist and she was then hospitalized for three weeks in May whereupon they sent her home without an answer to why she was having so much pain in her back.

When we learned that my mother was diagnosed with pancreatic cancer, we started groping around for solutions. There had to be a way to save her life. What about a second opinion? What about sending her to another country? It was too difficult to come to terms with but at the same time it was a truth that we couldn't deny. My dear beautiful strong mother had cancer.

Suddenly she was losing even more weight and before our very eyes we saw her decline. It was awful and we all felt completely powerless.

About four or five weeks after my return from Greece my mother was hospitalized again.

We visited her twice a day and couldn't really believe that we were going to lose her. We thought that the specialist would find a way to cure her. We thought that she would be operated on and that she would somehow recover.

In those days the medical staff thought it wise to leave relatives of cancer patients in the dark about the truth.

But when somebody is dying from cancer it eventually shows of course. My mother's hairline was receding rapidly, she could hardly eat anymore and the pain became unbearable.

Finally after two weeks seeing her lose more and more weight and living in perpetual dread and fear her main physician spoke to my father and us and informed us that my mother was very ill, that the cancer was rapidly spreading throughout her body and that they couldn't do anything for her anymore.

My poor father, he was so grief stricken. It was such a blow to all of us. We just couldn't believe it.

Our strong, vivacious mother was dying? No way!

My father wanted to take her home and although the doctors at first refused to let her go he stood his ground and on Saturday, November 8th, 1980, my dear darling mother was put in the ambulance and brought home.

We had put the marital bed in the living room so that she could look out the window and be with us all the time.

I remember how happy she was to be home again with us; a few days earlier they had by spinal injection stopped her nervous system from registering pain so she was peaceful and serene.

How was it that my mother was so brave and how could she accept the fact that she was going to die?

That first day at home I was alone with her for a few hours because my father, Lilly, Marjorie and Ben had gone to see the children who were left with their other grandmother.

I will treasure those moments alone with my darling mother forever. I lay next to her and told her how much I loved her, that she had always been there for me and my sisters, that she had always supported my singing and that she had sewn so many beautiful dresses for us girls, that she was the sweetest and best mom in the whole wide world.

'I was catty sometimes,' she said, and, 'I was always so proud of my three little girls.'

I sang softly: '*Hei molentje molentje hoog in de wind, wat sta je weer dapper te draaien, je doet of je het uiterst noodzakelijk vindt het licht van de zomer te maaien....*' for her and she smiled. It was one of the many songs she used to sing for my sisters and me when we were little. In Kindergarten I was put in front of the class often even though I was terribly shy but the grey-haired teacher insisted and prodded me on, 'Come on, little Stella, sing that Mill song for us.'

My beautiful sweet mother! To lose her...it seemed impossible.

She had already suffered a minor stroke a day before we took her home from hospital and talking was a bit difficult for her now, her mouth stood askew.

That night, my dear mama suffered a major stroke. It was strange; I awoke that Sunday morning at six o'clock with the words: Lord, why have Thou forsaken me, ringing through my mind over and over.

I intuitively knew something was very wrong and ran downstairs.

My father was awake and seemed baffled and confused.

He was stroking my mother's lovely golden red hair and looked up to me. I can't go on, I'm crying with the memory of my father's utterly forlorn face, saying: 'She won't talk to me...'

One look at my mother and I knew enough. I don't know why I knew but the reason she didn't answer my father was because she was in coma now.

I quickly walked over to the bed. 'We have to call the doctor, daddy; I think that she has had another stroke.' I said and walked over to the telephone.

The doctor arrived about a half an hour later while in the meantime I had awoken the rest of my family.

There we stood, my sisters and I in our dusters, Ben in his dark-blue bathrobe with disheveled hair, quiet and awestruck.

The doctor confirmed it; my mother was in a coma. The doctor put a catheter in place and made arrangements for a nurse to come each morning. He stopped by every day as well.

Sorry, I am crying now. I can't go on at this time. I will continue later on.

~

Chapter 23

Death in my family

My mother lies on the double bed in the living room, her face is peaceful and serene, and her eyes are closed. She seems younger, all the wrinkles have disappeared.

'You look like sleeping beauty.' I murmur while touching her cheek.

We don't go to our respective jobs anymore; my father is on early retirement since a few years and Ben who has his own contracting business goes to check on building sites now and then. We take turns sleeping on the sofa near my mother's bed.

On Tuesday my bossy aunt Trijntje arrives with grandma who is white as a sheet with grief. Her oldest daughter, Geertje, died from leukemia only thirteen years old and now she has to watch her second daughter, my mother, on her death bed.

My father grumbles, he definitely doesn't like having aunt Trijntje around.

We put ice-cubes in a tissue between my mother's lips and talk softly to her. My sisters and I also sing to her. We all feel that she can still hear us.

Once I swear I could feel her squeeze my hand, Lilly is sure she saw her smile and Marjorie says that she may come out of the coma yet.

We don't contradict her, we all want mama to stay with us. As long as she lies here, cuddly and warm, we treasure each second.

The days go by as if in slow motion; it seems unreal. Lee calls from Spain and Josh also calls, several times. I tell him that we are with my mother, that she is peaceful and serene. Josh seems impatient; he wants to know when I'm coming.

'I am here with my mother, darling,' I say and forgive him his disrespect; he is much younger than I and how could he possibly know what it is like to see your mother slip away from you.

My grandmother is very quiet and withdrawn; she can hardly eat a morsel of food even though aunt Trijntje is practically force feeding her.

She wants to go back to her own house; she can't take seeing my mother like this anymore. Daddy is happy and relieved when they leave.

The nurse comes by every morning to wash my mother, change the bag connected to the catheter and in the afternoons the doctor passes by as well.

My mother slips deeper and deeper into coma, no squeezing of hands anymore, no smiling either. It is strange because although we all know that the end is nearing we seem to think that she will forever stay here with us, like the sleeping beauty she is.

My thoughts go in all directions, from my own childhood memories to the stories of my mother's life. She told us about how it was for her and her sisters and brother, my uncle Jaap, as children of boats people. Grandpa and his father and grandfather and great grandfather before him all had their own business in transport of goods by freight boat. My grandmother's family all were boats people as well.

'Often when we came from school, the boat wasn't there anymore because father had accepted another freight and the other boat people told us where they went and then we had to walk long distances.' My mother told us and how they were called names by other children because they were boat people and also because my mother, aunt Geertje and uncle Jaap had red hair. She talked about when her sister died, how grandpa had given blood several times and how she then looked all healthy again but one day father came home and had to tell grandma the sad news: 'Our little girl is no more, she has passed away.'

How my mother had nightmares and once while sleep walking was found in the loading deck between the coals.

'The war started when I was fifteen,' said my mother, 'and ended when I was twenty, my teenage years were ruined because of that awful war.'

She told us everything, from the food shortage to the mean woman who always asked about the meat ticket when my mother came on Wednesdays and ate with her and her sister, virgin school teachers. My mother worked as a maid.

'It was always the first thing that old hag asked for,' my mother said, 'while all I could think of was how skinny my mother was so…one day I had had enough and told her off. Here! I screamed and threw the meat ticket in her face, my poor mother is skin and bones, you fat cow!'

She was sacked on the spot but boy, how proud that story made me feel of my strong and courageous mother.

She also told us about that time when she was passing the headquarters of the Gestapo in Leeuwarden and a little boy was jerked off the back seat of his father's bicycle because he was singing a forbidden song about the *dirty Moffen;* and how she heard the poor child screaming and watched, horrified, when the little boy was delivered back to his father moments later, limp and dead.

Horrible stories but I am so glad she told us because it all has happened and it is good that we, the next generation, know about all that evil and ugliness.

'How did you and daddy meet?' My sisters and I wanted to know exactly how it went of course.

And my mother was a great story teller. They met shortly after the war on one of those dance festivals that were held each evening.

Mama also told us about what had happened to daddy during the war, how he was sent to a laborer's camp and that he escaped and managed to get all the way back home only to be picked off the street again two weeks later because his stepmother told him that it was too dangerous for her and his father to shelter him any longer.

She told us about daddy's unhappy childhood; his biological mother died of thrombosis when he and his twin sister, aunt Annie, were born. My father was sent to his grandparents, his five year older sister, aunt Alie, was sent to an aunt and daddy's twin sister to another aunt.

My father's first six years were carefree and wonderful, the old couple spoiled him rotten but then his father remarried. My father's stepmother was a witch who was jealous of the children's dead mother; they weren't even allowed to keep a photo of her in their room. My grandfather was sweet and harmless but weak of character. He never lifted a finger for my father and even though my father was very intelligent and only got high marks in school, due to the stepmother's influence he was sent to work when he was only fourteen years old.

That awful woman and my grandfather had four more children, a boy and three girls (two actually because the youngest one wasn't my grandfather's but from a friend of the family) who were all allowed to study.

I still get so angry about it even as I'm writing this. My father's childhood and career possibilities were ruined because of his unkind stepmother and mousy father.

She was against my father marrying my mother, because in her opinion my mother was not good enough for him, too lower class.

One moment of carelessness can cause years of great distress, was a favorite phrase of my step grandmother and my mother thought that she meant my father's mistake in marrying my mother by that.

My father's parents didn't attend the wedding either. However, years later when my step grandmother was already dead and gone for years one of her daughters, aunt Ellie, found step grandmother's diary and learned that she had become pregnant from grandfather's best friend and that's why she often used that phrase and perhaps that also caused her to become a religious fanatic. Aunt Ellie died of breast cancer just like her mother

and on her death bed she gave my step grandmother's diary to her half
sister Felicia, who told me some years ago that she always knew
something was off, she felt like she didn't belong.

My father left home as soon as he could and hated any form of
religion for the rest of his life.

The illegitimate daughter is the nicest aunt from that side of the family
even though she is no blood relation of us at all.

On Friday, November 14, 1980 at about nine o'clock in the morning
my mother breathes her last breath. I am with her, daddy also and
Marjorie; a little later Lilly and Ben come into the room.

We are all very quiet; the only sound is the ticking of the antique clock on
the wall.

When her last breath went out into the ether I immediately noticed
the change in her…now all there was left of my dear mother was a body;
her soul was gone. Up, up and away!

We just stood there, dumfounded. My father bent over and kissed her on the mouth.

How do you get through the days when your mother has passed away? I don't know. I remember that I began to vacuum clean the hallway until my father came by, patted me on the head and said: 'Stop it, sweetheart, it is clean enough.'

One image I wish I had not seen was when the undertakers came to take her body away and they put her in a grey sack. That's how my mother was carried out of our home.

The funeral was strange too, it all passed by like in a trance, you are there but you are not there.

We had a funny moment because all the time we were concerned about cutting off a piece of my mother's beautiful flaming red hair for my father and while we were standing in line to accept the condolences of all the people I bent over to whisper to Marjorie: 'We mustn't forget to cut off a piece of her hair' just as Lilly whispered the same thing to her.

We couldn't believe how many people came to the funeral service; they didn't all fit into the Aula.

We had picked out some classical music that my mother liked, the Va Pensiero of the Slaves Chorus of Nabucco by Giuseppe Verdi among others. To this day I can't hold back tears as soon as I hear the first notes of that tune.

My first boyfriend Johnny was present (Lee was still in Spain) and he and I talked for awhile; he had arrived in his Jeep and told me that he spent a year in African countries. As teenagers, in love and full of idealism we were sure that we would go to Africa together to work for the poor there.

My sisters and I were angry that two of our cousins came dressed in T-shirts and jeans.

When the casket was lowered into the ground my uncle Ted, my father's half brother, recited the Our Father while it started to rain.

~

Chapter 24

Life must go on

Time waits for no one.

How we managed to get through the days I don't know. We were in shock I guess and tried to carry on as best as we could.

I went back to work via the temporary agency at the Psycho-analytic Institute in Amsterdam. In a way the work there helped me to get my mind off the loss and the sadness that lay as a stone on my stomach. My task was to file the doctor's reports on the patients in the computer system and I took advantage of that opportunity to read the case histories of children, mostly from broken homes, with psychological problems.

About a week or so after the funeral a melody came to me; I quickly picked up my guitar from my bedroom and bumped into Lilly just as I was about to run upstairs to the attic.

'You are not going to play the guitar!' she hissed, 'you can't play the guitar now!'

I didn't answer and ran up to the attic, Marjorie's former bedroom, where I sat down and the song, *I am a stranger in this land,* was born. Within ten minutes, a quarter of an hour tops, the melody and lyrics were written down. I played and sang ever so softly so as not to disturb and upset anyone.

The music is reminiscent of Arabic melodies and the lyrics are a bit haunting. That song later was one of the tracks of my first album, Going Places, and again with a different arrangement on my album All of Me.

It was, is and remains one of my favorite compositions.

Josh called two or three times a week asking me each time when I was coming. Although I missed him and loved him very much it was also a bit annoying to me. Why couldn't he understand that I needed to stay with my father for awhile?

I didn't want to leave my father now. He was so quiet and so sad. Lilly wanted to stay put as well.

On December 8, 1980, John Lennon was shot dead in front of his home in the Dakota Building in New York; the world was shocked.

I don't remember exactly but I think that around the end of January 1981, I went back to the United States. Josh had rented a triplex apartment on East 26th Street near Third Avenue and since Lilly had told me that she was going to stay with daddy I figured it was okay for me to leave.

My story draws to an end now. Sure, I could go on and on because many more things happened of course but one has to draw the line somewhere.

I went back to New York and one day after my arrival Josh, I and a group of friends drove up to Vermont to go skiing. I had never skied in my life but was willing to learn.

I did my first skiing on the bunny hill while Josh and his friends went skiing down the slopes.

After my lesson I waited, margarita in hand, in the lounge of the ski-resort and just as I was beginning to wonder why it was taking them so long I saw some of Josh' friends come running towards me.

'Josh is alright!' One of them shouted and I immediately knew something was very wrong.

Indeed it was. Josh had suffered a severe accident and was rushed to the hospital. His injuries were rather bad; his left leg was fractured in several places.

Josh was a very good skier; when he studied in Boulder, Colorado, he often went skiing in Aspen with friends but this time things went very wrong. Because there wasn't much snow Josh had skied closer to the tree-line and caught an edge.

Friends of Josh drove me to the hospital. My poor baby, I was very nervous and quite distraught.

Later I called his parents who came the next day and practically ignored me.

It was touch and go whether or not his leg would have to be amputated. Fortunately it didn't come to that, a so-called Ace Hoffman device was put into place, a contraption of steel spikes that kept the bones in place.

It was a heavy blow to Josh and I felt so sorry for him; I spent many hours by his beside, bringing him juice and tea and keeping him company. Pretty soon the personnel knew me and let me go in and out of the kitchen as I pleased.

Naturally our triplex apartment was not a good place for him to come back to so I returned to Manhattan and began looking for another place to live a few days before he was released from hospital. His mother had suggested that he should go back to living with them in Great Neck, Long Island but fortunately Josh didn't go for that.

I found a great apartment in one of the luxurious Glenwood Buildings on East 75th Street in between Second and Third Avenue.

His convalescence took many weeks, months even and it wasn't easy for him; there was a possibility that he would keep a limp because the injured leg was a few inches shorter now, however, he recovered well and completely.

Life goes on in face of all adversity. Our relationship grew stronger and stronger. Sure, we had arguments and disagreements but we had so much fun as well.

I sang in various luxury clubs and did more television and radio appearances, we entertained and went to parties, made little holiday trips, to Taos, New Mexico for instance, and enjoyed our life together.

Lee came back to New York later that year and we met occasionally in a restaurant or diner to catch up; I was glad to have him close again because although I had chosen to share my life with Josh I always kept a warm place for the poet in my heart and we stayed close friends until the day he died on February 17, 2005 in Amsterdam.

I still didn't have my green card and this time Lee wanted to make sure I got it so he contacted Doctor Harrington who called his friend Senator Moynihan. A few days later Lee's lawyer and Lee and I had an appointment at the Immigration Office downtown. The same fat black woman who had interviewed us a year earlier asked the lawyer and Lee to step into her office; I was asked to wait.

She told my ex-husband and the lawyer that she was not prejudiced at all. Why it took so long to process my application for a green card was not disclosed by her but in any case,

I finally received that much desired document. So, I now could go back to Holland to spend some time with my father.

Those five weeks with him in the spring of 1982 were a balsam to my soul. It was lovely weather, sunshine and warm temperatures every day and that in April and May, it was absolutely fabulous!

We went to the beach in the artistic village Bergen almost every day and afterwards we did the grocery shopping together and I cooked a wholesome meal for us. Then we usually watched some television and later on daddy brought out the cognac and sherry (for me) and told me all about his adventures and difficulties during the war; from his time in labor camps to the burning of Leipzig in the end of the war and how he made it back home at last.

It utterly fascinated me, to be able to talk with my father and find out what it had been like for him. I will always treasure those lovely weeks we spent together in the spring of 1982.

When I went back to the States the whole family saw me off at the train station in Alkmaar and I remember vividly how my father hugged me tightly and said: 'Keep singing, darling, you have such a lovely voice, never give up! Promise me that!'

Josh was very happy to have me by his side again after five weeks and took me on a weekend trip to Vermont where he had rented a beautiful cottage in the mountains. It was total bliss.

But then on a bright and sunny day about two months after my return to New York, Marjorie called with very disturbing news; daddy had suffered another massive heart attack and she and Lilly feared for his life.

Naturally I wanted to go back to Holland right away, however, I let Josh talk me out of it and I shouldn't have.

'You were just there, sweetheart,' he said, 'your sisters are there, they will keep you informed, there is nothing you can do now.'

What did he know? To this day I regret that I didn't go back home because although daddy recovered completely, on September 4th, 1982, my beloved father died in his sleep of heart failure.

When Marjorie called and told me the sad news I cried out in agony and slumped to the floor.

Lilly who had spent the night with a friend, found him on that Saturday when she came home around two o'clock in the afternoon. She was surprised to find the newspaper still lying on the floor in the hallway. An eerie silence greeted her.

Quickly she ran up the stairs and knocked on my father's bedroom door.

There was no answer so she opened the door and found him asleep on his bed; however, he was not sleeping.

When she came closer she realized that daddy was gone and panic seized her. She let out an agonizing cry and rushed downstairs and out the back door straight to the neighbors.

Luckily, the couple and good friends to this day, were home and she was immediately comforted by them.

Josh and I flew to Holland right away of course. The funeral was solemn; family members, neighbors, somebody from the company where my father had worked and a few close friends of my father were present as well as Lee and Johnny, my first boyfriend.

'She has all her men collected around her.' One of my aunts was heard saying.

It made me feel very good to have Josh by my side this time and also that my ex-husband and first boyfriend had come to pay their respects.

My father was such a sweet man who despite a difficult start in life made the very best of it; he adored my mother and was a source of humor and kindness towards me and my sisters, never too busy to lend a helping hand or give a kind word of advice. I was indeed heartbroken as were my sisters.

To lose both your parents in less than two years time and both of them so young, my mother was fifty-five when she died and my father fifty-eight, was indeed a terrible blow. However, c'est la vie and life goes on and etcetera, etcetera. What can you do? You can do nothing but accept whatever life has in store for you and make the best of it. That is all you can do.

My sisters and I were lucky to have had such loving wonderful parents although they were torn away from us way too soon.

A couple of weeks after my father had passed away a melody came to me, I took out my notebook and the lyrics poured out of me; it was the story of me and my father and the happy time we spent during those five weeks in the spring. That song I have only been able to sing once and that was when I did my special show called From All Sides, on October 6th (my father's birthday), 2000, in the Romijn Theatre in my birthplace Leeuwarden. The Province of Friesland had given me a grant to produce the show and I had some great artists among whom a poet and a fabulous blind jazz pianist.

~

After all is said and done, life has treated me kindly. Now, as an older woman, I can only look back with gratitude. My greatest joy is of course the birth of my two sons, in 1986 and 1988. They are indeed the sunshine of my life.

Josh and I got married on September 15, 1982 in New York at nine o'clock in the morning. We did go downtown in a limousine and I wore a lovely blue silk organza outfit and beautiful light blue suede shoes, a sweet smelling gardenia in my hair and a lovely bouquet of orchids in my hands.

Josh was very dapper and awfully good looking in his off white smoking while my friend Bibi came with us and made great photos of it all.

However, after the marriage I had to be checked into Lenox Hill hospital because I was in sheer agony with pain; I had a slipped disk. A specialist from Australia injected a slow working medication into my spine that had to do the trick and it did, after about a month and a half the pain was gone and I could walk, run and dance to my heart's delight again.

To be able to marry Josh I had to be divorced of Lee first; he was in Thailand at the time and went to the American Consulate there to obtain an affidavit that stated that he had no objections to the divorce.

However, that was not sufficient; at that time a couple couldn't divorce by mutual consent in the state of New York yet so Josh contacted a lawyer to help with this. That fool suggested that I would declare that I had been beaten by Lee. Naturally I couldn't do such a thing so then the lawyer thought it a good idea that we went to the Dominican Republic where you can get divorced without much difficulties.

So, Josh and I went to Santo Domingo where we went with a Dominican lawyer to the Judicial Building and a few moments later or more accurately a few days later I had my divorce paper in my hand.

When we arrived in the Dominican Republic I was surprised that Josh refused to take off his jacket, it was scorching hot!

We checked into a lovely first class hotel and later we went out to dine. It was then that I learned why he hadn't taken off his jacket before. He proposed to me and I was completely flabbergasted. Then he held out a blue velvet little box; in it was an almost two karats perfect white diamond ring. I was awestruck and tears sprang into my eyes.

We took advantage of the opportunity to spend a couple of days there; it was nice although I didn't like the military men patrolling the beach and the terrible poverty of the people all around.

Although Josh and I were a married couple now I figured that it would be better for me to convert to Judaism. Josh's parents were very much against our marriage because I was not Jewish.

To make life easier for him as well as for myself I thought it would make the communication and acceptance of me more reasonable for them.

As it so happened there was a rabbi in the family, Josh's father's uncle, Rabbi Rose. I went for Judaism lessons to his house in Queens and instantly liked the old man and his soft spoken kind wife.

I told him that I had become a Unitarian and that I was a member of the Community Church of New York.

Rabbi Rose was very nice and it was not at all hard for me to convert. Now that I was an orphan I figured that I was not betraying my parents and my upbringing by them.

However, the conversion itself was difficult because you have to perform this rite and thereby forsake all other religions. It did feel like a betrayal to my parents and I couldn't hold back tears. My mother-in-law thought it strange that I cried; I heard her question Rabbi Rose about it when she thought I didn't hear her talk to him.

The in-laws rewarded me by giving me card Blanche to select any watch that I fancied. At the time my sister's friend Tonia was visiting so she and I went to Fifth Avenue, to Tiffany's and Cartier. I picked out a lovely gold watch of Cartier in the end.

On October 25, 1987, I lost that watch together with almost all the jewelry I had collected over the years when I forgot to pick up my handbag of the roof of our car on a dirt road between San José and San Antonio, in Ibiza, a bleak and awfully black day in my life.

Josh's parents organized a huge wedding for us, on December 11, 1982 at the beautiful Rainbow Room in Manhattan. My two sisters flew in as well as my aunt Wietske, one of my mother's sisters, who had lost her only son Richard at the age of sixteen in a motor accident a few days before my father died.

It was a beautiful affair; first the Jewish wedding ceremony performed by Rabbi Rose in a separate room; my friend Bonita played the piano afterwards and later we went up to the main ballroom where many round tables were set already and a big orchestra played standards of the American Songbook. I will never forget it, it was fabulous!

Josh had rented a suite in the Plaza Hotel on Central Park and Fifth Avenue. It was huge; my sisters and aunt plus my friend Claudia who did my hair, stayed there with us.

The next day Josh had rented the Zipper Discotheque on Union Square for yet another celebration; many friends were there among whom my old friend Vincent and my sisters and aunt of course and also Josh's parents and his aunt and uncle; it was really spectacular.

On Monday morning we flew to Jamaica, where Josh had rented a pink villa right on the sea, it was called Scotch On The Rocks, with stone steps cut out to a private beach and a very nice couple who lived in a house on the grounds to look after us. It was like a fairy tale. Our honeymoon lasted three full weeks and during that time my sisters and aunt stayed in our flat on 75th Street.

In October 1983 my first LP, Going Places, was released, a milestone for me, a lifelong dream come true and Josh had made it possible by producing it. Furthermore the participants on the project were all friends: Dwight who was producer at Radio City Music Hall Sound Studios and who was the engineer, the musicians among whom Marion Brown, Lee's friend from Georgia and Bill Yoscary who let us use his studio for practicing. Shouki did a fabulous lay-out of the album cover and Lee wrote a very nice piece about me on the cover plus Bibi made some excellent photos.

I was terribly happy and so proud; my only regret was that my parents were not with us anymore to witness it.

Over time Josh became more and more unhappy working in the family business and during the year 1984 discussion between him and his father started about being able to leave the company. Eventually, I believe in June or July he was bought out of the company and then he had the freedom to do exactly what he wanted to do.

I was a bit sad because just as my singing career appeared to be gaining momentum (I had good reviews about my album, in Billboard for instance) I didn't really want to leave New York. I liked my life very much; a lovely apartment recently fully redecorated by Enrique, a designer from Puerto Rico, leisure and fun, shopping to my hearts delight, delightful lunches with my friend Lena from Finland, performing in exclusive clubs, going to have a manicure and a pedicure every week, what could be wrong? I was leading the life of a Jewish American Princess, a so-called JAP.

However, we left New York and flew to Spain where we loafed about a couple of weeks, traveling along the Costa Brava and staying in the Ritz in Barcelona.

Finally we took the boat to Ibiza and naturally Josh fell in love with the little magical island. You have to! I had fallen years before, in 1967 to be exact, the first time I set foot on the island with my first boyfriend and went back there with him on vacation five years in a row.

Before we left New York I went to see my gynecologist, Dr. Amin, because I knew he was specialized in fertility problems. Josh had assured me that he didn't care that I couldn't conceive but while I was still there why not take advantage of the doctor's expertise? Perhaps something would be discovered.

Dr. Amin performed a laparoscopy whereby they inject a fluid into the fallopian tubes to be able to see what could be the problem. There was no problem, the doctor told me; the only thing was that the tubes were rather twisted. The reason that I had never become pregnant before was that the tubes were too twisted for semen to make it to an egg. So…I had my own natural birth control all those years.

Our life on Ibiza was wonderful. Josh enjoyed his freedom tremendously and we immediately organized a Show in Jesse's and Britt's house on top of the hill off the Beni Musa dirt road near San José. I had known Britt, a close friend of Lee, for years. He was in Afghanistan at the time when Lee and I were there and used to tease me, saying that while he had to make do in flop houses in Kabul Lee and I were living it up in luxury in the Inter-Continental Hotel.

Britt used to come to the island every summer and over the years also became good friends with Josh. My children adored him; Britt was such a sweet and very funny guy. Sadly he died of cancer a couple of years ago.

Our show/artist exhibition was a spectacular affair; we had horses and riders meet the invited guests at the San José road to lead the people up to the fabulous big house and a video team who filmed everything.

The invitations were done in calligraphy by little Josie, Alonso Bridges' (former sheriff in small town in California as well as stunt man in B-movies) eighteen-year-old Danish girlfriend and all of the preparations were done by Josh and I within two weeks time. We had created a buzz on the island and later El Diario de Ibiza newspaper wrote a fabulous piece about our event with the headline: 'Los Elefantes de San José', a huge compliment indeed.

We had twelve international artists and singers and musicians as well (I sang too) and the wonderful thing about the whole affair was that each piece of art was sold.

To this day I consider the years in Ibiza the best part of my life. I was so happy and even more so when I became a mother. Life was pure bliss and I will treasure those years forever.

The first year we had rented a huge villa in Jesus but because the landlady wanted so much money for July and August we decided to rent an old Dutch house on the Singel, one of the canals in Amsterdam for two months where Josh made a video of my song *Amsterdam's Magic* and where our first baby was conceived.

About three weeks before my son's birth in Clinica Dexeus in Barcelona on April 23, 1986, we bought our lovely house in the hills of San José, Can Pep Suñera.

The house is built in Californian Hacienda style with a big garden and an orchard with cherry trees, oranges and pears, sloping terraces, bougeainville and oleanders, an inner garden with honey suckle, a dwarf palm tree and a banana plant; a lovely swimming pool with mosaic of frolicking dolphin with ball done by a German woman, a playground for the children and marble floors and, it has a great view of the Mediterranean Sea; on clear days you can even see Formentera.

Two years and four months later our second son was born, also in Clinica Dexeus in Barecelona, on September 19, 1988 and Josh and I were over the moon with joy.

Life was relaxed and so much fun, everybody who lives on Ibiza knows what I'm talking about; the island is pure magic.

With the birth of my children my biggest wish had come true at last; I was a mother now and there is no greater gift than that in my opinion.

Tanya, our Pilipino housekeeper/nanny who came to live with us (in her own studio/apartment downstairs) was fantastic. I loved her and am happy to say that she and I have remained good friends over the years.

Doting on my two children, playing golf at Roca Lisa with my three English friends every Wednesday followed by exquisite lunches with bottles of chardonnay on a beach nearby, dinner parties, the pre-openings of the disco's like KU and Pacha…it was a dreamlike wonderful life.

Josh had bought an eight-track recording machine for me and a Canon word processor as well so I kept working on my writing of songs and short stories and I also performed now and then in clubs on the island and in radio programs. I went into a recording studio in San Mateo with Mike Thompson, an English guitar player who used to work with Donovan and together we recorded a couple of songs among which *Ibiza Fun* (Alonso Bridges with his lovely sonorous voice says: 'Baila, guapa, baila' at the intro of the song) and it is one of the tracks on my album All Of Me.

I worked with several other musicians as well among whom a fantastic gypsy guitar player, Bee, a black American musician and René, a Swiss guitarist with whom I went back into the studio in San Mateo to record the song *Still*, also a track on my album All Of Me.

Our friends were of all sort of plumage, most of them mad as hatters but that's what made our life on Ibiza so much fun and laughter. Josh also got involved with two Swiss guys who organized the Ibiza Sun Festival in 1987 with stars like Nina Hagen (Josh flew to London to contract her and she spent some hours in our house, a hysterical but very nice lady), Dr. Feelgood and others. I performed at that show as well.

At almost every dinner party I was asked to sing, in fact folks wouldn't take no for an answer but I loved it of course.

My first poems and short stories that were published in Literary Magazines in America, Canada and England were written in my cozy workroom in our home in Ibiza.

Once Josh and I gave a huge party at our house with many guests, four Philippines to serve and an open bar, a little

Show with a fabulous flamenco guitarist, a poet and me singing as well…God, how nice it all was. At that party my friend Mary (Pepsi Cola) brought along Robert Plant, the singer of Led Zeppelin who thrilled me when he said he very much liked my song *Something In Your Eyes*.

After the first year Josh started a warehouse building and renting company together with an Englishman and things were looking bright and promising. However, in 1991 the first Gulf War in Iraq began and because people were uncertain about the outcome and too scared to invest things went down the drain.

Nothing stays the same as we all know and unfortunately my union with the father of my two children fell apart in the fall of 1991. I don't want to go into detail about the why and how; it happened.

In September 1992 I left the island with my little boys and eventually settled in the North of Holland, in a small village in Friesland where I went right back into the swing of things and performed all over the province.

It was of course very difficult in the beginning; it takes time to recover from a divorce but luckily Josh and I were able to overcome t

he past and I'm happy to say that we have become good friends.

The children and I moved back to Amsterdam in 2000 to a nice apartment where I still live now.

My sons are grown-up and lead their own lives; I am so very proud of them.

All in all life has been good to me so far and I feel a very lucky woman indeed.

~

THE END

Printed in Great Britain
by Amazon